INTO THE HIVE OF SAARLATHESH

Johnny Toxin

ISBN-13: 9781492963004
ISBN-10: 1492963003
Library of Congress Control Number: 2013919320
CreateSpace Independent Publishing Platform
North Charleston, South Carolina

This book is dedicated to all of my loved ones and friends who aren't alive to see my first book make it to print. Everyone you run into in life is an inspiration and an influence, so I owe you all for being a part of my own journey. Here's to hoping that they sell books in Heaven. If they don't, just send me a shipping address. I'll be happy to mail it to you.

Horror from beyond
Powerful, great, and wise
From our sacred temples
Listen for our cries

We beseech you, Dark One
To open our mind's eye
Teach us alien ways
And be desperate to die

Terror of the depths
Tyrant of the skies
From a watery slumber
An elder god will rise

Rise.
Rise..
Rise…

—Ancient chant from *Saarlathesh, the Dark Almanac*

CHAPTER ONE
Old Friends

"**E**xcuse me."

I dreaded the face I would see when I looked up from the counter. There were only a few people in this town that would say "Excuse me" in my store. The first type was tourists who undoubtedly got lost on their way to a much more exciting place than this shithole and were looking for directions. They wouldn't ever stop in to browse for anything or, god forbid, purchase something for once. The second type was the weirdos. People who spent most of their time hiding in a dimly lit bedroom, pouring over their rare collections of shit, crap, pointless memorabilia and whatever else anyone, they decided, didn't "get."

"Um…..excuse me?"

Oops. It looked like I spent too much time thinking and I forgot to respond. I looked up into the face of my newest customer and my mind regurgitated half a dozen thoughts, several of which involved kicking this fucker through the window.

"Yeah, how can I help you?" I lied. I knew what was coming; he wasn't one of my regulars. Just another sweaty, bespectacled fat man who still saw a scrawny nerd when he looked in the mirror… and forgot twenty years had gone by since then.

1

"Hey, yeah, I was, sorta, wondering," he leaned in close before talking to me. I could smell the cheese puffs that were definitely his breakfast, lunch, and dinner for the past (god knows how many) days as he opened his mouth. The stink shot out and curled around my nose, holding me prisoner for the duration of his question. "Do you have any girlie mags, like, somewhere in the back?"

Motherfucker. I'm gonna dropkick this shit through the WALLS.

"Get the fuck out!" I had slammed my hands down on the counter, pushing him back a few feet and freeing me from the cheesy terror that wafted around him. "Get the fuck out of here and don't ask me for that again. There's **normal** people in here, asshole!"

At this point, my other customers had looked up, from the dozens of dozens of comics littering the tabletops, to stare at us both. My ever-so-disgusting bother took a look around and, fearing the attention, fled out the door. But not before tripping over a stand of comics and slamming face-first into the door frame. *Well, at least my walls won't have to be remodeled.* He fled out the front door, almost knocking over one of my regulars, and ran across the street until he was far out of sight. I pressed my fingers into my temples, either to relax myself or to concentrate hard enough to somehow telepathically kick that guy's ass. I wasn't entirely sure. Could have been a bit of both.

The customer, who nearly got steamrolled walking in, decided to be a good Samaritan and picked up a few of the comics that had spilled over in the fatso's getaway. He plopped them down onto the counter and smiled at me.

"How goes it, Luke? Attacking customers again?"

"You know I don't like talking about that little incident," I sneered at him. He knew damn well I already apologized to those two tourists. I never did checkup to see if they got to the hospital

2

okay, but I never got a letter from them, suing me for everything. So I just let it go. It's a story for another time anyway.

"Hey, sorry, man. Just saw the look on that guy's face," he said, pointing out the door, to the direction of the sad little man who fled. "And I wondered what you did to him."

"Fair enough, Rob," I said.

"Damn it, don't call me that! You know my name is Robin." Rob, *(er, Robin…got to remember, tired of being corrected, so tired…)* was a local kid who lived down the street from me. Found out when he was ten that I owned a comic shop in town and didn't have the good sense to stop bothering me about getting him free shit every day. He eventually stopped when I decided to give him some stuff every now and again, so he slowly became a tolerable regular. His name IS Rob, though. About a year after I met him, both his parents died in a drunk-driving accident. It was a common small-town newspaper story about the tragedy of a child. Except Rob was adopted. And his parents didn't like him. And his dad was the drunk driver in the accident. And his dad and his mom were in two different cars…

Regardless, Rob then started coming into my shop to lose himself in any comic he could find. When he was about fourteen, he struck a chord (somewhere deep, I guessed) with *Batman* comics and sort of related himself to his sidekick. Somehow, he managed to not follow the conventional choice of an idol in the billionaire playboy. He made everyone call him Robin since then, marking the first time that anyone changed their name to get made fun of, instead of the opposite. I never did ask him how he planned to avenge his parents.

Robin broke my thought process, "Got anything in that's new?"

"What, you mean besides another story about Batman fighting the Joker?" I said sarcastically. I wondered, with each new comic, how they would try to spice up the next. "Or do you want something brand new? 'Cause I just got *Breadfuckers #4* in today and, let me tell you, *bread gets all kind of fucked.*" Robin just looked at me and turned from the counter. He wandered around the tables until he picked up a niche comic and began reading. *I'm getting way better at this. Few more months of hard work and I'll be nominated for worst employee of the year.*

By the way, *Breadfuckers* is real; a comic series by an artist who grew up around here. He had made it big, but his publisher didn't care much for his personal concepts and characters. So he just designs the front cover of some big name titles. A few months back he contacted me and offered to send *Breadfuckers* over to my shop as some sort of "exclusive." It was drawn, written, and inked by him. Didn't even charge me for shipping and asked for ten percent of its profits. I just shrugged and accepted. I could look over at the cover and let you know his name, but I won't, out of respect for his continuing career. And your sanity.

I finally reached closing time without assaulting some of my unwanted regulars who shuffle in at night. Methodically, I locked the door to the backroom, closed the register, took my daily slice of the profits, and turned out the lights. As I closed the security gate, laughing at businesses with back doors (my shop only had one exit, the front door, and no back door), I reminded myself of how little anyone could possibly steal from the store. Years ago, I had sold off all my first editions and collectible issues online to a whole assortment of morons.

I won't tell you how much I made off of this. Let's just say my mortgage is paid, and I have enough to survive if the comic shop blows up. *How many twenty-somethings can say that?* I thought the number must be equal to the amount that still talk to themselves constantly.

As my feet began to leave the ground, I heard hurried foot-steps round a corner to my left, followed by a light bump into the side of the brick wall of my shop. A low, nearly inaudible "ow" emanated from there. After a long sigh, I stepped off the curb into the street, making my way to the Hammered Chipmunk. That was the nearest bar in town, though it certainly wasn't the best you could find. That bar was three miles over near Deer Country, nestled on a road in between two closed factories. Harry's Rest, it's called.

The town square was just ahead of me, and the footsteps behind me had followed me all the way. I knew it was the same person that had skidded into my shop wall, but I didn't bother looking; I knew who she was. Paying the footsteps no attention, I continued on past the numerous storefronts, all doomed to fail in a few months' time. Besides the businesses that have been here for generations, all shops in the square opened and closed in four month spans of time. One way or another, my comic store had managed to be one of the good few that lasted.

One recently-closed store was a fishing chain that only car-ried one brand and always appeared, to me, to be some kind of corporate test to see how many people bought Mighty Mike™ bait and poles. It closed in a month and a half, so I guessed not many.

Another was a McDonald's, which lasted about as long as the fishing store, to the surprise of no one in town. *Who gave a shit about fast food in a town of home cooked meals and one bum?* Probably just the bum. The McDonald's folded and became a Starbucks two months later. We laughed at them. Not to ourselves, mind you. We didn't huddle at home taking bets on Starbucks closing while around a generic, store-bought, twenty dollar coffee machine. We laughed right in their faces, standing in the front entrance, me and about four other guys who were the first to show up for the

"Grand Opening." The process of renovating the old McDonald's into the coffee shop took about three weeks; Starbucks closed in eight days.

Claude's Emporium of Stuff lasted the longest out of any place I've seen attempt to make a profit in this backwater town. He sold knick knacks and trinkets that he used to "scour the country for." This coincided with the time he spent out of town, gathering product to put on display in his windows, usually with a sign proclaiming how low the prices were. Claude's place closed about the time the FBI realized his novelty human skull candle holders were the genuine article, and Claude's cross-country American expeditions for product turned into grisly cross-country murders.

21st Century Ameri-CAN! was a tech store about two buildings over from mine that also went under quickly. I had heard an older woman fainted in there once, because of the blurring neon signs, bright displays, and strobe lights within. No one needed a tech guy in a town full of do-it-yourselfers, which held a double meaning in this community. The first meaning referred to people who fixed everything by themselves. The second was people who told you coldly to "fuck off, do it yourself." People tended to keep to themselves around here, myself included.

My favorite store so far, however, was a café/lounge run by this woman Maria and her daughter, um, Maria. *Maria Jr.?* I had a thing for Maria (the younger, not the mother), so I used to stop there for lunch almost daily. Every day, there were fresh-made sandwiches and coffee and a large screen TV. I'll admit, some days I forgot to re-open the comic shop, hurrying back from 12 o'clock lunch at two thirty. I'm not sure why it happened, but one day they closed up. Rumor at the time was Maria got knocked up and they skipped town to avoid a scandal. No one was positive who got in her bed, but I've taken a few guesses. And I'm sure their wives had something to say about those rumors.

The last place of interest became quite a joke in the past few weeks. Nothing more than a regular, small-town, local diner, which has been around for a number of years, that had recently fired an employee for reasons that haven't been so clear. Whatever the reason, the guy was angry enough to jump up a ladder and change the message underneath the diner's sign to read "Twice, there were rats in the kitchen," a message which most of the community found believable enough that the number of cars parked outside the place on a daily basis decreased. When asked why they didn't change the sign right away, it was found that the only person who felt comfortable on the rickety ladder that the diner owned was the guy who was fired.

A suggestion was made to one of the employees to just ask somebody else to do it, which none of them seemed to conclude on their own. That sign now reads: "April Fool's came early! Enjoy our rat-free meals!" Obviously, the number of cars outside the diner still hasn't changed since then. *The place will close after about another month, I wager.*

It was about two in the morning when I found myself in front of the large cardboard chipmunk that greeted all patrons of the "Hammered Chipmunk - Bar & Dine." Besides a few interior renovations, this was one of the oldest buildings in the square. As I opened the door and adjusted my eyes to the lighting, I happily saw the bar had its usual turnout; about twelve or fifteen people getting drunk off their asses or, alternatively, sipping lightly at their drinks. The bar counter was off to the right, ahead of me and far to the back of the place. The only bartender, the owner for what had to have been sixty years now, was a man by the name of Old Man Mills. Not to imply that his first and middle name were

Old and Man respectively, that is. I'm sure he had a pretty generic Christian name, but I never bothered to ask.

"How goes the business, Mills?" I asked.

"Louie! Good to see you again. I'm doing pretty well," was the response. I wasn't about to correct the guy over my name.

"Good to hear. Let me get a shot of the fifth strongest stuff you got."

Old Man Mills turned away to face the, quite impressive, collection of bottles and shakers you would ever see for three miles. By then, you would have made it to Harry's Rest and forgotten this place ever looked good in your eyes. Harry's was the spot that kids graduated to, after lying to Old Man Mills about their age for four years of high school. College kids would come over from the city west of the border to party there too. I don't know how many times I had people walk into my shop, talking about a drunken asshole playing in the middle of the road, not too far from the bar. Harry got them drunk and buying rounds fast; Old Man Mills would get you a beer and drone on and on about how old the tavern was, the history of owners all the way back to the 1700's, and downright boring tales of his youth.

In regard to his appearance, I guess Old Man Mills had a bit of a grandfatherly look about him that just seemed to radiate into his business as well. On the top of his head, he wore one of those English hats that you see in old movies, a flat cap I think it's called. A pair of white trousers hung about his hip; a good tell-tale sign of a person's age and generation (disregarding those younger adults like myself who choose to be outcasts) is the height the top of their pants reaches on their body. Older folks tend to buckle their belt somewhere above the hips but below the belly button, although sometimes they may cover up the belly button entirely. The younger the generations go, though, the more sag you'll see.

8

For a shirt, Old Man Mills wore a buttoned-up Bahamas t-shirt, which displayed a scene of a Caribbean reef (plants, wildlife, and two oddly-colored, giant seaweeds running up the shirt) and remained unbuttoned near the collar. From this gap in the shirt, his old, white and stringy chest hair attempted to escape. Around his neck hung a sterling silver necklace, which held a gold and silver medallion, of unknown origin, at the center of his collarbone. I didn't know what shoes he was wearing because they were down below the bar counter.

I ordered a beer before I downed my shot. Tomorrow was a weekend, and I liked to open later than usual. Mostly so that I could nurse a hangover for the better part of the morning and scare any potential assholes. *So that means one shot now, two beers later, more beer at home…* Nobody really wants to piss off the drunken management.

"Luke, take a seat, bro!" I turned to my left to catch a table full of some kids I used to hang with in high school. Most of them had gone on to college without me; some of them went up north to Empire, the others headed west to that city college that so frequently visited Harry's. They weren't heavy drinkers, so I could rely on seeing them in the Hammered Chipmunk from time to time. Usually, though, they let me know in advance. *Guess not.*

"Hey, you guys. When did you get back?" I said. I walked over to the table and pulled out a chair from another, wedging it awkwardly in between some redhead and my best friend from high school, Jean. Jean and I went way back to freshman year (ages ago now) when we shared a circuit-building class together. Class work was boring as hell, but we just fucked around the entire year. I can't even remember if I even passed that class at all, but I did remember that Jean and I were always paired for projects. The teacher hated our guts every minute of every day. Besides being loud and disruptive, Jean got on his worst side by soldering LED's into his circuit board in the shape of a dick. Every second, the lights in front of the dick would flash in a pattern of semen flying through the air. *Now that was a work of art.*

Obviously, our teacher promptly lost his nerve and screamed, right there in the classroom. Some bullshit about disgusting behavior and disrespect for the class. Jean got suspended for a shit ton of time that even I thought meant expulsion. But after about a month and two and a half weeks, he was back in class and making snide remarks at the English teacher. I could probably write an entire book of the insanity we created together. *But let's not and say I did.* I really didn't have the time to waste on building a useful skill like writing.

Jean was wearing a t-shirt from a local band that had played a few times around town before fading into obscurity. He played in that band, although he didn't have creative control of the material they played, which annoyed him to an extent. The rest of his outfit was uninteresting: blue jeans and black sneakers. Jean had recently cut his hair very short, probably shaved to a close length; from the look of it, it already began to re-grow in spurts, very unevenly around his scalp. He looked more or less the same from the last time I saw him, but a patch of hair on the tip of his chin was new. I rubbed at my own chin, feeling nothing but stubble.

Clockwise from Jean sat Raphael, a rather heavy Italian guy with a temper to boot. He wasn't much of the stereotype I was painting, but I wouldn't take any other person as backup in a fight. One cheap insult and Raphael was ready to break your face in until your eyeballs were caressing the back of your neck. Tough dude. But, when I got to know him, he definitely had a sensitive side. He put his friends ahead of a lot of things in life; maybe not the most important things, but hey, we were family a few years back. I didn't know the redhead that was hanging around his arm, but I put two and two together. Probably met her at Empire, she was too good looking for this crap town.

Raphael and his girlfriend were wearing matching blue t-shirts adorned with animals, not of the same image but of similar style. His portrayed a white tiger; hers, a leopard. They matched in the way that couples tend to match colors when they reach that tender milestone where most sensibility goes out the window in favor of doing what seems pleasing to the other person. *I think they call that marriage,* I joked to myself, taking a sip of beer.

Next up, to my left and across from Raphael, sat Wayne. Now, I never really had a problem with the way Wayne acted. But the guy had some issues long before I had ever met him. Wayne seemed to have, somewhere in his early days with our group, fallen on a belief that we had stumbled upon some great secret to cool that put us above everyone else in school. Shit, I couldn't blame the guy. The way all of us bounced off each other was phenomenal. If Jean or Raphael came up with a joke, I was ready to throw in some retort. If we laughed hard enough about it, that one joke would come up almost every time we saw each other. Life was fucking hilarious and good, even when we inevitably pissed off some teacher.

Wayne didn't think it came as naturally as we claimed. He always tried real hard to say something insane. Tried to throw in some outlandish shit we didn't see coming. Hell, sometimes that shit actually stuck with us. Most of the time, though, Wayne just listened and laughed his ass off at the jokes we made. We didn't ask him to do anything more than that.

He was wearing a pair of jeans, much like Jean's dark shade of blue, a rather plain, plaid t-shirt of the color white with orange stripes, and a sizable watch on his left wrist that faced the wrong direction. I didn't know if he did that on purpose, as part of some gag, or if I was tired and buzzed from the drink. Regardless, he dressed casually and, as much as can be said of people's clothes, about as normal as clothing on a college student comes. None of us had that much variety in wardrobe beyond t-shirts and jeans. *Maybe that's what made all the time spent together seem like one continuous memory.*

Jean said, "We just met up tonight, right outside. Raphael and Victoria drove down, me and Wayne carpooled from campus. How have you been, man?"

"Tired as shit. Been working in my shop almost every day. Still don't trust the new guy enough to have control for a day," I replied. The new guy was Bishop, and I only hired him because he had retail experience, unlike my other applicants. Guy was a hard worker, but I felt uneasy handing over the keys. *That's why you haven't scheduled him in over three weeks, Luke. But don't tell them that, you'll just get defensive.* I downed a bit more of my beer.

"Shit, Luke. Give yourself a break. You need a vacation, close down the store or something. Do that, uh, walking across the Earth shit that those monks do."

"Yeah. I might just do that. Take a bus to Empire and start hitchhiking across America with only cash and a backpack of clothes. See some new places, meet people. Come home to a fucking cornucopia of bills up to my neck. Great idea."

"Hey, it was just a fucking suggestion. Close shop and go fishing. Put a smile on and kill some poor fish's daddy," Jean joked.

"Yeah, send him to fish orphanage!" Wayne added.

"Well...yeah," Jean said to him.

"Hey guys," Raphael interrupted, "maybe Luke has a case of sexual frustration. Go fuck a fish." His girlfriend Victoria covered a giggle with her hand. I smirked, finding Raphael's statement incredibly funny but not wanting to catch the attention of the entire bar with my laughter.

"Yeah, maybe I will. Hey, Ralph, maybe you can give me some of your old booty calls," I snickered.

"Hey, fuck you buddy…"

"Now that would add more frustration," I said. Wayne was laughing into a seizure in his seat. *At least I wasn't the one to do it.* We let the laughing die down; I think Jean had to kick Wayne's leg to get him to stop. I worked at ingesting my first beer some more.

"Fuck. That felt good. Luke, get up from your beer. How have you been, man? Got any customer horror stories?" Jean said.

"Nah, just some freak trying to get a hard-on in my shop again. Nothing too special," I replied.

"Shit. I think that the last good story you had was Free Comic Day. What was that? Two years ago?"

Raphael chimed in, "Oh, those Asians bastards? It was three years ago!"

"Oh, yeah. Time flies, y'know? Those guys were a pain in the ass. They came in and just marveled at every free comic we had. 'Ooooooo, this one's got cute little animals on the cover!'" I imitated one of them, rotating the nearby menu in all directions, to the best of my ability. Jean promptly lost his shit and nearly spit up beer onto the table. He managed to grab a napkin (lightning fast) and hold it up to his mouth. I just continued, "Had one kid tug at my shirt and constantly ask me if the one he was holding was free."

"Yeah. Yeah! That fucking little Chinese boy! And none of the comics he had were the free ones, right?" Jean replied, wiping more beer from his newly-discovered stain on his shirt. He scrubbed at it.

"I couldn't fuckin' believe him! Everyone was surrounding this table of boring, generic, artsy, indie-dropout bullshit, and this

13

kid is coming up to me with All-Star Superman!" I explained, finishing the last gulp of my beer.

"Holy shit, man," Jean took a long gulp of his beer as well and swallowed, "fuck that kid, haha!"

I was feeling a bit tipsy by this point. *Old Man Mills must be giving me the strongest stuff.* I couldn't even tell what kind I was having; at this point, it was like gulping down a drink and not having a sense of taste. Old Man Mills made his way to our table, taking my empty bottle and replacing it with a freshly opened one. I took another swig from the new bottle, and rubbed my eyes a bit. It was late. *I definitely have to open later in the morning if I'm going to continue with a third beer at home.*

"So you must be Raphael's girlfriend?" I asked Victoria. She just nodded her head.

"We have a few classes together, hooked up at a dorm party," Raphael explained. Victoria gave him a short, weak punch to the arm, the way couples do when something "embarrassing" comes up.

"What about you, Luke? I see you brought your girlfriend in here with you," Jean joked. I looked over my shoulder to see a brunette, about my height, sitting on a bar stool. She was slurping at some fruity island drink with a red straw. Every now and then, her eyes darted my way and quickly back at the bar counter. She was alone.

"Yeah…I kinda still have that problem." That problem was Tracy Gunther. Tracy followed me around whenever she could. Tracy liked to know where I was, liked to be where I was. Tracy… was a bit of a stalker problem I couldn't get rid of. Not that I tried very hard, mind you. It was hard getting someone interested in you when half the town knows you as that asshole that runs the only local comic shop. Tracy had a thing for me since high school, though, so it was getting a bit creepy by this point.

Jean whistled a low, disdainful, um, whistle. "I thought you said you were gonna tell her to leave you alone?"

"Yeah, well, I can't just waltz up to her and tell her to fuck off can I?"

"You can tell her to fuck off, do it herself," Wayne added. He completed the imagery by making a fingering motion around his crotch area, quite noticeably to anyone within eyeshot. I rubbed my eyes again, I saw Jean do the same. More frothy beer touched my lips, this time in a larger quantity. Raphael just coughed and sipped at his beer lightly. Victoria didn't seem to get it; she wasn't from this town, wasn't there with us from the very first joke. *Fucking Wayne, bro.*

Much of our time together, back in high school, consisted of many conversations such as this one. There was a time when the four of us were like brothers, inseparable after school and on the weekends. Summer breaks were always filled with adventures, or misadventures, as Jean often preferred to call them, around the town or heading down the shore. Oftentimes, my mother or my father would ask me what the four of us were planning, never assuming that I was going out on my own or with a new friend. It wasn't that we didn't have other friends at all. Those friends were the classmates we saw day-to-day at school; they were never a part of our extracurricular activities.

Old Man Mills had forgotten if we ordered a new round, but none of us felt the need to correct him. I was on a third beer, enjoying the nice warm feeling it gave me and the courage to speak to long-time friends. We didn't make an effort to contact each other in recent years. I thought of my old friends as too busy, too focused on pursuing a future that our close friendship just drifted apart. I looked down to see that my third beer was finished. I had noticed that the people in the bar had been slowly shuffling out for the past ten minutes. Looking at my phone indifferently, I pretended that I was attending to something other than checking for the current time.

Raphael yawned a bit into his beer, so I took the opportunity to lift my head up to say, "Hey listen. It was good seeing you guys again. If you're in town for a while, come visit me at the shop. Or at the house. Door's always open."

"Thanks, Luke. I'll probably stop by," Jean said.

"Yeah, later Luke," muttered Wayne.

Raphael put a hand up to wave me off into the night, using his other hand to block a massive yawn that had decided to escape.

CHAPTER TWO
Ghosts, Shadows, and...Bees?

I pulled up to my house just as the sun decided to drop below the horizon. The family house sat at the top of a short cliff, hanging over Lake Clearance below. The cliff was real short in height; I'd say about one story deep from the base of the house. I had lived here since I was born. The dusted white house at the cliff was the only home I have ever called my own. When I was in high school, I did a lot of research into apartments up in Empire, daydreaming of attending college with Raphael or Jean. But about two years into community college, my parents walked out on me. Didn't wake me up to tell me, didn't bother sitting down to talk. Just woke up one morning and they had left everything, especially a note on the kitchen table, "Sorry, we need to move on with our lives," scrawled on a partially torn sticky note. Fuck...that was depressing.

I walked into the kitchen, popping open a cold beer, my fourth for the night. I remembered the last thing I heard my dad say: Disappointed. That was it. Didn't really ask what he meant by saying that; didn't remember being in trouble at the moment. Not like I cared, or, more realistically, was able to ask him the next day. Just picked up and left with clothes and some other stuff. I never even bothered to chase after them either, although I did plan, once, to go to the police. That was the day that they were re-screening *Die Hard* at my local theater. I forgot about going the day after. *Sometimes, maybe mysteries just don't need to be solved.*

I suppose I should go into a bit of history of the comic shop. I worked there when I was in high school. My uncle owned the place and taught me a valuable amount of business sense that I promptly disregarded whenever a hot somebody would either walk in, either with their kid or past the shop window. *Comic books just didn't bring in my preferred type of woman.* When my parents left and I was just ending high school, he left the shop to me and told me that he was retiring. Just like that. It felt like my parents leaving all over again. I was pretty much running the place by myself though; my uncle's mind had mostly checked out by then. I once asked him about where my parents had gone and if they were even alive, but he told me not to fuss over it. I believe his exact words were: "Don't worry, they probably will be back by morning." They weren't and I rarely visited my uncle since. He didn't care.

By now, I was already flipping through channels on the couch, a new beer in my hand and pants someplace around the living room. Nothing was catching my eye on TV. Murderer on News-Flash 7, sitcom on 5, Spanish dub of *MacGyver* on 18. I noticed my digital recorder flashing, so I clicked to open up my instant video queue.

The only new recording was a new episode of *Tales from the Outer Darkside of the Twilight*, a science fiction show that Jean had recommended to me over the streaming digital service we shared. Jean liked mooching off my subscription, but I reasoned that Jean introducing me to the existence of *Tales* more than paid for his share. We would both send each other episodes each season. Not because they were particularly good, but because of how ridiculous the premise of each was. Jean called it the "finest entertainment available on television in years" while I called it a four-way lawsuit waiting to happen. I was surprised to see that he had sent me an episode, especially since I hadn't seen a recommendation pop up in over seven months.

The show was a complete rip-off of the three other series that it stole its name from. And its host was Jack "Buffalo" Johnson (no, no one you know), a rotund man who looked like Alfred Hitchcock and impersonated the late Rod Serling. Jack was an Empire man who moved all the way west to Hollywood with dreams. Like a sad, lonely waitress tending a late-night diner in the middle of Reno, having run out of money for bus fare and making do with what fate handed her.

Well, Jack Johnson found a way to make his dreams happen; I don't know if he met the right people or had some good ideas. Whatever the case may be, nothing changed the fact that I was staring at a digital recommendation for an episode titled "Nocturnal Submissions." *Quality entertainment.* I thought it to myself, but Jean's voice came through in my head. I reluctantly pressed play on my remote and sat back.

I took a swig of my beer, just in case. I thought I was too sober.

Outer Darkside began as it usually would since season two. Shots, in black and white, of random backdrops for the episode. This time, a typical suburban house over there, fading to a couple of shop windows in the sunlight, cut to a long-distance shot of a non-descript freeway during rush hour. The camera then faded in to the face of a generic nobody looking for his big shot in a shitty sci-fi show. The color slowly transitioned into color, because… well, fuck if I know anything about filming. *For nostalgia?* The guy was sitting in his car, sweating in a suit. He wiped his face on the sleeve of his suit and then looked further on into traffic. Random guy beeped his horn a few times, putting on his best frustrated face. *It sucks, I could have sold this scene way better.*

Cue the voiceover of Jack Johnson.

"Seymour Smith. A man with an alliterative name, who, in a comic book, may have been a superhero. Who in a film, one may call the protagonist," Jack droned on, "but tonight, Mr. Smith has become something completely different. Tonight, Seymour Smith is a witness, and victim, of the supernatural. Because up ahead on the road, he will be taking the familiar off-ramp to the quiet suburb where he dwells…An exit that to him will read 'Home,' but, to us, is one of the many exits that leaves our reality and whose destination is…one more *Tale from the Outer Darkside of the Twilight.*"

I rolled my eyes at the title drop. Jack had been on a streak of "good" writing; I was almost sure that the same guy who wipes his ass gave him a pat on the back for this one. The familiar title scrawl of the show now officially began. Unlike *Twilight Zone*, there was no Jack Johnson telling us that we had entered a world of bullshit and fucked-uppedness. Instead, the beginning sequence showed a silhouetted man, sitting naked in a wooden chair in a room that was too dark to see anything beyond him. Above him, a dim light bulb flickered and finally went out. The man in the chair then looked up through the darkness and his chair gave way underneath him.

Slowly, the unknown man in silhouette spun backward down through a starry background. To the right of him, the typical producer-executive-writer credits faded in and out. Then, "Created by Jack Johnson" in white text appeared, followed by the title, *Tales from the Outer Darkside of the Twilight*, and ending with the episode name. This time, the name read "Nocturnal Submissions."

The screen faded out to black, then back. The man who was in the car was now entering his home from the door on the left of the screen. His wife was sitting in the living room, drinking what I thought looked like a dry martini.

"You're late for dinner, dear," she said to him.

"Traffic is insane out there. I think I'm the only one who doesn't rubberneck at every little thing on the side of the road," he replied.

"Well, it's a good thing you are **so** punctually late. I didn't even bother to make a dinner that would get cold."

His eyebrows dipped and his mouth dropped into a half-frown, half-scowl. He said, "Is there anything to eat?"

"No."

He stood staring at her for a time, and then she took a sip of her martini and said, "I'm going to bed. Will you join me?"

"No, I have some paperwork to finish."

"Good night."

"Good night."

"Good night," I said to the TV set, watching my eyelids close over my eyes until…

BZZZZT!!

"OW! FUCK!" I shouted. I had just received a shock to my right thigh that jolted up my body and snapped my eyelids open. Many summers ago, Jean and I had set up this novelty shock-device that we had found in a flea market. We had used it like two stupid teens would, finding ways to shock random passersby and each other. Eventually, he left for college and I got stuck with it. I lost it a couple of days ago in the living room, when I had been using it as an alarm clock to wake me up. It wasn't a very good alarm, so I knocked it off of me a few days before. It had evidently imbedded itself in the side of my couch.

I was clawing for the damn thing when it went off and shocked me again. I bit my finger, and turned to the screen. Seymour Smith was typing away and looking at papers at his desk. Suddenly, a man came out from behind the curtain in his study and gravitated over to behind Seymour's chair. It was cheaply done, but I could guess from the effects that the man was supposed to be a ghost. The next part startled me a bit. The ghost grabbed Seymour by the wrists and threw him forward onto his own desk. Then, I kid you not, the ghost began thrusting behind him.

I went into hysterics, an insane momentum of laughter swelling up in my throat and releasing into the world of my living room. I tried everything to stop, but I couldn't while this ghost was just pushing and pushing against Seymour Smith. The scene was positioned so that Seymour was facing the camera. He was doing his best impression of a guy getting in a very uncomfortable situation with a ghost, and, to my surprise, it wasn't that bad at all. *Jack finally found a rising star in his auditions and he's going to be known for being ass-raped by Casper.*

The ghost was gone when I finally regained my composure. Seymour Smith was crying as the screen faded into a commercial for a late-night sex hotline. Typical for this hour, but completely inappropriate in the context of what had just occurred in *Tales*. When the show came back on, it went through a number of scenes of Seymour frightened at work, frightened on the way home, frightened near his wife. Each night, he would attempt to stay up and defend himself, but the ghost would find him. Through walls, through windows, popping up from objects in a room. Even one scene where he was at his office late at night and the ghost took him in the employee restroom.

Eventually, the man spoke to his wife, the complete unbeliever, to explain what was keeping him on the edge of madness and away from work. She couldn't understand what he was try-ing to tell her and he looked so ashamed. From behind his wife, the ghost materialized, with low-grade special effects, through the wall. With a look of terror on his face, Seymour ran out of the house and the next shot opened up in a police station. It faded into the interior, with Seymour sitting across from a detective in a dimly lit room with a cliché hanging light bulb, much like the setting with the naked man in the title sequence. Seymour Smith was telling this officer about his assault and the guy looked skeptical.

"Mr. Smith, couldn't there be some other explanation?"

"What other explanation is there?! How can I make you believe me?" Seymour said between sobs.

"Mr. Smith, I have dealt with many cases like this. Certainly, you are the first adult to fabricate a tale around your assault. Usually, only the kids do that. They're the weakest, y'know? The most frightened of what might happen if they tell the police who did it."

"Are you insane? Can't you see I'm not safe? He can get to me anywhere, anytime!"

On cue, the ghost appeared behind Seymour in the darkness. Less appeared, and more just walked in from the darkened edge of the screen. The detective couldn't see him, but the ghost immedi-ately gripped Seymour by the wrists, like before. The ghost tossed Seymour onto the steel table and began his daily routine. The detective jumped out of his chair at this point and stood fright-ened at what was happening. The ghost eventually made an exit from the screen and Seymour crumpled slowly to the floor. The detective then considered helping and put a supporting hand on his shoulder. The screen faded to black for the last time, and the "Starring" list played.

"Holy fuck," I said, half-laughing and half-disturbed. I picked up my phone and slid the screen upward so I could type on the keypad. I opened my texts to Jean. My last text to him was labeled as from a little more than a year ago. *Time flies, Luke, when you're too busy.* I hammered out a quick "fuck you for that episode" and closed my phone. I rubbed my eyes. The clock on my TV said it was already four in the morning. I rubbed my eyes again, took a swig of my beer and found there was none left. I plopped the bottle on the stand next to me, where it knocked over another one. Thankfully, it didn't roll off. I took a look at the trash scattered around the coffee table, the stand next to me, and on the TV.

"I need to clean this place up," I said, to no one at all. My phone played the first ten notes of *Smoke on the Water*. I flipped the phone open and glanced at the screen. From Jean: "Your welcome :) nice c n u dude." I closed the phone and dozed off.

I woke up to a start. At first, I thought the novelty buzzer had jolted me up from the couch again, but then I realized that I wasn't exactly alone in the room anymore.

Standing there, in the middle of my own living room (*of course*), was a man. He was in his early thirties, maybe a little younger. From the quick glance I made of his person, he was wearing a rather stuffy-looking suit jacket in gray, with a ruffled white undershirt and a reddish-brown tie that dangled loosely around his neck, like in the way all the sitcom dads loosen their ties when coming home to their nagging wives. And all the real-life dads who use said ties to strangle their wives after twenty years of the same shit. As if to spit in the face of my expectations, naturally, he was wearing nothing below his waist but a set of white boxers, which was decorated with numerous hearts. Making my way down, I saw on his right foot what could best be described as a rotting sock, missing the entire front, exposing all of his toes. Did I mention this guy was a semi-transparent red and I could see my furniture behind him?

Now, I know there are times where men attempt their best to remain the strong, masculine heroes that the media normally reveres. These men will laugh in the face of death and punch the fuck out of any obstacles that will prevent them from saving their wife/child/children/dog/cat/man-eating leopard pet. And when it comes time to finally face heavy personal tragedy, they will shed one manly tear and punch the fuck out of tragedy too. Because screw tragedy, that's not bringing this motherfucker down one bit after he just jumped through the air firing two guns like a badass and killing all the terrorists in the room.

I mention this because every guy I know, and every guy those guys know, jumps at the chance to fuck shit up without fear. To stick their necks out of the car window and spit at death for even daring to stop the speeding bullet driving down the highway at two in the morning, drunk off his ass. Metaphorically, that is. Spitting forward out of a speeding car is grounds for a Stupidity Arrest Surcharge. And if your town doesn't have a legally grounded tax, added to the tickets of people breaking the law while doing something stupid or life-threatening to themselves, congratulations on living in a crime-infested shithole of a place. Email your senator about it.

But I didn't jump at the chance to perform a flying kick off the couch and at the semi-transparent man in front of me. This is because, even though I totally picture myself being the hero of my life on a day-to-day basis, there was no way in hell I could suppress the girly shriek that escaped my throat after taking in the current situation. I also could neither stop myself from leaping over the couch like a crazed lunatic, nor could I stop my feet from turning me around and sprinting, eyes closed, toward the bathroom door. I slammed headfirst into the door frame and spun, remarkably, into the bathroom. With some strange extrasensory reflex, I kicked the door closed during my tumble in. I wasted no time jumping at the door knob and twisting the tiny metal lock. I sighed heavily, thankful that I had escaped. Then, a ghastly forehead poked in through the door. Then, the rest of the head came into view. The ghost man looked at me slowly and pushed the rest of his body into my bathroom.

Cornered and trapped, visualizing scenarios of ways I could escape, I realized I had backed my way into a room I had previously thought about escaping from. Showering in an empty house over a span of years leaves a lot of work to the mind; namely, I had come to the realization that if I had ever been the victim of a burglary, the bathroom would be the worst place to run to. And here I was, facing something completely unaccounted for in those scenarios. All my thoughts pointed to thieves and murderers, not the supernatural. I was wholly unprepared to fight and the ghost took small steps forward. *Careful, Luke, he's got rape in his eyes!*

"Fuck you!!" I'll admit, I don't know why I was shouting at a ghost, but the episode of ghost rape was still fresh in my mind. And I wanted to delay that possibility as long as I lived.

I backed up quickly into the bathtub itself, clawing at the decorative window that sat at about waist-high. I say decorative because, in all my time living here, I have found no way to open it. I was still convinced this was a penis window, from which I was expected to shake my naked body in front of, for the neighbors. Why else had they built it at such a height? For a family of small children? *Or for one lonely pervert?* But more importantly…

"Why the fuck won't you open?!" I shouted at the piece of glass that neither felt nor gave a shit for my predicament.

I spun around to face the ghost and raised my fists in a pathetic show of force. When he continued to walk closer, with a faceless expression, I dropped to my knees, clasped my hands together and started groveling to the supernatural dickwad in my home. His face did not show any malice or anger or even a slight twinge of being upset. His steps merely carried him forward, speechless and unnerving, to the edge of the bathtub. When he was not one foot from me, the ghost stopped dead in his tracks.

He scared the shit out of me by speaking up. "Oh, um…I'm sorry. Are you…say, are you taking a bath, or something? Because I don't mean to interrupt, I'm going to go wait outside in your living room." He began drifting towards the bathroom door again.

"The FUCK you are! Get the fuck out of my house you transparent fuck from fuck nowhere. Fuckin' out of here, dick waddle!"

In retrospect, never shout at a ghost that just told you he was leaving. I am almost positive that is grounds for a supernatural whatever to come back and ass-rape you repeatedly. At least, on TV, it's the way it goes. The show I watch, at any rate.

After some time spent pathetically clutching at the shower curtain and trying the window again, I decided to regain my composure. I filled the sink up with water and then splashed some on my face. I briefly considered drowning myself in five inches of water, but kept coming up for air with nothing but a soaked head for my troubles. I grabbed a towel off the rack and dried myself off.

Carefully, I made my way through the bathroom door, checking the corners of the hallway for any sign of my new guest. The coast was clear, so I tiptoed my way through until I reached the living room again. It was there that I saw him. The ghost was sitting on my couch, watching the static TV image that displayed my instant download queue of bizarre B-movies and strange television shows. I didn't see the remote in his hand, so I assumed he was confused about what he was looking at. *Maybe he's trying to crawl back into that episode I just watched.*

I crept up slowly to his back and coughed. He didn't seem to notice.

"Um, excuse me?" I said to him.

He looked up and behind him to answer me, "Yes?"

"What are you doing here?"

"Just sitting."

"No, I mean in my house," I was starting to feel sweat build in my forehead. I didn't know whether or not I could convince him to leave. My experience with the supernatural amounted to a working knowledge of how to die in horror movies, how to run away and fall in horror movies, and how to survive the ending of a slasher flick. Unfortunately, that last point required me to change genders; only the women ever really survived. But thankfully, it looked as if I currently found myself in a real-life recreation of *Ghost* rather than *The Frighteners*.

"Oh."

"Oh?"

"Oh, I…seem to like it here."

"You like it here? How long have you been here that you can say that?"

"Hmm," he drifted off into thought. I considered asking again, but I decided not to agitate him. I watched him sit there, near motionless, on my couch where I had fallen asleep. The idea that he was sitting there all night in the same spot, inside me so to speak, made me shudder and mentally swat the idea away like a fly buzzing around my consciousness.

Some time had passed, and the ghost still sat there. I coughed. Then I coughed again. I moved from my position at the back of the couch to directly in front of him and looked into his face. He didn't seem harmful; if he had wanted to scare or hurt me, he wouldn't be staring off into space.

"Hey Ghost-Man," I said, "how long have you been in my house?"

"I don't remember," he said.

I rubbed my palms into my eyelids. A quick glance at the TV told me that it was already eight in the morning. I rubbed my eyelids again. I had slept for most of the night, but I felt like crap, a result of being startled awake. I knew that I needed to rush over to the shop if I wanted to open on time. I glanced again at the ghost sitting on my couch. *What's with this guy?* There was a pressing need to get rid of him, but I didn't have the time.

"So, I need to go work and I need you to get out of my house," I stopped and assessed my situation, "please?" No answer from him.

"You can't stay here all day," I explained, but decided to clarify, "with all my stuff." I stopped to think about what I had just implied. *What was he going to do with all junk you have lying around? Can he even pick things up?* He still wasn't answering.

"Alright, alright. You don't remember how long you've been here. What about something small, like your name?"

He broke the silence with, "My name?"

"You can't remember that either?!" I was almost shouting. Considering that I was face-to-face with something most people would consider to be impossible, I was surprisingly sane. Or maybe I was desensitized from all the 21st century media I consumed on a daily basis.

"No, I do remember it. I'm Michael."

"Michael. Nice to meet you, please don't touch my stuff or eat my food," I said, "or drip ectoplasm everywhere. I'll be back later and we can talk about this more."

My feet graced the sidewalk near the comic shop at around nine thirty. The store was scheduled to open at ten and yet there were a couple of people standing around already, waiting to get inside. *Don't any of you have jobs?* Before the security gate was even all the way up, one guy tried to weasel his way in through the front. I managed to slip into a small crack I made before I slammed the door shut again. His knee hit the glass panel on the door, causing him to swear under his breath. I held out five fingers and mouthed out the words "five minutes" and headed to the back of the store. Ten minutes later, I had the register running and some new comics laid out in the "New Arrival" standee by the register.

I unlocked the front door and let in the first of them, the man who had banged his knee.

He said, "Five minutes, my ass."

"Just get in," I replied.

The day rolled on without much incident, unless you consider the constant stares I was getting from random window shoppers. Throughout the day, I was pouring over a bunch of horror comics in search of some sort of answer to my ghost troubles. I was flipping through anything remotely close to having "ghost" or "haunting" in the title. When I had run through my stock, I decided to flip open my phone and browse the Internet for a solution. The customer in front of the register looked annoyed, though, so I put it down.

"Are you going to be on your phone all day, or are you going to ring me up?"

"I was going to ring you up when I found a solution to my…rodent…problem," I stammered.

"You're rude."

"You're…not particularly attractive."

She had her mouth agape at my insult, "You are an asshole!"

"And you're annoying, please go away."

She slammed down the comic, which she had been holding, down onto the rack of New Arrivals. On impact, the standee shook and four or five comics tumbled out. She continued to stomp her way through the store until she reached the front door, turned around to flip me off, and then slammed it shut. The front shop windows shook. *Very mature for your age, lady.*

I sighed. I sighed long and hard. Over the years, I came to the conclusion that most people I met through the comic shop were not worth stressing over. I saw them once in a while if they lived nearby, weekly if they were kids from the town and once in my lifetime if I was enough of a pain in their ass that they would vow never to return. Plus, when you own the place, you really do have a better say over exactly how far you can go when dealing with the rudest, most unappreciative shoppers in America. When I started working the shop with my uncle, he drew the line in customer service for me. When I took over, I covered up that line with a giant plaque above the wall behind the register that read: "Don't be a dick."

Groups of kids shuffled in with the regulars, knocking over comics, mixing them up in other sections, leaving them on the signage around the store, and so on and so forth. I quietly prayed behind the counter for a legal precedent to kick a child out of a privately owned store. They continued their rampage, and I sat behind the counter with a nervous twitch in my eye, a single violent impulse for every single act of vandalism. When they had gone, I realized the day was dragging forward at a snail's pace; I contemplated closing the store for the day. The need to keep the place running with a nice, cool influx of cash changed that idea, however.

That was how it was in my life. There was always a pressing need for money that kept me coming back to the shop, day in and day out. The days dragged, but gave me a lot of time to think, in a philosophical way. I could say that I practically created my personal beliefs and formed my opinions under the glare of the florescent lights above the counter. One thing you notice when you work in any sort of retail chain, any type of store involving customer-cashier relations, is you start to see a horrible truth in people. Namely, that each and every one of them thinks they are the sole owners of some common thought, that they are unique in their way of thinking. Around the first year of my employ, I always had this exchange with at least two customers on a weekly basis:

"Hello, how are you today, sir?"

"Comics cost too much! How can they charge four dollars for something I can finish while taking a dump?"

"Well, sir, the amount of effort in drawing and writing contributed by the artists and writers dictates the price."

"Because it's so hard to make a comic book." *This was usually followed by a lengthy eye roll to annoy me.*

"That's not how the industry works. People need to make a living."

That's how every conversation went. Like not one person was able to open up a web browser some day of their boring lives and do some research into pricing. I felt bad, knowing that they came to the conclusion on their own and thought that they owned it completely. I made the mistake of thinking that customers would change or would realize that people in the same environment think similarly. The only change I ever saw to that conversation was slight differences in wording. Never a civil conversation about the current industry pricing, just arguments because people love to complain. Over time, I managed to increase the speed of each transaction:

"Comics cost too much! Do you think I'm going to pay this price?"

"I jack up the prices when I see you come in because I want to screw you over and pocket as much money as I can from you without you noticing."

It's a win-win situation. I save a breath or two, and they never come back to complain. Or at all.

By three o'clock, I had gone out to eat at a local diner and come back to mull over the ghost problem I was having. Lunch had soured my mood further than before; a new waiter had the pleasure of taking my order, which he incorrectly wrote down. Instead of getting a Monte Cristo sandwich with a side of fries, he brought out a plate of mozzarella sticks and a grilled cheese. I feigned sincerity, then promptly left the smallest tip that my good nature would allow. *Maybe shouldn't have tipped at all, but there's that overbearing public guilt that comes with not tipping.*

While fixing up the clutter and mess left around the store, I happened upon one indie comic I hadn't read before. The cover of the book read "Late Night Haunts: The Insect King." The interior read like a cheap sci-fi movie, one that came on in the middle of the day for stoners, old people, and the unemployed. According to the comic, the Insect King ruled over the Planet Nylos, subjecting all the human slaves to cultivate the land and care for the Great Hive (his throne or castle or something).

About the same time as the last page flipped through my hands, Robin walked through the front door and greeted me at the counter.

"Hey, Luke."

"What's up?" I replied.

"Are you alright? You don't look so good, and the store is a mess."

"I'm fine. Some kids were in here earlier."

"And you've been ignoring that guy in the corner since I walked in, maybe before that," Robin said.

I peeked out of the corner of my eye to my left. I witnessed a grown man snap his fingers in my general direction, lips curled downward in a needlessly menacing frown. I continued to watch him, one hand snapping and the other holding a graphic novel, until he eventually gave up and slammed the book back down. He stomped out of the store, each heavy boot shaking a few of the cheaper (read: cardboard and Styrofoam) standees. *God, what a wonderful assortment of adults I get in here.*

"I'm not worried about that guy," I piped up, after the man's exodus.

"See? You didn't even bother coming up with an insult," Robin complained.

"So?"

"So," he chirped.

"So I'm missing your point here, Robin."

"Simple. Something's bothering you. I can tell, I've been coming in here for how long? Come on, tell me what the problem is."

"I've a-I've got a bug problem at my house. Yeah, that's it," I said, stuttering.

"A bug problem?"

"Got an issue with that?"

34

"Yeah," he began, "Not half a year ago, a fly made its way into the store, planting itself around the register. Right here."

"Yeah, so?"

"Do you remember swinging the newspaper you had, like a morning star over your head? The times you missed and knocked over papers? Swinging around the register in front of startled customers?"

"I mean, yeah. That would be kind of hard to forget. But I-," I started to say.

"The customer you accidentally hit in the face, when you spun around and swatted through the air with your fly swatter?"

"Vaguely."

"The old lady who nearly passed out when you leapt the counter to throw your stapler against the wall to kill it?"

"Seems unlikely."

"The absolute hell I gave you for weeks after that?"

"Get to your point, Robin."

"My point," Robin stated, "is that you have either an intense fear of insects, or you hate the bastards. I doubt you'd be in this store right now if your house was infested. You would have closed shop and dedicated a week to house cleaning."

"You exaggerate…but I guess you have a point," I replied.

"Aha! So what's really going on?"

Do you really want me to tell you, Robin? Are you prepared to deal with the supernatural? With the unbelievable?

"I've got ghosts."

Robin ventured to the side of the register. With both hands, he grabbed one of the few folding chairs I had beside the counter. He flipped the seat open, and then sat completely wrong on it. And by that, I mean he sat on it facing backwards.

"Tell me more."

35

I hesitated for a minute. I didn't know whether Michael the Houseguest was a danger to myself or my things. If I told Robin about him, he might want to take a trip over to the Thornton residence to see for himself. *Screw that, just tell the kid.*

"Well, it's just the one ghost, actually. He came out of nowhere the other night, and just took up housing on my living room couch."

"Has he tried anything?"

"What? Tried wha–No, not a thing."

"Is he haunting the place? Rattling window panes, slamming the toilet seat, that sort of thing?"

"Well, no," I lied, last night's scare fest replaying in my mind, on loop. *I really did scream like a girl, didn't I? Definitely not a dream, or things may have played out a bit more heroically.*

"No?"

"He kind of just…sits," I said, "on my couch. Stares off into nothing for hours."

Robin got up, took a few steps forward and planted a sweaty palm atop my forehead. I recoiled from it.

"Well you're not running a fever," he said.

"Are you two finished yet?" questioned a voice from behind Robin. He pivoted on his foot to face the man behind him. He wasn't anyone special, just looking to check out some of his selection for the past ten minutes. I had spotted him coming up to the register around the same time Robin had walked into the shop and after the previous customer stormed out. This guy was perusing the back aisles for the past hour, crouched down to see our collection of "Low Price-Low Quality" titles. I didn't bother telling Robin to move out of the way; the man wasn't a regular, so losing his business wasn't too much of a concern. That, and I could see from the front covers that he picked some of the lowest of the low priced comics.

"Who's your manager?" he continued.

"I am my own manager," I replied, "I own the place."

"That explains why it's such a hell hole."

"Thanks for the compliment. Can I ring you up now?"

"No, not yet. I still have a few more choice words about your mother." I saw Robin escape from the corner of my eye over to the bookshelves. He scanned the pages of a few volumes before pulling one out and scanning the contents.

"…And furthermore, I sincerely hope that you lose this business and learn a lesson or two about respect for the world," said the man, finally having finished his speeding train of insults.

"That'll be seven fifty," I told him.

I closed up shop early, around 7 pm, to the loud protests of some kids who had wandered in. Some of them threw a tantrum, so I threw them out onto the sidewalk.

"You can't do that!" yelled one of his friends.

"I'm sorry. Our operating hours are ten to seven. Please stop by tomorrow if you wish to continue shopping," I said, in a proper and polite way.

"Your sign says you close at nine, asshole!"

After getting the store re-organized and counting the profits for the day, I closed out the registers, sealed up the safe, and drew the gate down. I shoved the store key into the front door, and then made my way across the street towards the town center. I had planned to walk around the area before I made my way back to the house. Beside me, most of the shops were getting ready to end the night. A couple of the owners saw me and waved; others looked on and hoped I wouldn't go in. A few of the latter used to be customers when my uncle ran the place, but they decided they didn't enjoy the company of the new management.

Time to go home, grab a beer, and pass out until tomorrow. The thought of returning home ran a shiver down my spine. What was Michael doing all day while I was at work? I spent most of my time looking through comics and through my phone for some kind of exorcism and came away with nothing that I was willing to try.

Sometimes, you get the feeling that you shouldn't be home. I remember this guy at a bar had maybe a little too much drink in him, and he began telling me about the feeling that he would get coming home late at night. A feeling like maybe he should turn around and just drive off to someplace else or head over to the bar for an after-work beer or park his car somewhere quiet and just sit there waiting for something. He didn't listen to the instinct, to the nagging feeling clawing at his brain.

He said, "It's a feeling of repetition, I said to myself. I'm waking up every day to go get coffee, to go to work, to come home later, jack off and then sleep. Every single day, with a little change here and there. But mostly the same coffee, the same work, the same home. One time, I tried to force myself to buy a different coffee. One of those fancy latte shits, the ones that they load with sugar and cream and give out to all the teen girls. But the feeling was still there when I stepped through those glass doors and sat down in my cubicle. The same fucking feeling, y'know?"

I said I did know. I told him I owned a store and I was trapped into opening it, day in and day out. It was a life of being trapped in monotony.

"Yeah, you'll think that feeling is a feeling of repetition. I told myself that, y'know? Oh you do know? I told ya? Well that wasn't the feeling. I tell you, there are things that we just know. That nobody tells us, but we can feel somewhere deep. Something amiss or something going on. Well, I tell ya that feeling is fuck-ing supernatural, some kind of human ability that we all forgot when we started building houses and making laws. Early cave man powers that we didn't use much anymore but show up sometimes on instinct. I came home early one day, trying to break that nag-ging feeling, and my wife is banging the valedictorian of the high school she teaches at. Sure, the kid helped my wife with school events, and she tutored him on the weekend. But I never knew he was dicking her. The little fuck…"

I had given some form of condolence to that guy at the bar, buying him a shot of some strong stuff and moving myself to another seat. In the present, I sighed. I had stopped walking because I noticed that the sun had gone down. I took a look around and found that I was standing at the corner of a Franklin and Lincoln Street. *Very patriotic*. The only place of interest here was the Express Station corner store. It was owned by a Mrs. Hill. She was a pleasant enough lady; she didn't have any relatives in town that anyone knew, and her house was on the border of our town and the next one over.

I took a swinging detour from my walk, went toward the Express Station and slipped through the sliding doors. The place was bright, brighter than the darkened street that I had come in from. Right at the entrance, a sign greeted all customers with a big, cardboard smile of Mrs. Hill and some text that read:

> "Welcome to the Express Station! We have all
> your mini-mart needs at a lower price than any
> other mini-mart in the area! Be sure to grab a
> coupon book from Mama!"

A stack of coupon books were resting on top of a rather lopsided cardboard hand, which curved outward from the life-sized Mama Hill standee. Someone had attempted to half-draw a moustache on the cut-out, and I could see that Mama Hill had tried to remove the ink with a wet paper towel. It was smudged and looked sort of like an old-fashioned greasepaint moustache. I grabbed a book, just in case, and flipped through it casually. From behind the counter, a voice called out to me.

"Hi, Luke!" said Mrs. Hill.

"Hello, Mama," I replied.

Mrs. Hill had gotten a bit of a reputation as a "mother-away-from-home" running a store for all the "kids." The name "Mama Hill" became a moniker of hers. The thing about Express Station that separated it from a Tiger Mart or a 7-Eleven was the homeliness of the store. Mrs. Hill tried her best to remodel the place into a sort of expanded kitchen that you'd expect to see in a typical, 1950's nuclear home. When you entered the place, on your left was the standard metal racks and shelving, with name brand candy, chips, sodas, and whatever else stacked neatly in rows. But to the right, near the register, you could find a coffee machine with condiments, a full spread of baked goods (fresh every morning), and a row of plastic-wrapped sandwiches.

I walked over to the metal shelving and looked for any deals on chocolate bars. *Hey, now. Buy two, get one free!* I grabbed two of the bars from the box, and then wandered over to the baked goods. Mama had baked up some bagels with cream cheese, so I snagged one from the table. Completing my circle back to the front door, I ducked my head into the sandwich display, picking out a turkey club. As I reached the register, I placed down all the items onto the counter.

"How ya doin'?" Mama said.

"I'm alright."

"You look worried, baby. Something the matter?"

"Just working too hard, I guess."

"You should take a vacation," she offered. Then she reached behind her and handed me a pamphlet. "I'm taking a cruise in a month to the Caribbean! Me and some of my girls are gonna enjoy ourselves."

"I get seasick," I remarked, "but thanks for the offer."

"Not a problem, hon. Twelve fifty, please."

I dove into my pocket and extracted my wallet, dropping a penny to the ground. I ignored it. Inside, I didn't find any cash, so I handed her my debit card. One swipe, a printed receipt, and a goodbye, then I was out the door. I feel it is as good a time as any to mention that I lived off of other people's cooking, be that at a diner, at a restaurant, at Mama's, or just a fast food joint outside of town. I didn't take much time to learn how to cook, even though it had been sometime since my parents decidedly took off on a grand adventure to somewhere. My body moved more like gelatin than I would probably have preferred, but I wasn't obese or over-weight in any sense of the word. If anything, popping my body open would reveal all the garbage and microwave dinners that were floating around my system. I quietly wondered how clogged my arteries may have gotten over the years.

Sometime later, I worked up the courage to open the front door to the house. Michael wasn't sitting in his spot on the couch, so I dipped into the kitchen. He wasn't there either. I put one of the candy bars in one of the holders on the door of the fridge, then cracked open the other. I jammed it into my mouth, and then stood contemplating whether I was going to eat the bagel for dinner and the sandwich for tomorrow's breakfast, or vice versa. That's when I heard it. At first, the sound seemingly came from out the window above the sink. It was a fluttering noise, like the beating of wings. My second thought was a fly was buzzing around my ear, so I swatted at air around my left ear. I moved away

41

from where I was standing, getting an overall view of the kitchen, but I found that there was nothing buzzing around. I turned back to face the living room, creeping slowly out of the kitchen, when I realized the sound was coming from my bedroom.

I took a gulp, and then bit off another piece of the chocolate bar. Step by step, my legs inched me closer to the bedroom door, which was slightly ajar, but only betrayed how dark the room was in the night. I couldn't make any details out from the crack in the doorway. Carefully, I raised my hand to the door and pushed it open. The buzzing was louder now. My hand met the light switch on the wall, pulling upwards and bathing the room in warm light.

Hovering above my bed stand was a yellow and black bee, about the size of a watermelon. Rather than a set of eyes, the bee's sockets were lined with jagged teeth that clenched and opened in a strange replication of eyelids. At first, I thought that maybe Mama Hill had put something in the chocolate and I was having that sort of hallucination that one gets from the combination of sleep deprivation, stress, a sense of paranoia, and rotten chocolate. Then I remembered that a day ago, a ghost decided to make my humble abode a bed and breakfast. The supernatural things in my life had quickly gone from television and comics to a tangible, floating insect, with a not so friendly face.

Without making a sudden movement, I inched slowly into the bedroom, sliding my socks across the carpet. *Slowly, don't startle it and maybe you can open a window or something.* I looked over to the lone window, and then put on a look of doubt. *Yeah, open a window and have to push the gigantic thing out with my bare hands.* My body shivered at the thought of touching small hairs on the bee's body. Something caught the bee's attention, as if it could see me shuffling my way into the room. My fears were confirmed when it turned its body completely toward me and emitted a screeching sound unlike anything I had ever heard before.

In an instant, the bottom half of the insect curled upward and a sharp dagger-like protrusion reached out from inside it. I winced at the thought of the stinger entering any part of me. And just as quickly as the thought entered my mind, the bee rushed stinger first at my head. I instinctually jumped a half step to the right and slapped with the back of my left hand toward the charging creature. My hand connected, sending it flying against the wall behind the TV set in a loud clatter. The insect rose once again, dazed, yet still aiming its stinger toward me. It attempted another charge, missing me by an inch or two and imbedding itself into the closet door.

I stood in shock at my blind luck, and I watched the thing desperately struggle to pull itself out. I jumped toward it, gripping it around the thorax, which I noticed felt strangely prickly to a disgusting level. With my arms surrounding it, I pulled the thing out of the closet door and started to stumble backward. The back of my right foot hit the metal frame of my bed, loosening my grip on the creature. It stumbled, attempting to regain some semblance of flight, which it was able to faster than I was able to stand. With swiftness, the bee lunged at me again, but I was able to catch it around the thorax once more. Both of my hands were gripping the sides of the thing, with its stinger in the direct middle of both of us, thrashing and waving in an attempt to stab me in the chest.

About the time I felt my grip loosen on the thing, a hand axe flew into my bedroom from the living room, through the open door, where it impaled the bee on the left side. The force pushed the bee out of my hands, with the stinger scraping the inner forearm of my left arm. I covered up the wound with my right hand, letting out a low hiss of pain. The bee dropped dead onto the floor, spilling a sickly green-blue ooze of blood onto my fresh carpet. I looked over to the doorway to see who my hero was, only for my jaw to fall completely. I was nearly convinced that it had detached itself from my face.

Standing at the doorway to my bedroom was Robin, in all sense of the name, sporting a yellow cape, a red tunic, an emblem stitched onto the tunic of the letter R in a black circle, and a pair of Robin Hood-esque green tights. The image was completed with a domino mask straight out of Carnival. For a moment, my brain decided to shut down completely, less I found myself howling through the night in a frenzy of madness. *What the hell did Mrs. Hill do to my chocolate?*

"Are you alright?" Robin finally said.

"Oh, good. So you are really here. So I am crazy," I answered.

"I just saved your life! Probably…" he drifted off, staring at the blood soaked bumblebee on the floor.

"Let me be the one to say, I'm glad you decided to forgo the short shorts in favor of pants," I decided was the appropriate comment.

"Shut up. You're lucky I was even here."

"Why were you here?"

"I realized at the comic shop that you were in trouble. The look on your face worried me. I haven't seen you look that serious in a long time. So I ran home and got together my outfit," he said with an embarrassing look, "and ran back to the comic shop at closing time. I saw that you had already closed for the day, so I went looking around your usual spots."

I said nothing.

"When I noticed how late it was getting, I figured you went back home to face the ghost in your living room. I looked into the living room window and saw you slowly pushing the bedroom door open. You look scared."

I still said nothing. I was staring at the bee on my floor, kicking it a bit with my foot to see if it was still breathing. It didn't even squirm. To my annoyance, it dawned on me how much of a pain in the ass it would be get insect blood out of the carpeting.

"So I ran out to your shed, sorry, and grabbed your hand axe. I heard noises coming from the house when I left the shed. The front door was locked, so I tried the back door and here we are."

I was staring angrily at the insect on the floor. The blood had seeped under the bed frame, staining the carpet heavily. I turned to face Robin.

"Get the bleach from under my sink, a plastic bag, the spray bottle and the entire roll of paper towels. It's starting to set in."

CHAPTER THREE
An Unpleasant Introduction

"So, does Burt Ward know you raided his wardrobe?" I said.

"Who's Burt Ward?" Robin asked me.

I just shook my head and muttered, "Damn kids today." The bee's blood was deeply soaked into the carpet, so much so that all my scrubbing would probably result in a missing chunk underneath my mattress. I gave up. My lip curled as I stood, staring down the deep, dark stain. Robin just stood around awkwardly, holding a roll of paper towels and a tiny spray bottle that read "SuperGone," in my handwriting, in black marker.

He was still wearing the Robin outfit, which he explained away as not bringing a change of clothes. You know, in case I didn't feel comfortable having a teenager dressed as a superhero in my bedroom. Robin ducked out shortly after we had rolled the bee into a bed sheet, which he chucked into the lake outside. After realizing my futile attempts at cleaning and temporarily considering scrubbing my skull, I told Robin to go home. He complained and argued to stay for the night, to keep watch.

"What about your ghost problem? Had I known at the comic shop it was a bee infestation, well, I–"

"I still have the ghost problem. I just haven't seen him anywhere tonight. Maybe he went for a walk or something," I replied.

"Why would a ghost need to go for a walk?" Robin questioned.

"Maybe he wanted to get a view of the lake," I theorized.

"Couldn't he just stick a head out of your wall?"

"He could, I guess."

"What if he's upstairs?"

I looked to the door next to my bedroom that led to a short staircase. I hadn't gone upstairs since my parents left; the only rooms on the second floor of our home were their bedrooms and a bathroom. There was no need to be up there. Nothing to see but loose scatterings of things they left behind and painful reminders of a couple of losers who abandoned their only son. I shook my head at that staircase, and then remembered I once drunkenly promised myself I'd board up the doorway to it. *Time flies, you forget to do things.*

"If he's up there, he can have that half of the house."

"C'mon, Luke. You need someone to keep watch. We can grab some tools and-and force him out of here."

"Robin, go home. I'm fine."

"What if you need my help?"

"If I'm in need of help, I'll call the police. Or Green Lantern."

I closed the door on Robin, closing my sight of the sour expression on his face. I was grateful on the inside about his rescue, but that level of gratitude didn't rise high enough in my throat for me to utter out a thank you. I just wasn't that kind of person, or that nice of a person. I didn't approach a stranger and speak to them with kindness in my voice; I was the kind of guy who took a serious discussion and tried to make a joke out of it. Outward, I tried to blame this solely on Jean; he was the smartass, having a comment for every little thing, a snide remark for a simple conversation. But inward, I felt that I had just become jaded over the years from my own lifestyle.

My attention returned to my house, to the place of security that had, in the recent week, become a place I was afraid to live in. Two uninvited guests had broken in, and one of them had just tried to kill me not a few moments before. My plan of action directly after closing the door involved grabbing my coat, turning on my car, and driving to the other side of the continental United States, abandoning my home to a ghost. *No one will find you out there. You can start fresh and have another comic shop.* I considered, for a second, that I was crazy for suggesting to myself that I could remain in retail comfortably. This fact left a disgusting taste in my mouth.

I returned to the bedroom doorway, afraid to enter a place that I normally would have spent an entire day in if I didn't have obligations. The blood-stained carpet was still an eyesore; I had just dropped the paper towels and the SuperGone. With a frown, I slowly closed the bedroom door, flipping down the light switch as the door made its way closed. My back was up against the door, and I searched for answers in my ceiling. After a minute of receiving nothing in the form of an answer to a prayer, I leapt over the backside of the couch, landing with a rough thud into my familiar position in front of the TV set. As if to continue my discomfort, I had landed atop the electric, novelty buzzer that had found its way back between the cushions.

Leaping into the air, I looked back at the couch, angry and stressed; I tore off the couch cushion, revealing the buzzer that had knocked me away from my own thoughts. With contempt in my eyes, I grabbed hold of the damned thing, chucking it against the wall. It didn't so much as break as it did clatter, detonating another discharge of low-level electricity as it fell to the floor. Sitting upon the couch once more, a glance at the table next to me revealed an unopened bottle of beer, one that I must have left untouched from the previous night of drinking. I popped the top open, downing a large gulp of stupid juice into my mouth. If I was going to get any sleep, I needed to pass out from alcohol. After getting up for a few more beers, I did just that.

I had heard this story once of a guy in Arizona who died in a tornado. Dude was sitting on a toilet, giving it his all, when it came through his neighborhood. Most sensible folks would pucker up and sprint as fast as they could, shit trailing behind them or building up in their trousers. Not this guy. Not him. This was a battle of his bowels that, goddammit, he was gonna win. A local news crew was nearby, looking for career-changing reporting, when this dude's trailer lifts off the ground. At this point, the tornado was right on top of it, spinning and turning the thing slowly upwards. The entire time this guy is fighting the urge to look out the window and see the clusterfuck of fuckdom he was engulfed in. So, the trailer eventually begins pulling apart from the force of the winds, into pieces. Like a computer simulation that, I'd imagine, some dropout architect would make to get hired by whomever the hell made a career out of trailer design.

On the ground, the news crew sees the thing break apart and, lo and behold, the guy on the toilet comes into view and he's straining with all his might. Because Mother Nature about to fling you miles on a porcelain toilet wasn't enough for his bowels to evacuate and call it a day. The news crew gets one good look at the guy, and they all break out into laughter. He's about to be eviscerated by the very power of God and they're standing there, clutching their sides. All because, rather than the absolute hell breaking loose around them, the reporters can only see the most embarrassing moment of this guy's life.

I relate this story to you because at two in the morning, after my late night meet-and-scream, I was sitting with my pants around my ankles, pushing out a rather uncomfortable dump. From a nearby rack, I had grabbed a porno mag to read. You may call that needlessly placed fluff exposition, but I call it setting a mood. I was going over a poorly edited blurb about the rising stars of the smut scene when I saw hair, then a rather broad forehead, then a set of transparent eyes peek over my nudie mag, scanning the page like a curious toddler.

"Luke…" Michael said to me. "What are you up to?"

In the span of a second, I envied the guy in the twister for having such a normal moment of shame, and then cursed him repeatedly because of it. I screamed shortly after that thought. On instinct, *or stupidity,* I rolled up the porno mag and began swatting at his head like I was trying to overkill a fly who dared to land in my presence. The magazine went right through his cranium like he was a hologram floating through my bathroom floor. The girl on the cover seemed to be enjoying it. A look of worry and confusion appeared on Michael's face; it was the first time I would ever see my unwanted roommate display any emotion other than the blank stares I'd grow to hate.

He said, "I'm going outside now."

"You do that!" I yelled at his now disappearing form, leaving through the bathroom door. *Jesus, I yell just like my dad used to.* For a few minutes, I considered opening up the magazine to continue reading, but instead I threw it aside. It landed with a thud at the edge of the garbage pail, toppling it over. A collection of used tissues and toilet paper sheets spilled out. I concluded my business, got up, buckled my belt, washed my hands, and headed into the living room. Michael was sitting upright on my sofa, staring at the black screen of my TV set, or the wall directly behind it, or through the house at the lake behind my house. Fuck if I know what ghosts see, and I wasn't about to ask him.

"Luke." At my entrance, he turned to face me. Like I was the director saying "action" and he was beginning his take.

"Yeah, what happened in there…I'm gonna need you to forget," I said, gesturing at the bathroom. I'm almost positive my cheeks went red at the thought of the entire town greeting me in the street with giggles, the kids at the comic shop snickering behind their *Aquaman* #500, and the countless retellings of the event that eventually evolve the story from how I was caught in the bathroom taking a dump while reading porn articles to how I was caught in the bathroom beating off. *You'd be run out of town or have to hide in the house all day to escape the ridicule.* I was getting too old to be worrying if I looked cool to the people in town, but I guess that feeling follows you into adulthood.

"Okay," he responded.

"Absolutely no one."

"I understand." I wondered if he was being sarcastic with me, knowing full well no one else could see or hear him.

"And you need to leave." I figured if he was agreeing to demands, maybe I could squeeze another one out. Instead, Michael the Rather-Annoying Ghost turned back to face the wall again. I felt my jaw unhinge in disbelief, and I had to put effort into not looking down to see if I had dropped it to the floor for the second time. This was one stubborn ghost. He sat there motionless and I was already bored at making angry faces at him, hoping he would turn around to see them and feel sympathy. Or just realize he was trespassing. *Can a ghost trespass? Maybe he never lived here. But then… how and why did he show up in my house?*

It was no use, though. I never heard of anyone who convinced a ghost to leave by asking it. Any interaction with a ghost seemed to end with no survivors and a quick cut to the credits in the movies. I decided to call an exorcist in the afternoon. Right then, I needed to get back to sleep. My head was spinning (the start of a terrible hangover) and he seemed harmless enough that I trusted I could fall asleep.

I went to work without incident. I took my lunch at the appropriate time, closing the store and sitting on a chair by the counter, not forgetting I had to re-open eventually. By the time I closed for the night, life seemed to have changed back to "mundane" as a daily setting. It was late again when I unlocked the front door to the house and threw my coat down near the door mat inside. I looked through the dark hoping to catch a glimpse of Michael in the living room, but saw nothing remotely like him. I turned to my left and flipped up the light switch, illuminating the area in a bath of light. My stomach growled. I had spent the whole day in the shop, snacking on the bagel I had bought from Mama's as my lunch. A small sigh escaped my mouth.

When I had reached the kitchen, I headed straight for the refrigerator. The contents were as followed:

> Half an inch of milk left in a carton
> A bottle of local brand soda, empty
> One slice of cheese in its wrapper
> Yogurt, expired a week ago
> One packet of Instant Ramen noodles
> The turkey club from Mama's

I picked up the instant ramen noodles, forcefully pulling open the wrapping so hard that the "Secret Thai Seasoning" packet flew across the kitchen and landed in the sink. I walked over, pulling up the now-soaked seasoning, and then tossed it back on the counter near the microwave. I filled the noodle bowl with a half-filled bottle of room temperature water nearby, and then threw the bowl into the microwave. The noodles sloshed in their container, spilling some water around the microwave interior. I sighed again, and then hit "Preset Four" on the microwave.

I took a few steps back and planted myself in a seat by the wall. The low hum of the microwave cut through the house. Besides the microwave, I could hear the additional hum of the overfilled power strip in the living room. My hands went up to rub my eyes. I still don't know if I had somehow tapped into some innate instinct, lying dormant since the early days of man like that guy at the bar once said, or if I just hadn't been fucking paying attention. *How long had that noise been there?* It wasn't the microwave, and it wasn't the hum of the fire hazard in the living room that was my power strip, filled to the brim with electronics. *How long had I heard the chewing?*

I didn't stop to ask myself any more questions upon the discovery of the chewing sound. I leapt out of the chair, my foot catching on the chair leg that I wrapped my foot around. It toppled over to the ground, clattering to the floor and taking a nearby charger out of the wall socket. My next act of self-vandalism was to shoulder-tackle the kitchen door as I made my way into the back porch. I fell onto the floor, but managed to scramble myself up quickly. *Horror movie rules taught me that running and falling is a quick and painful death.* I'm a clumsy person, so I had much practice with pulling myself off the floor as fast as possible, lest someone point a finger in my direction and laugh at my misfortune.

Throwing open the screen door of the porch, I sprinted down the pathway that winded down the hill of my backyard. I heard the doorknob of the porch door crash into the siding, most likely imbedding a round hole into the exterior of my house. A few seconds later, though, a second crash followed. The door slamming back into its frame. I didn't dare look back to see if I was still being followed or to glimpse an image of what I was being followed by. I continued down the path and saw Michael sitting on a small tree stump in the grass, playfully plucking and rubbing his ghost fingers onto the pedals of a nearby daisy.

"Michael! There is something chasing me. Can you get rid of it?"

Michael the Unhelpful Ghost just sat there in a trance, as was the norm. His eyes were transfixed on the pedals. Seconds ticked by in my subconscious. Slowly and surely, a number of increasingly more brutal deaths conjured up in my mind. I stopped thinking to realize I had begun chewing down on my thumb, and I was already getting close to taking it off completely.

"Michael, get the fuck up from there and do something!"

Before he could react, I heard the same chewing from inside the house grow closer behind me. My body leapt forward three feet and took off in a run, leaving my thoughts behind. Eventually, I took myself off autopilot and dug a hand into my pocket. I fumbled behind my wallet to grip onto my car keys. Swinging around the grassy yard toward the front of the house, I found myself closer and closer to the driveway; closer to outrunning (and hopefully out-driving) another creature of the night. My hand finally clenched around the key ring, which I hoisted up and out of my pants. I ran about ten more feet before the leg of my pants caught underneath my shoe, throwing me forward into the gravel.

With the wind knocked out of me, I raised my torso up, just in time to see the keys had managed to slip from my palm and slid under the car door to pitch blackness. I scrambled in the dark to find them, scratching at the ground like an animal desperate to hide. The longer I took the more scenarios jumped into my head of the ghastly demon behind me. It wanted to either take me or kill me, *where are the keys?*, but I wouldn't let it. I felt metal and grasped hard, pulling back until I was scraping the side of my driver-side door with the top of my arm. I cursed. The key found its place, and I pulled on the handle, throwing myself into the driver's seat as hard as I could.

…And promptly overshot my trajectory. My lower ribs made contact with the upright parking brake, nearly shattering them. A surge of pain made its way up through my chest; my heart reaching its maximum pace. I sat back upright and jammed the car key into the ignition. Wasting no time, I peeled out of the driveway. I was driving recklessly down the darkened road. My tires screeched across the asphalt and bucked at every small pot hole I managed to steer into. I was looking back at my house, looking for the demon that would undoubtedly follow me.

I turned back to face the road and managed to catch a breath or two. *Nothing there, Luke.* I calmed myself, lowering my shoulders and loosening my grip on the already-peeling material that composed my steering wheel. There was no destination in my mind, no place for which I wanted refuge. I was driving far away from where I was before, and that was the end of the matter. All the reason I needed to not pull over and hang myself from any one of the trees I flew past.

Calm down, you're safe now. I told myself this over and over. The silence of the night began taking a toll on my psyche. I began slapping at the dashboard in a mad attempt to hit the power button on the radio. It finally worked; the radio buzzed on, bringing to life some heavy metal song that a late-night trucker had called in to request.

Suddenly, the car lurched forward, then to the right, then forward again. The radio began to wind down like an old-timey record. Nothing but static remained on the station, so loud that I began to feel nauseated. The steering wheel ripped itself from my grasp through its unpredictable flailing, and I found myself being driven by some invisible entity in complete possession of my car. The radio flipped channels again and White Zombie's "I, Zombie" filled the countryside. If you haven't heard it, about thirty seconds into the track a woman screams. As if on cue, my car began hitting the throttle so hard that I felt my head slam into the headrest behind me.

I was barreling down the road, slowly building more and more speed toward my phantom car's destination. The speedometer lurched forward to 75. Then it made its way up past the 90 mile per hour mark. Not three seconds later, the meter reached 120. Then, something so bizarre happened that, to this day, Jean still doesn't believe me. The needle grew in width to about three times its size, and then proceeded to break through the glass casing that housed it. With incredible precision, it reformed itself into what, I swear, resembled a human hand flipping me off.

It then began to point upwards with the index finger, so I followed its direction in time to watch the tree in the headlights grow close. Then, my head slammed into my steering wheel, and I was officially out for the count.

I opened my eyes and was not where I found myself minutes ago. I was lying on a bale of hay in some random barn I had never set foot in before. I took a look of my surroundings as I propped myself up in a sitting position. Wooden beams held up the second level, and roof, of the building. Hay bales littered the place in strange arrangements, some stacked three-high and others simply tossed into the barn without care. There were pens for animals, but they hadn't been used for what appeared to be decades. That didn't stop the common smell of a barnyard from wafting about the place, a stench one may commonly find at a petting zoo or at an actual fucking farm.

I eventually noticed it. Before me, five feet away at most, was a strange break in the air. I couldn't properly define it or comprehend its shape. It was like a break in our dimension. A rip in the air that just lingered and changed from a lighter shade of dark blue, to a dark black, and back again. The color was almost metallic, reflecting the hanging light in the barn when I shifted in my seat to look around it.

I sat in front of the ripple in space for some time. I felt a strange, compelling urge to leap inside, to take a look in the interior. I needed to breath and assess the situation. Not ten minutes ago, I was being chased out of my living room by another unholy piece of fuck. It could be standing on the other side of the rift, waiting for me to jump through to catch me. I began running scenarios in my head. Scenario one was walk into the portal, greet whatever unholy alien being I met on the other end, and talk this out like a gentleman. Scenario one was sort of wishful thinking. Scenario two was me entering the portal, which would lead directly back into my living room to be killed by what I escaped from in the first place. More wishful thinking. Scenario three was walk into portal, and get deeper into shit than I wanted to be. They were all looking equally terrible, but I didn't even know if any of this was real.

So, I rose up from my temporary seat and walked straight into the slit in space.

Do me a favor. Go grab a few friends and have them knock you out with whatever kind of chemicals they can find. Then, have them cover your ears, eyes, and nose, drive you off to the airport, fly off to a piece of shit neighborhood in a piece of shit third-world country, remove everything blocking your senses, and have them wake you up. That is the best way I can describe being where I found myself.

The blue portal had teleported me to, what I could only guess, was a completely different dimension from where planet Earth may be found. I was standing on nothing; the air below me continued down until a distant spattering of purple, blue, and pink melded together and slowly drifted in a direction behind me. It reminded me a hell of a lot of a colored picture of the Horseshoe Nebula. And it confused me just as much, I think.

Wait, I'm standing on air. As I stood on nothing, I looked up from the colored stream to see a man in a tuxedo, bow tie around his neck, standing in front of a small, white marble podium that held a very odd black leather book. *Who are you? Help me, I've been in some kind of accident.* He seemed to be on the same level as me, on some kind of invisible flooring beneath both our feet. I tested the waters by taking a step in front of me, and found that my foot landed on the pocket of air that my other foot remained on. *Must be flat. Flat and invisible.*

Where am I? I took another few steps forward and hit an edge of nothingness that propelled me headfirst into the podium. The only sound I made was a low grumble, a sound which may have echoed through the void around me. *What am I doing here?* The podium shook a little, and I looked up to see the strange man hold it in place.

"Mind your step," he said to me.

"You speak English?" I replied to him.

He said nothing to me. I suddenly felt my brow curl; I was here for a reason. *What was it? Why did I come here? Why did I think this was a good idea?* Somewhere in my head, I felt something pulling at me. *Wasn't I just in a car accident? Wait, no I was home, in my living room. Watching Tales from the Outer Darkside of the Twilight. Yes, that's it Luke. You must be dreaming.*

"I'm glad to have you here, Luke."

"No." *Why was I here? What just happened to me?* A deep pang of dread echoed throughout my entire body. Something was happening to me in this place; it was messing with me, changing me in some way. I felt alien to myself. *I have to remember.*

"We need to talk."

"No. Who are you?" The past few moments rushed me in a way that took me by surprise. Then it was gone. Like having an idea at the tip of your tongue, except about where you were two seconds ago. So, like amnesia, but I knew who I was and where I grew up. The events of my life were still mine to hold onto, except for the past hour.

"We are not enemies, Luke Thornton."

"Oh yeah? And who the hell are you again?" I replied.

"Luke Thornton," he said. "Do you forget what just happened to you?"

"I was in some sort of an accident. I think. Everything is very confusing right now…my head hurts…"

"At your house, Luke Thornton. By the lake." He raised his eyebrows, attempting to get me to add one and one. But it was like I was currently expected to do math in the middle of getting open heart surgery. It wasn't happening.

"My home? No, I took a car. I left."

"Please, Mr. Thornton. You are very clearly not well. I need you to think a bit harder. Where have you just been?"

I sunk into the nothing-floor that held me aloft in the place. My hands slumped to the side, my entire body shook. This wasn't real; not a week ago I was minding my own business in a small-town dump I called home. Now I was most definitely…

"I'm dead?" I said to him, no strength in my voice.

The strange man walked over and placed a comforting hand over my shoulder. *Can he feel comfort? Does he know what it is?*

"Guess I shouldn't have made so many jokes about hanging myself in the comic shop, huh?"

"Dead? Do not despair, you are not dead, Luke," the creepy stranger said, while still holding his hand in place. It felt like a rock, a great weight pressing down on me.

"How can I be alive?" I asked him, or it, "I remember. I hit a tree…"

"I tell you, you live. Not in this reality, however. In another world. A place so similar to this one that it is nearly indistinguish-able…except for one fact."

"Another world?" I blinked a few times. I considered that maybe I was just having the worst drug trip of my life. The only problem was, I couldn't remember how anything that happened tonight could make that true…unless I had eaten the other candy bar from Mama's. I tried to imagine that both events were linked to some rotten batch of chocolate or some spiked chocolate from a prankster factory worker or just a bad shipment of cocoa. *Can cocoa make you hallucinate?*

"Luke Thornton, perhaps there is a way to simplify it for you…" He drifted off and began rubbing his chin. I realized that he wasn't human long before he decided to try to comfort me; I could see that all of his mannerisms, his shape even, were a sort of veil. Or a relatable form he took for me. I shuddered when I tried to think of what his natural state of being was. "One called Thornton, have you ever heard of Quantum Immortality?"

"No….maybe?"

"I am sure you have seen it on one of your news broadcasts or on your Internet. Basically speaking, it is the belief that one may be able to jump between parallel universes."

"Parallel universes? What are you saying?"

He sighed, *like he once saw a human do.* "Let's backtrack a bit then. Do you know of Hugh Everett III?"

"No."

"Hugh Everett was a physicist who proposed that, for every little detail of change in one universe, there is a divergence from some kind of main timeline, so to speak. There are parallel universes to your own that, combined, make up what is known as the multiverse."

"This stuff is kinda going way over my head, buddy," I replied. Multiple universes? Quantum stuff? Who or what was this thing wearing a tuxedo? *You're still shuddering, you know you don't want to know.*

"Listen," he said, "every time some little event happens in your world, it doesn't happen in another. Understand?"

"So…you're saying to me…that I am alive and well…right now, because of a thing called Quantum Immortality?"

"Yes, exactly. It is a simple fact in reality that once you are deceased in one universe, your consciousness will transfer to a second."

"When I'm deceased?!" I let the revelation sink it for a minute or two. He seemed to be okay with letting me have the time. "But, where am I now?"

"Well, you are currently in between universes, as it were," he stated, "awaiting a jump into another universe."

I felt a shiver go down my spine and some tears escaping. "But, it's another me from another parallel universe…" My body slumped again. My heart was punching my ribs so hard I thought it was trying to commit suicide. I felt the hand go back to the spot on my shoulder.

"Do you not see it yet?"

"What do you mean?"

He chuckled. It honestly made me uneasy; it was forced, in a way. "You are perfectly okay. On your way to being alive and conscious again."

I thought about it long and hard. I thought about the scenario as it had just played out twenty minutes ago. How hard had I hit that tree? Hard enough to dream up all of this? But then, why did the pulsing in my head feel so real? Was I stuck in the crash with a concussion? Could I be vividly imagining these many things at once, in this much detail?

The strange man said, "Your philosophers and scientists and thinkers are barely scratching the surface, but they do have one theory that many of us here know to be true. Upon the hour of unnatural death, of any creature of any universe, the mind will deconstruct, enter an adjoining universe, and join with the consciousness of your parallel double. You see, instead of witnessing death firsthand, the body and mind conspire to trick you and move into another reality. You don't end up dead, and you have no recollection that you have met that end somewhere else."

"But then why do I know where I am now? Why am I not already in another universe blissfully unaware I didn't survive a car accident?" My head hurt, but was it from simply being in this strange place? Or from the things that the stranger was telling me? Or because no one had come to pick me out of the wreckage yet and I was bleeding from my skull, delirious and near-death?

He stood up again, removing his comforting hand (which I began to notice lacked heat) from my shoulder. "It is all very complicated and involves higher brain function and awareness than your species will ever obtain. You were pulled into this middle ground."

"Wait, wait. If I died in my first reality, wouldn't it be true that there should be several universes where I live and some where I die?"

"Hmm. Yes, that would seem to be the case."

"But what happens to the new reality I get? The new body I get?" I thought I finally had a grasp on it, "What happens to Earth-Two Luke? What happens to his consciousness when I decide to move in?"

He chuckled again, "The most ingenious minds of Earth are scratching the surface of such a theory - and it is, as you know, merely a theory in your world - and small town Luke Thornton believes he has understanding. I admire your attempts to put your current situation into perspective, but I believe we have dwelled too long on this topic."

"I don't even want to argue because I can't even tell if what I just had could be called a coherent thought. I feel sick to my stomach, my head hurts, and I'm still confused as shit." I clutched at my sides, at my head, at everything. Shit. I thought the multiverse in comics was confusing. "What the fuck is going on?"

He had moved back to his place behind the podium. I stood back up again, and walked forward a few paces to reach the leather-bound book that still sat there. While walking over, I tested the space in front of me, recognizing that I had previously tripped on invisible steps. I looked over the book, but couldn't quite understand the title. Like reading a clock in a dream, I knew I could see it, or rather, that my eyes could read and understand the words. But my mind had fumbled interpreting it.

"What is this book? Can it get me back to where I was before? Can it teach me to Quantum-whatever across the fucking stars until I reach old Earth?" I contemplated for a second, and then said, "Is this some sort of archaic time machine?"

"This book….is *The Compendium of Shadows*. It holds secrets to all of the darkest horrors that exist in any reality, across a multitude of dimensions. It is an encyclopedia of those things that scared your primal ancestors and now take the form of big-headed aliens, unstoppable killers, and cosmic terrors that taint most of the media you consume day-by-day. This book is one of a kind, although from where it originates is as mysterious as the contents. This book has existed since long before I came into being, Luke Thornton. This book…is the key to one of the most important global events yet to occur in the history of your planet. It can be the key to unlocking your mind and freeing your soul."

"I think I once heard a Jehovah's Witness pitch it to me the same exact way." *There you go, Luke. You're dead not half an hour and it's already crack-wise-with-the-supernatural-freak-show time.*

"Listen close, Luke Thornton. There are two other books, much like this one, around the world. Two others are in possession of the books; you must unite them and their respective volumes."

"And I'm going to do this because…?"

He paused, then gave me a stern look, "Because then you will get whatever you want. And more. You will be rewarded, gifted with knowledge as well. Your life will have purpose, for a time…"

I thought about it for a hot minute. I decided to play nice with the transdimensional tuxedo man. Considering my current situation, being agreeable was a better solution than trying to fight my way out of here. "Where do I find them? And how do I convince these other two that I'm not some nut job?"

"The first book keeper is the Librarian. I will instill, upon leaving this place, his location to you. The second book keeper is known as the Salvager."

"Since I get a book, does that give me a flashy nickname?"

"You are known as the Collector, in this realm."

"Great. I'm guessing the Librarian and the Salvager are nearby, like ten miles or so?"

"You have a ways ahead of you. The Librarian is also known on your world as Professor Southway, in the town of Dartford."

"That doesn't sound close to home."

He smiled at me. It creeped me the fuck out, and I wanted no part of whatever happiness he was dreaming up. "Try England, Luke Thornton. Now, it is time for you to leave this place."

"C'mon, man. England? I have a store to run," I said to him.

"The wheels are already in motion, Luke Thornton, and you are not in control of a car or your own two feet. You are on a train, and the conductor wills you to move forward with him."

"And who is the conductor?" I asked, but he merely smiled at me. I gave up asking questions; I had been offered a way out of the realm. It was time to take it.

I turned around with the intent of leaving through the break in reality I came in from, but off in the distance was something incomprehensible. I finally saw where all the wisps of color were heading so far below me, what stood behind me this entire time while I spoke with the strange man. It was massive in size, about the height of the Space Needle. Of course, that wasn't taking into consideration the distance it stood from me; I found myself trying to comprehend the actual measure of the hulking thing. But my head hurt with the same pain and uneasiness that I had first felt when I entered this place.

My eyes narrowed into a squint and this is all I can remember seeing: its head was black, but seemed to be writhing. It had a spider's eyes (two large on top, four small below them) that were not round globes, but little teeth that opened and closed asynchronously. I realized in horror that they were mouths, not eyes. This head was mounted atop a body of an insect-like thing, like a grasshopper or cricket, with four wings fluttering from the abdomen in a proud display. Surrounding it, numerous large insect creatures swarmed and dipped around the massive thorax, coming from god-knows-where to encircle the massive beast. It was opening night at Broadway Theater, and I had won front row tickets to *Clive Barker Presents: Disney's Fantasia.*

I collapsed at the sight, unable to move any part of my body. I was looking up, terror and sweat pouring down my face. The strange man walked from the podium, I saw, to my motionless body, where he knelt down and whispered into my ear.

"We'll be watching you closely. Take care of yourself, Luke Thornton." The air-floor below me finally gave way to nothingness and I fell, further and further into the blue-purple stream below. I thought I would fall through, but the stream caught me violently, like I had landed on brick. My entire body felt broken, and the stream carried me in its direction to the thing. The demonic horror out in the distance. The speeds increased and I felt myself being ripped apart by high winds. As I got nearer, the thing turned to face my direction. It casually gazed into my eyes, it felt, and then tilted its head upward to let out an inhuman wail that pierced my skin and deafened my senses. The pain surged. My body ached more. I felt something deep within me rumble. Something inside of me began calling towards it…

Saarlathesh…
Saarlathesh…
Saarlathesh…

And then there was calm. I awoke lying flat on a hay bale, staring at the barn ceiling. *Fuckin' hell of fuck shit.* I was home, sort of, and away from that thing. And in my hand, gripped at the binding, was *The Compendium of Shadows.* I looked at it, discovering that I could finally read the title.

"I should just fucking throw you in the lake and take a day off," I said to it. I quickly thought that I should apologize. Maybe it would eat my face off, like everything else I seemed to meet this week. I positioned myself to stand up, but I could not lift my weight. I tumbled backward onto more hay bales and then…

I awoke to a loud, repetitive beep. My eyes opened, and I was staring at a tiled ceiling. I couldn't move my right arm or my legs. Everything came in to focus; I was on a hospital bed and my head was still throbbing…

The nurse had told me everything I needed to know about what happened to me. She had come in, surprised to see me awake. Apparently, an unknown caller, female, had called the hospital, describing the crash and where to find me. I was carefully removed from the car, found to be alive, and rushed to the emergency ward. Despite the damage to my vehicle, all I suffered was a bruised and cut knee and a few broken fingers. A mild concussion had disoriented me enough that I could not remember the ambulance ride. My saviors had told the hospital staff that I was raving on the way over, saying strange things and talking to an invisible man and yelling as if I was in immense pain.

A bag of my personal effects was found in the backseat of my car; a small knapsack that held a few scattered college papers from back in the day, a notebook with doodles and notes, a ruler (bent into the shape of a boomerang from high school graduation, when Jean decided to have a little fun), and a leather book. When I questioned the nurse about the book, she said that they hadn't taken anything out or rummaged through it. When I told her that it didn't belong to me, she became quickly offended, reiterating that she hadn't gone through my things. I let it go.

I feigned dizziness and asked the nurse to let me sleep it off. When she had closed the door behind her, I got up from the hospital bed, hopping on one foot, toward the knapsack hanging on the visitor's chair. Inside, I found it. *The Compendium of Shadows.* When I returned to the bed, I looked around the hospital room suspiciously. I couldn't tell you why I did this. A patient reading a book wasn't beyond reasonable activities, but I somehow felt like I was about to unfold a three-page spread in a swimsuit magazine and be comically interrupted by an entering nurse. I cracked open the cover to the introduction of the book: *The Other Gods.* The intro read as follows:

> We have all heard the legends and mythologies of the many peoples inhabiting the Earth. Heroes of might and magic. Legends of lost treasure beneath the waves of the Caribbean. Damsels in distress in ivory towers awaiting the medieval knight. Dragons and Griffons. And we hear the tales of gods and demigods from old and new civilizations. The Norse Asgardians. The Greek Pantheon. Osiris, Set, Anubis. The Modern Christian Myth.
>
> But there are other divine beings that inhabit our universe that very few mortals can claim

intimate knowledge of. These beings have found their ways into the cultures of the very isolated. Natives of islands in the most remote regions of the Pacific, where the journeys of explorers and conquistadors of the days of old met a grisly end, worship such gods as part of their creator myths. Other natives fear the gods; their worship and sacrifice is appeasement from lowly creatures to the darkest forces their minds have conjured and passed down from grandfathers to fathers, fathers to sons.

Further still, one can hear these beings mentioned on the tongues of whisperers and the hushed voices of the devil-worshippers. From travel and the poor, immigrant element, these devils have established a place in the world of civilized man. Called upon by foolish youths and imprudent groups of suicidal men, they live on as legends and myths, passed on in secret meetings in the alleys between buildings and in darkened basements of even the most prestigious and prominent figures of our time.

For it is the allure of the unknown and the hazardous that drives men into the shadows; the oft-repeated gaffe by the curious mind that causes him to explore the realms of forbidden wisdom. Wisdom whose only purpose in the hands of mortal man is to corrupt the mind, leading to a rampant series of mad ravings and violent actions that one may read in the newspapers. Evidence of man's desire to play in the domain of gods can be seen also in the filling asylums; the remnants of the dark rituals can sometimes be heard in the mumblings of such men.

It is important to note that it is not necessarily the fault of these seekers of truth that their meddling with the supernatural inevitably causes disaster and misfortune. The form of wisdom that men must whisper to each other in the dead of night is, simply put, not for the ears of such laughably insignificant creatures. No, it is not the business of the humble ant to know it is living on an orbiting rock in the middle of a vast ocean of nothingness, interspersed with pockets of gases and planets and the occasional sighting of life. So too does the civilized man not possess the know-how of existence beyond the cosmos; inner workings and plans of organisms that seldom take notice of our insignificant occupation of their realm.

To the Other Gods, we are but ants, staring up at the heel of a larger, more capable creature. We laugh and step atop the creatures of our planet (tangible life sharing a home with us) because we have crowned ourselves the rulers of our dominion. But we are the ants of the Gods. We crown a miserable ant hill in the garden of very watchful keepers. Keepers who sometimes find

themselves in the need of a fumigation of the
hill we have built up for ourselves, only because
the hill has grown to block the view of flowers
they hold dear. For on our hill, we can only see
the throne we have erected, ignoring the plans
that other beings have for the space we dwell in.

Beside the hospital bed, I placed the *Compendium of Shadows*
down on the end table, jostling the lunch that the nurse must have
placed sometime in my sleep. *She didn't even bother to wake me.* I
inspected the green lunch tray with a bit of suspicion, being that
hospital food, much like airline food, does not have the highest of
reputations. Something that I never could quite understand was
the desire to cheapen the only comfort that a person could have in
two situations, which required good food to alleviate the stresses
put upon a person.

The first situation is undoubtedly in a hospital, a place of rest,
recuperation, and, in many cases, a fight for survival on a very
basic level, namely between death and the human body, struggling
to hold on to a degree unseen before in life. For the third case,
patients aren't subjected to the hazards of hospital cooking as
much as the first two. A good number of hospital patients must
traverse another path of survival, a fight against the mystery ingre-
dients of the Lunch Special, which today consisted of a tiny slab
of steak (most likely produced from the ass of a cow, rather than
a more delectable piece of muscle), boxed mashed potatoes with
little to no butter utilized, a single spoonful of corn (regrettably,
the only salvageable part of this meal), and a plastic cup of green
gelatin.

The second situation, traveling on an airplane, is much more
commonly experienced by the public at large. If a person is lucky,

their flight only lasts a few hours at a time, where meals are not served but replaced with the on-flight snack of a pack of peanuts and complimentary refreshments. If you're lucky. If you're unlucky, you are given a plain pack of pretzels that have long gone stale sitting in the middle of an airline warehouse somewhere on the runway. Either that, or purchased from a pretzel truck by the ton. For the long distance flyer, the stewardess will offer a false illusion of choice in the meals selected to appear for the day, or night. A series of options dreamed up by a corporate board upon receiving the question: "How cheap can we make the food before someone starts to taste the dog food in the beef?"

Still inspecting the tray, I decided to take a spoonful of the gelatin, before reconsidering and realizing that I was safer with simply drinking the cup of water beside it. *Blech!* The water was most likely from the tap in the room's bathroom sink. I leaned forward into the cup and replaced the water from my mouth. I rubbed my tongue on the back of my hand and coughed out what little I thought I swallowed. My throat was not dry, a fact that was reason enough for me to abandon the water altogether. With nothing else to do besides lay in the blinding flares that were the hospital lights, I shut my eyes to the sensory overload overhead.

I started to dream. In my dream, all my friends have distanced themselves from me; some leaving to far destinations, some disgusted by my presence, some dead for years, some never appearing again, as if their existence was removed from the fabric of time and space. I have no family, no business to run anymore, and my luck had finally run out in the worst way possible: my bank account was empty. My ambitions have become muddled and confused, and I lack the aspirations to achieve any of them. There is nothing for me in the world, nothing that I can produce as a benefit to society and nothing I can take in an act of selfishness.

All at once, the planet Earth no longer is a plane I walk, replaced instead by the void of space. I am at a loss to myself.

A room of darkness envelops me; I kneel on the floor like a dog. There is only one voice that I can hear, one voice that reaches out to me through the void. And I know its true face, for it is a face that is etched into the folds of grey matter in every newborn child. I look up to see it, to see the monster that beckons me from my personal darkness with the intent to draw me further underground. He has seen my true weaknesses, he knows how to tear down the walls of my comfortable life and shackle me to the chains of infinite horrors beyond my understanding. Saarlathesh. It beckons. He calls. It plots to subdue me. He asks me to leave myself behind and cast myself into the void, blissful. Saarlathesh calls…and in my dream, I nearly answer…

Some hours later, I arose from my nightmare, drenched in sweat at the base of my neck and with a painful feeling running along the palm of my left hand. With effort, I raised my hand into my vision to find the source. My fingers were wrapped in bandages and stiffened through the use of a small splint, interlocking my index and middle fingers. The bandages were stained with dull red, blood from beneath the wrappings. With haste, I slammed my right hand, with a flurry of presses, at the button designated for "Nurse." For over three minutes, I sat up, in pain, waiting for someone to approach the room door in a rush, eager to prove to their superior the swiftness of their patient response-time.

When a figure finally materialized in the doorway, I nearly shouted into the hall, but I found my voice cut off at the throat as the figure came into focus. It was a man, about forty-eight or forty-nine, dressed in a brown business suit with a yellow striped tie. He looked up from his palm pilot as he passed my room, looking from the bloodied hand raised in the air, to the look of pain on my face, to the hand once more. He then lowered his head to his device, resuming his path through the hospital halls.

"Wait, you fuck! Get a nurse for me!" I shouted. But he did not return to my room. I grumbled out some slurry of cave-man grunts as I held my damaged hand with the other. *Why do you stick around this town? There isn't a single situation, person, or place you believe you have something positive to say about.* I pushed the thought away as a nurse finally appeared at the door.

"My fingers are bleeding," I said.

"Yeah, I can see that."

"Are you being sarcastic with a patient?" I said. She just rolled her eyes, and then proceeded to remove the bandages. I witnessed enough of the damage done from the car accident, so I turned my head away as she performed whatever treatment she learned from paying a substantial amount in loans to a school, which had a good chance of not properly instructing her in how to be a nurse.

"It's done."

"What is? What happened?"

"You aggravated your wound. You shouldn't mess with the bandages."

"I woke up like this."

She sighed. "Please don't touch the bandages or the splint again."

"Is it customary to treat the patient like an idiot?"

"Excuse me?"

"Oh, and your response time is awful. If I was dying, they would be reading my eulogy by the time you would be able to find out which room called you."

"I am trying to help you, sir," she said, with her nose upturned at me, "Don't get upset with me."

"Can I have a different nurse? One who won't watch me bleed to death?"

"Well, you're **welcome** for the assistance," she growled, as she disappeared into the hall.

A second later, the small frame of Tracy Gunther, current resident Luke-stalker, entered through the same door, looking back into the hall with the same worried face, the default expression of her timid nature.

"Um, Luke, did you yell at the nurse?" she asked.

I was shocked to see her, so I said, "Uh, a little."

"You shouldn't do that. I mean, they want to help you."

"She was being rude."

"Oh," she said, but not in an agreeable tone. People said "oh" when they disagreed with a person's actions or an event at hand. This time, it meant "Luke, try to be nicer to people." But, although I didn't talk to her much, I knew that Tracy wasn't the confrontational type, so she wouldn't say that outright. Tracy Gunther was the girl who apologizes to you because you were stepping on her toes in the middle of a dance, while she was holding onto them in pain. That was Tracy, and I found it completely unacceptable.

"How are you?"

"Bleeding, for one," I joked, forgetting I wasn't in the proper audience for such a joke. Tracy was too timid for black humor. "I'm doing okay, just a few broken fingers and a faded concussion," I added.

"I was worried."

For a moment, I considered escaping off the hospital bed, but the tubes and cords hooked up to me would no doubt create an obstacle in that regard. I decided to play the situation straight, in a nonchalant way. "I know you called in the accident."

She had been sitting on the bed, but now turned away from me to face the door she entered from. I heard a bit of whimpering.

Tracy may have just been my stalker, in my mind, but she most definitely saw a bit more between us. "Hey, stop that. I'm doing alright, honest. Just banged up a bit, not even that badly," I said, trying to console the crazy person at the edge of my bed.

"Sorry."

"No biggie," I said, "How's my car?"

"It's wrecked," she said, "Dad took a look at it, said you'd better just junk it." It was at this point that I became concerned about how far Tracy believed she was involved in my life.

"Your dad?"

"I, uh, called him after the ambulance came. He picked me up at the accident."

"How did you find me?"

"I brought my bicycle. I was, um, heading to your house when I saw you speed off the driveway," her eyes looked away from me, hoping that I wouldn't question the reason. "I pedaled really fast. I think I broke the chain."

I scratched at my head, felt a small bump which I massaged with my thumb. "So you called your dad to drive you?"

"Yes."

"Lucky me. Guess I'll live another day."

Tracy sat in silence for a while, before she decided to try and lay in the hospital bed with me.

"Hey, yeah, don't try to do that," I said.

"I'm so sorry. I just thought–"

"You might aggravate my wounds, y'know? So thanks for calling for help and thanks for the visit. I'm going to try to get sleep now. I haven't slept much."

"Oh…of course."

"Yeah, cause I'm still in pain, so the sleep helps, y'know, and it would be better if I rested."

"I understand," she said, getting up from the bed, "I'll come visit you later on in the week."

"No, no, you don't have to," I stammered, "Because… because…you've done enough and I'm sure I'll be out in a day or two. I just have to heal up a bit."

She simply smiled a bit, taking steps away from the bed with her hands behind her back. She seemed to be a bit cheerful, I thought, as she left the room in a bit of a skip. I took a gulp. *The last thing I need to do is lead that girl on or something.* Tracy was a stalker who didn't quite comprehend that her fascination with me had just escalated from 'weird' to 'creepy' in just about an hour. I silently hoped that I was discharged earlier than she could come back and have another conversation with me. I would rather have her find an empty bed in the hospital than risk getting to know Tracy on a more personal level.

I shifted in the bed a bit, finding that hospital beds were as uncomfortable as I had imagined. I looked around the room, inspecting the area within my reach. Regrettably, they hadn't installed a television in my particular accommodation, so I was without entertainment. To my right, *The Compendium of Shadows* still sat closed on the end table. Not wanting to produce more nightmares, I turned over to face the other direction and closed my eyes.

CHAPTER FOUR

Homesick

My head slammed back into the head rest of my seat, causing it to sway slightly. I rubbed my eyes and moved my legs a bit, to try to get some feeling back in them. Flying in coach meant cramped spaces and the strangest cast of characters ever to pack into an airplane. I was sitting in the window seat, closer to the back of the plane. Sunlight trickled into my lap and chest from my right. I looked out the window, and saw that we were still over the water.

It was about a week before the hospital discharged me, billing me a nice sum in the process, when they had deemed me fit to leave. I waited for my fingers to heal up a bit before doing a bit of research on the man that the stranger wanted me to find. Professor Southway was a professor of South Pacific memes, characteristics of cultures that were passed from generation to generation, and mythologies. The man wasn't a highly prestigious and celebrated figure; he taught courses at universities, was known to travel the world occasionally (without any sort of specific location, which reasonably meant he took vacations more than business trips), and managed a small library inside of his own home. I didn't find a photo of him online, even though I searched through a number of professors who, strangely, shared a name with him. *How common was the name Southway?*

His library, and home, was in the town of Dartford, in the county Kent, England. The flight was estimated to take seven hours; I would leave from the local airport in Empire and reach London City Airport, where I would get a taxi to take me the rest of the way. Dartford was across the Thames River, so the distance from the airport would be no more than half an hour, barring the traffic conditions of Kent. If traffic was anything like it was over here in America, I would probably have a faster swim across the Thames than sitting in a stuffy cab, listening to the unpleasant sounds of European car horns screaming at one another in frustration.

I hadn't been sleeping for too long on the flight, but to finally be awake was a godsend considering that my dreams were far from what I would call normal (for dreams seem to commonly lack normality in any sense of the word). My experiences were leaving me with nothing but nightmares. Behind me, I heard two college girls practicing their English accents. Because when you visit another country, they love when you mock their accents and giggle about it. The seats on the plane were only three by three, three on the right half of the aisle and three on the left. I was surprised to see the old woman, who had been assigned to sit in the middle seat next to me, was missing. I looked through the crack in the seat in front of me and saw a flabby arm placed on the middle armrest. The guy in the seat next to the person owning this arm was attempting to move it, but he couldn't budge it. Eventually, he gave up and tried to doze off.

On the left side, across the aisle, was a kid playing one of those LED handheld games that were popular in the 90's. I had no idea where his parents might even have gotten one, then considered it was a hand-me-down. He glanced up and to the right. His face met mine, and then he turned to whisper to his dad. His dad looked up at me with such hate in his eyes, then whispered something, most likely a sternly worded mention of "not talking to strangers, especially the ones that look sick in the head" back to his son. The son went back to playing; I could tell that his dad had added something to the effect of "don't look at him." *Because I'm a real threat on an airplane, pal.*

I hadn't been out of the country for a long time. The last time I had even found myself on a plane was with Jean and Raphael. We had planned a long trip to the Caribbean. Even had a whole itinerary, hitting Bermuda, the Bahamas, Aruba; all the big name island spots that rich Americans liked to vacation in. After Bermuda and Bahamas, we ran out of money and had to call my uncle to send us just enough to get back. Raphael was caught up with buying everyone back home a gift, like some silly souvenirs with the island name on them, t-shirts that did much the same, and knick-knacks of so many varieties that you would think Claude's Emporium of Stuff moved to the Caribbean. Jean found his own little cash sinkhole in his attempts to try as much fresh cuisine as he could find.

Because of Jean, we dipped into nearly every restaurant we came across, from seafood to fried food, from breakfast to dinner. "At least one thing from the menu, Luke" were the words he said to me, dashing away to the nearest street vendor, who was cooking mystery meat on a stick, or to an establishment that promised tourists "The Finest Caribbean Meals." As for myself, I felt peer-pressured into following in both their footsteps. Still, the trip was nice and the resorts were beautiful; the perfect vacation for a couple of college freshman and a loser with no future. That was one of the last times I had seen the two of them before everyone decided to find careers and leave me behind to tend the comic shop.

I shifted in my seat and felt the knapsack at my feet jostle around the floor. It was in there. The book had made me feel uneasy, sick, just looking at its cover. I hadn't even tried to open it up a second time; I was afraid of whatever was inside, whatever strange passages and phrases I would find. After the first few days at the hospital, I started to think it was causing my nightmares; my dreams had never before taken on such a grisly, depressing tone. All of them began in some darkness, with me feeling uneasy or lost or at the verge of death. And I could hear its name each time. *Saarlathesh.* My skin crawled. I pulled up one of the rough, cotton blankets they kept on planes. The kind that you woke up itchy from after a rough sleep in a speeding pressurized container. It didn't bring me much warmth, but my trip was almost over. Soon, I wouldn't have the book anymore, and I could be on my way home.

I wasn't getting better at lying to myself.

The cab pulled up to a plain looking building toward the back of a dead end street, only a short drive away from the airport. The house was colored dark beige, two floors high, and featured a chest-high, white wall guarding the front yard. Alongside the wall were two garbage cans, one of the color black, with the, I assume, house number on it, while the other was green. Up one step was a small, black gate, which I opened without any resistance. This led to a red brick walkway, which itself led to three more red brick steps, then a blue-painted door. I tried to peer through the glass door windows, but could see nothing beyond the drapes on the other side.

Instead of a doorbell, I found a knocker hanging in the center of the door. It was a bronze mold of a hand, outstretched, grasping the large ring. I pulled back on it and slammed it. My face went white; I had left a dent in the wood that would probably be noticed from across the street. I was placing the ring directly over the damage when the door swung open.

"Can I help you?" In the doorway stood an American (his accent was nowhere near European and I detected a bit of Mid-West America in it) in a custom-fit two-piece suit, that he probably stole from a vintage photograph of a rich 1930's aristocrat. His clothes betrayed his rather thin frame. Above his lip and below his nose sat a strangely perfect moustache, the exact length of his top lip. He was well-groomed, well-dressed, and well-off. I was in a bleach-spotted *Alice in Chains* t-shirt, baggy jeans (ripped on the left knee), and brand-less sneakers.

The man did not fit any description that I had conjured up in my thoughts on the way over. For a professor, he was rather young-looking, barely into his late thirties and his hands were large and coarse as they held the doorframe. In my mind, I saw white hair, a hunched over back from years leaning over books in a dimly lit library, a wrinkled face that held a bit of that knowledge that the golden years were finally in full swing, and I even expected a cane or some form of support he would require to stand. However, his vintage clothes, the only part of him I pictured correctly (to an extent), were in stark contrast to his appearance, which led me to believe that this man might have discovered the Fountain of Youth.

"Um, hi."

"Can I *help* you?"

"I was told to come to you. Bring you this," I said, while I was rummaging through the knapsack. I presented the demonic book to him. The man removed it from my hand, inspected the front and back cover. Slowly, he pried open the book. I tapped my foot on the ground while I waited for his assessment. There was no traffic on the street, no vehicles, and no people walking down the sidewalk. Not too notable, though, as I was on a dead end street in a fairly quiet town; to expect the hustle and bustle of Empire would be a mistake. It actually had a bit of the same feeling as an American dead end street, except for the architecture and arrangement of the front lawns. I bet to myself that all the fun was on the opposite end of town, a place where more people of my age and younger got drunk and found themselves at the sour side of the law.

"Come inside," he said, abruptly. By the time I looked back at the doorway, he had already disappeared. The door hung open, and for half a minute I stood there confused. *Do I go in?* Against my better judgment, I took a few steps forward toward the doorway, looking around once more at the daylight that I was leaving and looking into the poorly lit house. I walked in and closed the door behind me.

The man's house (I assumed it was his house, although I had no reason not to believe I had written down the wrong address) was plain-looking and much smaller than it had looked from the outside. The entire room was carpeted red, up to and ending just before the kitchen at the opposite end of the front door. The kitchen didn't look that furnished; a mini-fridge and a microwave, coffee machine on the counter near a plain sink. The room I was in, however, contained the occupant's desk. Loose papers decorated open books, which were lying on top of travel pamphlets. I shuffled a few of them, scanning the titles and headers; topics ranged from biology to astronomy to newspaper clippings of events around the world.

The man appeared next to me by the desk. I jumped a bit, but realized he must have come into the room while I was sifting through his notes. I muttered out an apology, but he didn't seem to hear it. He was focused on the papers on the desk, picking them up and viewing their contents. Then he placed each paper in a pile on the desk until he stopped at one in particular. I hadn't seen it; it was one of the papers below the books. He placed it down with the rest.

"Where did you get the book?" he asked me.

"Some weirdo in a suit gave it to me," I answered, honestly.

"A 'weirdo in a suit?' Where was this?"

"It's….a bit complicated. There was a car accident, I went, somewhere, and then I woke up in a hospital with that book. It was in this bag," I said, pointing to my back.

"You went somewhere? Where did you go?"

"I don't know. A really strange place. What is that book anyway? Why did that guy send me here?" The room was kind of humid, most likely because his thermostat had jumped a few degrees on its own, like thermostats are known to do. *Or maybe he liked it that hot?*

He spoke again, saying, "This book is ancient." He tossed it lightly onto the stack on the desk. It wobbled slightly, causing him to extend his hands as if to catch it. It didn't fall, so he was left standing with his hands extended awkwardly. He straightened up and continued, "It comes from a civilization that died out around the time Alexander the Great thought he could be King of Earth."

"That's pretty old," I said, adding absolutely nothing to the conversation.

He just shrugged and took a seat at the desk. He fiddled through a drawer for a few minutes. I was left to take a second look around the place.

The nearby bookshelves in the man's study held just as many books as the floor they stood upon. He was extremely busy; someone who had no time to notice the small things in life, the everyday necessities of proper hygiene and organization. But he didn't smell or look disgruntled. The owner of this house was clean cut, properly groomed as if he was of royalty or in front of a Hollywood camera for most of his day. Had he not opened the front door, I would think he killed the homeowner and threw him down the basement stairs. *Go ahead, Luke, go find the basement door and crack it open.*

I pushed the thought away from my mind. *This was his home, he wouldn't answer the door in the first place if it wasn't.* I continued my surveillance. The place was rather small compared to the two-story home I came from. I could see into the kitchen and that the kitchen sink held not one single object. *Probably likes a lot of takeout.*

"I bet you order a lot of takeout," I said suddenly, feeling my brain attempt to murder my lips for slipping out a thought.

"Occasionally," he muttered from behind the desk, "Ah, here it is."

"Can I at least know who you are?" I said, "Um, sir," I added. I wanted to make sure I had the right address. It occurred to me that I hadn't even bothered to ask his name at the door. For all I knew, this man was the professor's neighbor. *Off to a great start.*

"My name is Professor Southway", he responded, clutching what I could see was a book rather similar in appearance to mine.

"Southway isn't a very common name, is it?" I asked, with a lack of tact in addressing my host.

"I didn't pick it," he said nonchalantly, "I believe it to be likely that whomever sent you to me with this tome is either an acquaintance of mine or knows of my library. *The Compendium of Shadows* is very similar to a book that was offered to me when I was studying in Burma."

"Was it the same man in a suit? That offered it to you, I mean," I questioned.

"Hardly," he answered, annoyed in a reminiscent way, "Some street vendor kept pestering me to buy the damn thing. He followed me down the market, left his stall completely! The idiot kept raving about how rare a volume it was, how I 'looked like a man in search of a great find.'"

"So you bought it?"

"Not even then. I told him that he saw 'a man in search of a great loss of money.' But he would not leave me alone!"

"How did you get stuck with it then?"

"He had been asking for one hundred dollars for it, so I gave him a twenty dollar bill to leave me alone. I found it later in my bag," he said, sighing. The Professor sat down and put his feet up on the desk.

I whistled, or tried to. It came out more like a broken tea kettle, or someone failing to produce a sound while blowing across the top of a plastic bottle.

Then I said, "Can I see it?"

"First, how about an introduction?" He looked up into the back of my skull and out the other end into the wall behind me. *Jesus, dude. Stop staring.* I became aware of the fact, at some form of uneasiness, that Professor Southway was inspecting me to a degree, probably attempting to draw a conclusion from my sudden arrival with a mystical object. I cleared my throat a bit.

"My name is Luke Thornton," I offered.

"Where are you from, Mr. Thornton?"

"America," I replied. I didn't want a European pen pal any time soon, so I spared him my address.

"What do you do for a living?"

"I run a comic shop."

"You run a comic book shop?"

"*I run a comic book shop*," I repeated, enunciating each word a bit, but not enough to make him stand from his desk and slap me in the face for it.

"Alright. Good enough. I won't pry into your life. You don't seem interested in telling me," he said.

Damn straight…can I leave?

Professor Southway picked up his book from the desk, clasping it firmly in both of his hands. He extended the book to me, giving me the first real glimpse I had of it. He was right. The hardcover resembled the one given to me, down to the font on the cover and the texture of the cover itself. I traced my hand, in horror, over the gold lettering adorning the front. A lump formed in my neck, drying the center of my throat and choking me. I tried to swallow hard a few times, but it didn't alleviate my fear. The title of the tome was *Saarlathesh, the Dark Almanac.*

I felt a sudden loss of self-control, like a puppeteer had taken me from my resting place to begin his performance. The puppeteer seized my right arm, raised it to the edge of the tome, and opened to the index. My eyes tried in vain to scan the words contained within, but my sight grew hazy at the sight of Saarlathesh's name emblazed upon the top of the page. Fear ran up my spine, leaving chills at every disc. Fear gripped my heart, squeezing hard from all angles; my heart galloped to the finish line of life. Fear made my sight blur and blind, making the text down the page become incomprehensible, even though they were right in front of me. A headache permeated the frontal lobes of my skull, pulsating like a snake weaving through my brain matter.

The puppet master beckoned my body to perform the will bestowed upon it. Nerve centers in my arm flared, telling me my fingers tracing the edge of the page would soon turn it. And turn the page they did. I was stricken blind by my owner, who collapsed my body at the knees, and I fell to the floor. When I hit, my sight returned in time for me to see my body above me, lying on a pile of books near the Professor's desk. The Professor was caught in freeze-frame, reaching toward my lifeless body. But I was still falling, somehow, into an abyss below the very fabric of the world I lived in. Below, a familiar stream of purple and blue caught me and slammed me hard into an invisible-something. I was knocked out cold.

I awoke in someplace strange, yet stranger still from the abyss I had dropped into. Below my hands, I felt the touch of grass, wet from the early morning dew. I lifted my head to see that I had been moved, or had fallen, into someone's lawn. Looking up, I saw a typical Colonial-style house with a porch. The porch contained a wooden bench, a wind chime above the short stairs, and several potted plants, spread out amongst the railing that ran from one side of the house to the other.

My feet found traction on the grass, lifting me from the ground. I walked over to the porch, taking the steps slowly and reaching the front door. I didn't knock. I didn't have to. The interior door opened, revealing a familiar face in the form of Jean. He opened the outer screen door, which I grabbed, then said to me:

"Come on in, it'll be the best episode yet."

I tilted my head in confusion, but he slipped back into the house before I could mutter a 'what' or a 'the fuck'. The interior door was cracked slightly, so I pushed it open fully before I stepped inside.

Jean was nowhere to be found. The foyer I walked into was empty; devoid of life, devoid of furnishings, devoid of any color other than a muted blue on the walls and floor. A staircase spiraled upward to my right, while a long hallway stretched itself to the back of the house to my left. I didn't recognize any of my surroundings so far; the exterior of the house could have been any rural community back home in the States, while the interior didn't even bear a resemblance to anyone's residence. Not any residence I knew. I was somewhere foreign, somewhere alien, for the third time in the past week. Disoriented, I walked to my left, daring the possible dangers of walking deeper into the realm.

About halfway into the hall, I heard the loud buzz of an insect's wings in my eardrum. The sound wasn't deafening, but it was as though a fly had planted itself inside my head. I grabbed my ear, trying to block the sound or shake it out. My disoriented situation became worse; I fell against the wall, holding myself up with my left hand, while my right hand was placed over my ear. Eventually, the buzzing stopped. I took a few deep breaths, and then stood up again.

I was taken off my feet almost immediately. Something had run into me from behind, knocking me further down the hallway into an empty room. Empty, except for a single wooden chair in the center. Picking myself up for the millionth time in this decade, I turned back to face the hallway, and then broke into a sprint at another nearby empty room. I had seen what hit me. And it was chasing.

The thing tackled me from behind yet again, slamming me into the wall ahead, face-first. I spun on my heels, taking in the horrible sight before me. The thing was about thirteen-foot tall, green, possessing two spiked forelegs, standing on four posterior legs, with the face of a humanoid creature. Its eyes were empty, black spheres. From behind the creature, two wings fluttered. It sprang up on me, pinning me to the very wall it had thrown me into, with its two forelegs. The skin of my arm crawled as it made contact with the boney exoskeleton of its arms. I felt helpless.

The lower half of the creature's face unhinged, displaying a wonderful assortment of razors, ranging in size yet symmetrical. I kicked at the creature, hoping to bury my foot deep within its abdomen or loosen the piercing grasp on my arms. I didn't succeed. A burst of screeching pain emitted from its mouth, the same screech that had deafened me when I first met the tuxedoed man in the other realm. In a flash, I caught sight of the creature's left foreleg pull back, and then thrust forward into my shoulder. I let out a howl of pain, a symphony of curses, and pleas emitting not too far after. The pain was immeasurable. I was never the one who could handle pain, and, at that moment, I whispered to the creature, asking for mercy.

The creature screeched again, deafening all of my remaining senses. It was unnatural, alien. It was the call of a successful hunt; the lion roar at the end of a bountiful kill, the rumble of victory. Life was draining from me at an alarming rate. I felt my fingertips grow numb, then my hand, then up my arm. I let go of the creature's forelegs and hung limp against the chipped and cracked paint wall. The creature pulled me off by my pierced shoulder, following this by bucking my body off of its leg. I hit the floor hard, closing my eyes before impact. The creaky, wooden floor of the house felt awfully soft and carpet-like underneath my flayed limbs.

My eyes opened at the sound of footsteps coming near. A pair of well-polished, black shoes reflected my cowering visage back to me. I lifted my head up to see the thin man in the tuxedo, smiling down at the pathetic lump before him. The creature resumed a position above me, pinning my arms to the ground with its own and hanging its mandibles over my face. Wet saliva dripped onto my nose, causing me to thrash in a failed attempt at escape. The tuxedo man bent down near my head and said:

"Mr. Thornton, it would do you a world of good to make haste in your departure, as my master has expressed an interest in collecting his tomes before certain parties find themselves interfering with us. Or with you. Being that you have found yourself in possession of the first tome so easily, I trust that you will be able to do as we ask. Take care, Luke Thornton, for Saarlathesh does not like to be kept waiting."

The creature screamed into my face, splattering more saliva upon it. I gagged and choked as it pulled its head back, with the intent to strike. I shielded my eyes from the creature that drew near me and opened them back up to the sight of Professor Southway checking my neck for a pulse. I instinctively swatted his hand away, as if the creature from my dream was the one with its claw placed so close to my jugular.

After gathering a suitcase of clothes and toiletries, Southway met me at the front door of his house. Closing it behind him, he locked the door with a gold key, slipping it into his jacket pocket as he checked the doorknob. It was locked for sure.

"Where are we going from here?" he said.

"Back to America, I guess. That's the thought I had when I regained consciousness, no doubt an idea planted by the strange man," I replied.

"But from what you told me, he sounds like a threat to us. Do we really want to follow his directions?"

"I don't know. It was sorta like a dream and dreams tend to blow things out of proportion," I said. Southway looked doubtful. "Besides, I want to get rid of these nightmares. If going along with the stranger's plans will do it, I just want to get this over with."

"I'm still not sure this is a good idea."

"Where's the airport from here?"

"Don't worry. When I was packing, I called for a taxi."

"You don't have a car?"

"Mr. Thornton, I'm in the business of research. Thus, I rarely take leave from my house. If I do, it is to the local library just two blocks away. If I'm required to venture out of England, I call a taxi to take me to the airport."

"Jesus. Don't you have friends to visit?"

"Do you have many friends to visit that require you to go far out of town?"

"Touché, asshole."

"Don't be crass. Here's the taxi now."

The taxi was much different than one that you would see in Empire. Rather than the elongated, yellow Ford Crown Victoria cars that are so well known for crashing into themselves repeatedly, the English taxicab was a black TX4, as Southway explained. The taxicab was roomy and well-kept, a stark difference from the cabs I was used to riding in at home, the very few times I found myself in one. The driver did not speak much, just exchanged a few pleasantries with Southway regarding the weather and some sports event or two that took place sometime earlier in the week. The conversation was short and the driver resumed his focus on the road ahead of us. I was still very unfamiliar with the area, so I kept quiet and watched the buildings fly by.

"The airport is about half an hour away," Southway said.

"I know, genius, how do you think I got here?" I joked. By the look on his face, he didn't like the joke.

After a few turns, we found ourselves on a long, empty road consisting of wide open plains and the wonderful human addition of power lines and transmission towers. Further on, we reached two wide hairpin turns, which led us to A282 Dartford Crossing.

"This road," Southway explained, "takes us over the Thames River."

"I see," I replied, "I came from the other side, through Blackwall Tunnel."

"It's about the same distance, either way. We'd probably get more traffic on the A282 though." The driver scoffed at the notion. Continuing my streak of luck, we hit traffic right at the tolls on the Dartford side. I sat contemplating walking, or taking a dive in the river below, when the traffic lessened enough that we were traveling at a steady rate with no stops. It was relatively quick down Route A13 into Eastern London, where the taxi pulled into the London City Airport. When asked to pay the fare, I shrugged my shoulders at Southway, who grumbled a bit and produced some cash, which he handed to the driver with a thanks and some small talk. As the taxicab pulled away, Southway picked up his small, leather suitcase, and we entered through the main airport doors.

The plane I had arrived in, Southway explained to me as we walked forward, was a jet airliner, the model being an Airbus A318. More than likely, he continued, we would be leaving for America on the very same one. London City Airport was small; in comparison to major airports, of course, the entire area seemed to be no larger than an American shopping mall. The main difference being that an American shopping mall can contain more people in one building during a weekend than this airport. As I glanced down to my left and to my right, I only noticed a light presence of other people.

We were making our way through the airport, bags checked and tickets verified, and began to aimlessly wander. Southway was wholly focused on following the signs to find our particular gate number. After scratching his chin, I can only assume he made an educated deduction and began walking away. I followed. There wasn't an enormous amount of shops like I had seen at the Empire Airport back home. McDonalds wasn't at the corner of each four-way hallway, Starbucks had yet to make a sizeable appearance, and only two small bars caught my eye in the time we had to glance around.

Upon reaching our gate, Southway approached the counter, making small talk with the woman standing behind it. She was about my height, had a dark complexion, rosy lips, and, from what I could see above the counter and in her face, weighed a bit more than the average. Southway continued his talk; I found a seat nearest to me, dropped my bag on the adjacent one, then sat myself down. I began to take in the quiet of the place, hushed murmurs and footsteps only occasionally interrupted by the sound of a woman on the loudspeaker, who had the luxury of addressing the entire airport from whatever office she may have been sitting in.

Southway seemed to shift demeanor, although it was difficult to tell from my angle of him. All I could see was the arm, that he was using to lean on the counter, straighten out, and Southway stood upright in front of the airline worker. His voice rose a bit, but I could not make out the words. Whatever the exchange, he thanked the woman politely, and then turned around to find me. I wasn't too far away. He picked up the one case of luggage, which he had brought with him, and began to walk towards me.

"What's up?" I said.

"Bad news. Since this is such a small airport, our flight has been delayed."

"I thought you actually had bad news. In America, we still call that 'on schedule.'"

"That's not funny. We're going to be here for a couple of hours."

"Good thing I brought a book with me."

"Really? What are you reading?" Southway questioned. He didn't have an upturned nose or a look of anger on his face, so I could tell that he was being sincere.

"*The Compendium of Shadows.*" It's too bad that I wasn't. From the speed at which Southway's face dropped, I could tell my humor was not well received.

"Lighten up," I added.

"That's not funny. I suggest you avoid making that book," he said, pointing to my knapsack, "a leisure activity, Mr. Thornton, as I believe it may be hazardous to your health."

"Hazardous to my health? I've already perused a bit of it."

"Yet you nearly dropped dead at just the mere sight of my tome. I still do not know if you are just a very good actor, but I don't think you should be reading any deeper into this. If what you say is true, do you really want to know more about this situation?"

I had filled the Professor in a bit more on the details of my experiences back home. He listened quite well, even though I couldn't shake the feeling that he was mentally reciting "bullshit" with every sentence I ran through. *But he's here with you now, Luke. Either he believes you word for word, he doesn't know what to make of it and has time for a trip, or his own book has been giving him nightmares too.*

"Has anything strange cropped up since you've gotten your book?" I asked, as he was shuffling through a few of his things.

Southway looked up from his luggage and said, "No, nothing supernatural or bizarre, beyond you walking into my home earlier today."

Okay, so a bit of a dead end there, Luke. I turned away from Southway to the rest of the airport, wondering how I would be spending the next few hours, the last few hours of my time in England.

"How long have you been teaching, Southway?"

"About ten years, perhaps. I lose focus on my time at the university. I'm much more heavily involved in my research. Teaching is just a way for me to make ends meet."

"You seem to be doing quite alright for yourself. You got a cozy home."

"Yes, I suppose you can say that."

"Do you know anything of the occult? Of this *Saarlathesh* figure?"

The Professor said he did not, which he followed by producing a small, paperback novel that he had packed. I wasn't familiar with the title, but the action itself spoke much about Southway's feelings on the present conversation. I dropped the topic, turning back to the large, glass windows to the right of me. I watched planes being taxied around the exterior, planes docking (with passengers, I assumed, shuffling through the loading bridge, greeting the on-flight crew at the door), the cityscape, reflecting sunlight into the airport, in the distance, and the swiftness of the exterior airport personnel, running around the tarmac.

After about ten minutes, I grew tired of this, so I turned my attention into the present area surrounding me. There weren't many people America-bound at this time; waiting with us at the gate were a mother and a boy of no more than seven years old, the latter being reprimanded by the former for jumping out of his seat to wander aimlessly around the sitting area. Behind the row of seats that Southway and I shared, a man in a brown business suit had somehow managed to slip himself atop four seats: one contained a bundle of garments, which he rested his head on, two supported his body from underneath, and the fourth propped up his feet in a rather uncomfortable looking fashion. He was squirming and shifting in the makeshift bed of his.

In my mind, I imagined he was a moderately important man in his early fifties, not young but not yet exhibiting the white hair and wrinkles that accompany old age. The way that his stomach seemed to bulge and push out his white undershirt gave away his portliness. I struggled to picture the image that I was connecting, only concluding that he reminded me of a cross between J. Wellington Wimpy from Popeye (in body) and a young M. Emmet Walsh, the actor. I dreamed up that he was coming home from a long business trip, one that had taken him a bit of time (from negotiating a deal to establishing a new branch of a business in England), and he was about ready to go home to his wife and three kids. I was interrupted by a loud snore that echoed around the sitting area and originated from the businessman. Evidently, he had stopped shuffling some time ago, beginning a restful sleep wedged between airport seats.

I wracked my mind for better ways to keep myself occupied, which resulted in me flipping open my cell phone, which I had removed from my pocket and which I had been rolling around in my hands. I had deactivated the wireless signal, out of fear that my provider would undoubtedly begin adding roaming charges to my bill, to be discovered upon my next month's payment. With nothing to pass the time with, I turned on the phone. *Somewhere, in some office, a man is adding charges to my bill and grinning sadistically as he slides his mouse over to whatever electronic form he uses, fingers sensually rubbing the mouse button in restrained glee. The sick fuck.*

Opening up my messages, I scrolled through texts from a number of people. A scan through the chats with Jean and Raphael revealed that I had not been invited to any sort of get together. I thought about sending Jean a text about the bee that attacked me and the car accident, but I just didn't feel motivated to involve him in my insane life anymore. Closing out my messages, I flipped through the applications I had installed before I left America. A mobile game lit up my screen and was closed just as I found myself dozing off in the middle of playing. I glanced at the time display. It had only been half an hour. I sighed, leaned back on the chair in a position that no man, or woman, could call comfortable, and closed my eyes.

Altogether, there were about ten of us currently boarding the flight to Empire Airport. Southway had fallen asleep in his seat, much like I had, but the stewardess had woken me up personally when the flight was ready. I kicked Southway in the foot, a gesture that he neither appreciated nor knew why I had done it, to which I answered him that the flight was ready. His face lightened a bit, *probably glad to be leaving*, and he gathered his small luggage bag.

I cheerfully remarked to Southway that the seat we had been assigned was only two rows from where I previously sat during my trip. He yawned in boredom, telling me that, considering the small size of the plane and the amount of planes available for travel in such a small airport, the likelihood that we may be sitting close to my previous seat was high, as high as getting the same exact seats.

I frowned at him, then jumped into the window seat and yelled "Dibs!"

"How old are you again, Mr. Thornton?"

"Seventy-six. We age differently in America now."

"That's not funny."

"Doesn't matter. I have the window seat."

"Are you aware that the window seat is much more dangerous in the event of an accident? That you may go flying out of the side of the plane into a grisly death?" He said.

"Oh well, at least it'd be quick."

The mother and her child, those who I spied in the airport gate with us, had quickly changed seats upon hearing the conversation that was unfolding. She was whispering to the kid, who seemed to be on the verge of tears. I speculated that he had wanted the window seat, and the brief exchange between me and Southway had scared him. I motioned my head over to the two, which the Professor turned to see. He chuckled to himself, and then took a seat next to me.

"I don't think the stewardess will mind that they changed seats."

"I think they like being called airline attendants now."

"Oh. Right," Southway said, in a manner that said to me that he missed the old days, when a man was in the right state of mind to call a woman a woman and a man a man, without the necessary consideration of checking the current and proper form of address for the person. It wasn't too long ago that, as long as the conversation and tone were of a polite and relaxed nature, a person could greet another, or speak about another, person without being called out on using archaic and insulting terms. Yeah, it seemed lately that treading on a person's toes was as easy as leaving the house in the morning and finding that they had placed said toes underneath your welcome mat, ready to be crushed the moment you left the comfort of your home, the last bastion of sanity and freedom.

The Airbus took to the runway, and then we were in the air without much of a hassle. Usually, I expect to wait another hour or two on the runway; a nice refreshing reminder that Empire Airport had as much difficulty coordinating flights as did a baby in the attempt to walk those first few steps. It was late in the day, meaning that from the window seat of the plane I was able to spy the immense pathways of light that humans have established around the planet. *I wonder if we're just one giant light bulb to the universe.* After some time had passed, however, all I was able to see were the stars in the nighttime sky, both above me and reflected down below in the waters of the Atlantic.

Southway had taken to reading his book again; when or where he had pulled it out from, I have no clue. I asked him for some light reading material, to which he responded that he had brought only the single book, expecting to be finished with this business in America as soon as possible.

"What about your other book?" I said, hinting at the tome in his luggage.

"Luke, you passed out in the middle of my study from just browsing the table of contents and you want to do the same on a plane?"

"I had jetlag," I lied.

"Come now, jetlag? At least choose your lies a bit better next time."

"Look, I want to see what's inside. I'm thinking I passed out because the stranger I told you about needed to contact me. Maybe these books have some sort of power of communication to the next realm. Or something."

At this, the older woman murmured a complaint of some sort and moved herself and her child as far from us as possible. I moved in closer to Southway to reduce my voice to a whisper.

"Just let me read a bit. If it looks like I'm about to drift off into the void, just knock it from my hands."

"No, Thornton. No way am I taking a chance with this. If everything you say is true, if you collapse on the plane or go into a delusional rage, I don't want to be responsible for your actions. I don't think opening up that kind of power on a plane screams 'safety regulations.'"

"What does it matter? Say, for instance, that the plane does become endangered in any way. According to the stranger, you and I, and the people on this plane, will just survive in a separate universe!"

"And, Mr. Thornton, have you given thought to the possibility that only you or I survive and not both together? That in my safe universe, I awake from a crash by myself, you having your head removed from the impact. And you," he began to whisper a bit more, realizing he was getting slightly irate, and thus raising his voice, "wake up amongst the jellyfish, no plane in sight as it has sunk to the bottom of the ocean? We may survive, yes, but slightly worse for the wear, I do say."

"That's, like, worst case scenario."

"With you, it is likely case scenario."

"Have you ever read the book yourself?"

"Merely once. I skimmed through it, but, as I told the peddler in Burma, I did not think it was of value. The only information you'll find in that book is some amazing work of fictional prose by an author with far too much time on his hands and far too many gullible readers who enjoy such a thing."

"How can you say you are a researcher and dismiss this so casually?"

"Don't test me. Leave the book and try to get some sleep. Or twiddle your thumbs. I don't care, either way."

Feeling defeated, I let Southway swallow his win and delve back into the novel he had brought with him. I finally was able to read the title, but let me tell you that, from the title alone, I could tell it was a novel of very dry humor, a sensible plot, nothing supernatural or beyond reality, and with an ending that closed the book in the same way it opened: dry and devoid of bringing anything new to the world. I was restless on the flight, having spent the majority of the past four and a half hours in an airport and sitting in a cramped flying tube, counting seconds go by as my sanity slowly slipped away from me.

I found nothing of interest out of the window. Instead, I realized that, without being involved in the sights (namely splashing and diving in the water below), the waters were really nothing marvelous to look at for long periods of time. *Those aliens sure do avoid this planet for a reason. That and we keep shooting at them in our movies and books.* I silently joked to myself that tomorrow could be the day they make the decision to vaporize us for our own good. I then wondered how I would survive into another universe with the planet blown up. I would have to ask the stranger the next time I saw him, if I had the sense to ask before I strangled him to death.

When I heard snoring, my mind snapped back into reality. *Who is that?* I looked over to see my companion, Southway, slipped off into a dream state mid-sentence, no doubt from boredom. The novel he had been reading had collapsed near his feet, split open in the middle. I leaned over to pick it up, finding that Southway used no bookmark to trace the last page he read. *Guy must have a great memory.* I flipped through a few pages, and then read the following:

Auk had been on the hunt for only an hour, having kept sight of her prey from afar and having been careful to hide her presence from it. She jogged gracefully through the brush with feet so light that the blades of grass beneath did not crumble but merely parted, as if they carried her quietly through the forest. Auk glided across the green sea, bow at the ready and quiver on her back. She caught sight of the animal's head sway to the side, to which she responded by using the trunk of a nearby tree to hide. The trees, as her mother had told her, would conceal her completely, having been old enough to witness the hunt for many seasons, from the times of her days at the hunt and her mother's and her mother's mother still.

Auk was patient. A far cry from the days of her youth; days marked by brashness and frustration. The days of training. The days that taught the youngest of the tribes the proper way of the hunt. The sight of the hunt. The speed of the hunt. The feel of the hunt. It was her first hunt alone, unaided by the other girls of the tribe. During the training, it had been her mother who held the title of mentor.

Auk shifted from the sturdy trunk, observing the pond at which the game had stopped for a drink. The scene was peaceful, quiet; there existed in nature those moments of pure, child-like calm that can be encountered from the shadows and during the bright, moonlit nights on the plains. For most animals, the calm was norm insomuch for the relative ease that the herbivores found themselves when amongst others of their kind. Moments ruined by the stalking and pouncing of predators or through the innocent pull of a bowstring that so often ends in the impalement of a young buck.

'Humans,' Auk's mother had said, 'have no place in the natural world. We are from chaos; we are from a world so foreign to the one we now call home. Thus, we have no right to belong, no right to pine for the calmness that is the forest. We are the hunters. We engage the hunt, the disruption of peace and quiet. That is why we give thanks, young Auk, to the beasts we slay.'

'But I want to drink with the deer, mommy,' young Auk had replied in a childish manner, which contained a hint of that all too familiar feeling of the want of the forbidden.

'Child, when you grow older, you will understand.'

Auk had grown older. She had visited the forest for seven seasons now, but this was the first in which she was to be isolated from the tribe. She took this opportunity to weep softly at the scene before her; weeping for that feeling she had held as a child, a feeling that she now knew, being an adult, to be unattainable. So Auk wept for the animal, wept for the last drops of water it would consume. For, by virtue of the hunt, Auk would consume the animal, continuing the cycle.

Auk reached into her quiver, grasping the feathered tail of an arrow and positioning it on the bowstring. She steadied herself. To feed her tribe, she and others had been selected to be the hunters. While the others were far, vast distances apart, they were all to bring home game to feast upon. Auk began to sweat; first at her brow, then the pores of her arms.

Then the arrow was released, but not from the hands of Auk. Another hunter had fallen into her territory, had scoped out her game. Auk was prepared. None of her kinsmen could interfere with the hunt; this was something else entirely. Exhibiting the aforementioned grace, Auk slipped into a tall bush, neither rustling a branch nor disturbing a droplet of dew from the leaves therein. Auk peered into the glade.

She witnessed a sight that had only been taught to her in legend, in fable. A man, similar in clothing and wielding the weapon of Auk's choice, stood on the opposing end of the clearing. *He is handsome,* Auk told herself. *I have never seen his tribe before, yet they hunt in our woods. How strange.*

He gently made his way toward the writhing animal, still punctured by the arrow, protruding from the neck. The hunter returned his bow to the straps on his back, Auk witnessed, and then unsheathed a large dagger from his bootstrap.

Auk pulled her bow close with her left hand, pressing her mouth with her right as the tears ran down her face. Much as she had done before, she wept softly to herself. The man was cutting at the flesh at the animal, which struggled in vain to kick off its assailant. Auk saw the hunted squirm, eyes bulging in pain and wild panic at the slashing of the cruel man, until finally the deed was completed, roughly, crudely, and without care. Auk sat in the bush, crying out toward the glade, which now held a pond, trees, wild grass, and the bloody skin of her hunt.

I'll admit that I recoiled a bit from the passage, having no context for the story which I had delved into. *I should have started from the first page.* The novel didn't truly interest me; what value a professor like Southway saw in a fictional account, I had no idea. The man was fast asleep next to me. *If it had been interesting, he'd be awake to read it.* I tossed the book aside, having no interest in learning its title, nor the author of the piece. My mind was still restless, unable to think ahead to the next step. I hadn't told Southway we would be returning to my home to pick up Michael. To any sane person, I reasoned, the task at hand would be to find the third book, then call it quits forever.

I wasn't exactly in a mindset that anyone would say was a credit to sanity. I wanted Michael to be a part of this; whether or not he actually needed to be involved was questionable. *Then why bring him along? Because you want him out of your house?* The thought was not far from the truth.

The airplane did its best to maintain a steady altitude. I couldn't recall later if there had been turbulence on the flight, but, at one point, the woman and her son both exited their aisle, made their way past us (naturally, the woman held onto her son tightly in the same way that the man of my first flight instructed his spawn to avoid me), then vanished from sight upon entering the bathroom. I had an uneasy feeling around me, perhaps something in the air that didn't feel right or some form of subconscious premonition that said "Get out of here!" Or maybe it was the whispered words I swore I could hear from above me.

Rising from my seat, I cautiously shuffled sideways past Southway's knees, lightly knocking them into each other. *Still fast asleep.* I reached upward toward the carry-on baggage, pulling down Southway's bag carefully. From inside, I saw his book. I made my way back to my seat, being sure to avoid waking Southway. When I had been only an inch or two away, I threw myself at my chair. Southway lifted his head, grumbled a few words that may or may not have been of some English dialect, then drifted back to sleep. I sighed, turning my attention to the *Dark Almanac*. Like the book before, I cracked it open, not at the start of the tome, but somewhere down the middle:

> But from whence does such a foul creature spawn? Is It given birth like an animal? Kicked into the world in such confusion that It thrashes out and wails and yearns for Its mother? Is It born like a lizard, collected with Its brothers and sisters in a pit of eggs, hatched in the morning?

Does such a creature require a source of creation? Does It merely exist because the universe exists, does It do because it is in Its nature to do?

Saarlathesh may very well not be a tangible thing. Yes, many a man, even those that have been praised as the fiercest in the world, can wake up screaming in the night about the Insect King. And when questioned on the event, make claim that he has neither interacted with the godlike being nor heard of Its name before.

Can a thing be both tangible to man's eyes, yet intangible in matter and form? Can it be possible that a man may gaze upon Its writhing body and beating wings, yet men of science say such a thing cannot possibly exist and sustain Itself? Are the doctors and scientists and philosophers the ones who delve into madness? Or is it the man whose mind has shattered to so many pieces that the reassembly of his consciousness has created something dark, albeit entirely fictional? Or is he simply feigning madness for another purpose?

Does Saarlathesh indeed have a body? A face? A manner of breeding and a manner of consuming? Can such a being have plots and ideas and opinions and tastes? Is It above such human qualities? Qualities that we have taken for granted in our own lives and imposed on the natures of creatures that neither need nor desire?

Saarlathesh is very real, in the sense that an idea
can be as real as long as It exists in the minds of
man. Words, tales, poems, and songs speak, tell,
rhyme, and sing in praise or horror at the dark
entity that many have come to call Saarlathesh.

And where is Saarlathesh? Does he occupy our
world, a creature that must share our planet like
the fish must make room for the blue whale in the
ocean? Does he occupy our universe, seemingly
too far away to be noticed, yet having a profound
effect on the intricate events of fragile minds,
which are unaware, or unwilling to acknowledge,
that they do not control their fates?

I say Saarlathesh is not of this universe, not of
our dimension and our homes. Yet he has power
here. Control in a way that defies physics and
laws that only govern the celestial bodies of our
universe, without defining limitations to those
dark things that exist outside it. Saarlathesh, and
others, have minions here on Earth; those who
would do the bidding of false idols for a promise of power. Or a promise of death, of release
from their mortal existence. Thus is the way
of the Other Gods, as is transcribed in stones
of long disbanded cults whom sought out His
protection.

Saarlathesh was very real, in the sense that an idea can be
real as long as It exists in the minds of man. The sentence rose

something profound in me; an idea that frightened my core, which shook at the fabric of who I thought I was. *Saarlathesh is everywhere, sees everything, knows you all too well, Luke.* I felt myself reaching for an on-board puke bag from the seat pocket in front of me but came away with nothing. *Okay, get a grip. You read some trippy stuff out of a book. Books can be fiction, this is fiction. Got to get a grip before something…*

Like the norm, I wasn't able to finish the thought before my chair and me were pulled out of the plane and transposed into the starry, black realm that I had already ventured to far too many times. This time, however, there were no blue-purple streams or stars, and I found myself sitting uncomfortably in a black room that seemed to be illuminated by nothing at all. The stranger was smiling at me, sitting upon an invisible box of air for a minute or two.

"You're well on your way, young man," he said.

Then he vanished, popped out of existence like a bad cut between frames on a cheesy sci-fi show. I then saw myself sitting at home. From my airline chair, I had front row seat to a spyglass into my personal bedroom, watching myself begin to roll around in bed, rocking back and forth in uneasy sleep. I couldn't understand it at first, but I began thinking that the plane trip was just an insane dream. That I wasn't having some form of out-of-body experience was confirmed as I watched the stranger walk into my bedroom. He stopped at the edge of the bed, holding something in his hands.

My other-self sat up in bed, knees up to his chin and his arms folded around them. He slammed shut his eyes, tears beginning to swell on his face. *Something isn't right, this isn't real.* My dream worlds had ceased being my own for some time now, but I was still unable to shake a feeling of ownership. *I wouldn't be dreaming this. I don't think I'd be having visions of the stranger, smiling and reassuring.*

I realized that the stranger (and Saarlathesh probably) were showing me this as some kind of exhibition of the hold they had over me. My other-self had gotten out of bed now, moving over to the edge of the bed where the stranger stood grinning. The stranger's arms cradled something important, something I could not see from my perspective of the dream. But, as his arms outstretched, I could see the glint of a silver pistol being handed over to my other-self.

I screamed and thrashed in my seat, but the seatbelt on the chair pinned me tightly to it. *Did I put my seatbelt back on? Wait, am I still on the plane?* My other-self rose from the bed, gun in hand, and then walked over to the edge of the bedroom. He pried open the ammunition chamber, which I could see was empty. Opening a drawer of my dresser, my dream-self revealed the shine of six metallic bullets sitting atop a folded blue shirt. My hands gripped the airline seat, sweat forming beneath my skin and on the nape of my neck.

"Luke!" I called out my name, but the other me did not seem to hear.

The chamber was returned to its locked position, which my other-self seemed hesitant to do, which was apparent in the way he cradled the gun worryingly. He returned to face the stranger, whose face still held a sickeningly twisted grin. I could now see, as my vision rotated around the room, my doppelganger's face held that same grin. He seemed to be acknowledging whatever the stranger was telling him, words I could not comprehend.

"Luke, stop!"

But my other-self didn't stop. He held the disturbing grin on his face as he slowly raised the revolver up the side of his body.

"Don't do it!"

But he was doing it. Without further wait, he pressed the revolver up to his neck, propping his head up. His hands were shaking violently, a fact that frightened me more because his finger was so close to the trigger. My dream-self was smiling, ready to blow his own brains out while the stranger looked on in glee. It was sick and twisted, even for my sick and twisted mind.

"Luke, don't you think about it! I'm not even on a plane. I'm home, absolutely at home where this isn't happening. I'm dreaming this all up, I have an active imagination." I felt the straps of the airline seat begin to chafe at my skin through my shirt. *I'm being held in place*, I thought, *to watch what's going to happen here. I'm not at home, but I'm under their spell.*

The rocking in Dream-Luke's hand stopped, and then I saw a look of tranquility in his face. He was looking up at the ceiling and whispering words I could not hear at someone or something above him. He finished his speech, and then closed his eyes. I watched as the bullet entered through his neck, erupting in a small shower of blood and brain out of the top of his head.

"No! No!" I screamed, directed at no one and heard by no one as well.

Dream-Luke's body was limp against the bedspread, gun smoking on the floor and blood caking the majority of my sheets. Dream-Luke didn't have any expression on his face, a fact that bothered me as I was still sitting in front of the still scene. I shut my eyes to the aftermath, closed my mind to the pain, and denied that I had just witnessed my own suicide. *This isn't the real world, it's a stupid dream filled with stupid paranoid delusions. Snap out of it. SNAP OUT OF IT.* And I did. Southway was holding down my left arm, while the stewardess on the flight was fanning me with a pathetically-sized airline napkin, occasionally throwing water into my face from a plastic cup.

Southway didn't seem upset at the book on my lap, which sat open on the page I had fallen into a trance from. He merely glanced into my face and wore a look of worry that I could feel through the pressure of his hand on my arm. A bead of sweat was forming on his brow, a look that expressed his nervousness, directed at me for having another event, thankful that our earlier conversation on plane crashes hadn't been bad omens. I leaned back in my seat to look out the window and saw city lights in the far distance. There was a burning feeling on my forehead and I was drenched in my own body sweat.

I filled Southway in on the details of my nightmare: the reappearance of the stranger and my own suicide. He didn't say much of anything, choosing instead to listen carefully before attempting any kind of expression of assurance.

"It's okay, it was a dream. More importantly, one of the nightmares you've been having," he told me.

"I hope it's not true. I hope it isn't some deadly premonition of things to come."

"I doubt it. Maybe they're fucking with you, trying to scramble you up so you make mistakes or just because they find it funny."

"Yeah, I'm breaking out into hysterics," I replied.

"We are definitely at a disadvantage here. Your friends seem to want you to search for the books, but don't seem to be doing this as a mutual exchange. They're exerting dominance over you, control over your actions."

"I…shouldn't have read the book."

"That's also true."

"Southway," I said, "if I die and wind up in another universe, what happens if I cause my own death?"

"Why do you want to think about this? Hm? It's not going to be healthy for you to be worrying about things like that the entire time we're in this."

"I just want to know."

Southway sighed, "I suppose it wouldn't be very much different from death caused by anything else. Like the car crash, you'd move on to another universe, unaware that you transferred consciousness into another reality."

"Unless you're me. Someone who has seen the middle ground."

"Yeah, you would be a special case. Although, the idea of knowing you cause your own death doesn't seem like a healthy way to live. Every day, even on good days, you would sit thinking about how you ruined yourself, left loved ones to cry over you. That knowledge would elude the ones you were alive with, but it would eat away at you, seemingly without cause. And then it would eat away at those closest to you, when they can't figure out a reason you are miserable. One by one, they would slowly begin to leave you, thinking you to be selfish and self-pitying."

"Oh," I said. "So how does one get out of the loop? How do you move on permanently?"

"My father had an idea about that. He shared it with a group of people, of intellectuals, that he met with once a week."

"Yeah? What did he think happened?"

"I was raised Christian, Luke. My father said when you pass on, you enter heaven."

CHAPTER FIVE
Meeting the Team

L anding was not as swift as I'd imagined. Some new worker decided that he had a much better time driving half-asleep and half-drunk, taxiing colossal planes through the airport tarmac in figure eight circles. We were forced to circle above, with the pilot repeatedly lying to us about the state of affairs on the ground.

"There has been an incident on our runway," he said over the intercom.

"Damn right there is," I said back toward the cockpit.

"It seems that we'll have to maintain altitude before we get the all clear."

"Are you kidding?"

"We have been ordered to land in ten minutes."

"That's bullshit."

After twenty minutes, we heard: "We have been ordered to land in twenty minutes."

"Now that's horseshit."

A bit later, we received the reassurance: "We will be landing shortly."

"Like hell we are," I said to the stewardess, standing nearby Southway, "Get me the hell off this plane."

When we finally landed, we got a glimpse of the man who was responsible for our delay. From the windows of the loading bridge, the sight of a supervising manager screaming loudly at the half-drunk loser was perfectly visible, and audible. That's where I was able to glean the details of his drunken escapades.

"I'm tired of this, Thomas! I gave you a chance for a reason!" the supervisor screamed, "How many times am I going to cover for your addiction? Do you think that I can this time? What am I going to say when they ask me what happened today?"

I felt sorry for the guy, but not sorry enough that I was willing to mentally forgive him for the headache I developed on the flight. He just stood there, tilting ever so carelessly around the mid-section: his body in the need of remaining upright while he was being lectured. The supervisor was pulling at his shoulder every now and then, ensuring that he didn't lean too far in one direction. The man, although not audible, was mouthing 'thank you' after every grab by the manager. Eventually, he looked up at the staring audience at the bridge. We were being scolded by the employees of the airport, who were shouting for us to leave the area. When the supervisor caught sight of the distraction, he moved himself and the drunken worker off the tarmac and through a doorway to our left.

When he had disappeared from sight, Southway and I began discussing the event at length, while the woman and her son laughed to themselves and the fat man whispered complaints. The other members of the passenger list talked amongst themselves; about the delay, about the man who would be fired for the whole incident, then onto their plans for the trip (talk of attractions, local relatives, and the last time they had flown into the country).

When we made it into daylight, the two of us waved down one of the yellow cabbies. The taxi driver had an accent that I couldn't place as Middle Eastern or East Asian or African. As far as I was concerned, he had taken a boat from a strange island in the Atlantic to America, fulfilling his lifelong dream to chauffeur unappreciative Americans around in a bright car and stick his neck out every time he risked a late-night passenger. The one passenger, whose actions are reflected in movies and books, brought to life by a warped writer. The psychopath who would sooner stab or shoot the taxi driver before paying for his fare and wishing the man a good day; the sick bastard that everyone goes to the cinema to see.

I don't know if it was due to the judgment I passed on him, but the taxi driver skipped on most of the familiarities, like discussing local events or the weather. Although, if I really thought about it, the drivers in this country were more concerned with finding the most fares and delivering them the quickest than speaking with travelers. Drivers in smaller countries were more focused on giving you the entire package: the quickest routes through the city (that only they know of, kept secret from the other drivers in the company), the best sights to see in town (spots that tourists like to visit or spots that threw a dollar or two the driver's way for each white family that takes the offer), and generally a favorable conversation that would leave you laughing one minute and listening intently to the history of his career as a driver the next.

In short, American taxi drivers liked to make the most money, the others prefer to grab hold of your ear and entertain. The latter wanted to give you an experience instead of a journey. Besides, when you need a cab in the middle of a city you found your dumb-self lost in, you'll reach into your pants pocket to grasp that taxi company number. You'll dial that number on your cell phone (or local pay phone, if you, like me, like to avoid roaming charges and find yourself in a country that hasn't yet heard of an iPhone), and you'll ask for What's-His-Name the driver to rescue you from your predicament. And he'll be sure to tell you another humorous story on the way back to your hotel.

In quick order, by which I mean the span of an hour or so of near silence and complete sweat-riddled seats, we had finally reached the location I had given the driver. We pulled up to the familiar lakeside house of mine, paying the taxi driver more than he probably would charge on an honest conscious. Both of us removed our luggage from the trunk, which, having completed his fare, resulted in the taxi driver speeding off. He allowed the momentum from a pothole to slam shut the trunk lid. We stood not quite surprised at the scene, due to the 21st century mentality of "having seen all that the world could offer" and declaring proudly that "nothing can surprise me."

I strolled up toward the house, pulling open the white fence that surrounded the front yard, when Southway decided to stop me.

"What are we doing at your house?" he said.

"How did you know this is my house?" I said, at a loss.

"You walked right through the gate like it was yours. Wasn't too difficult."

"Oh. I did, didn't I? Well, at least I got you this far."

"What are we doing here, Luke?"

"I had a stop to make. We need to pick up Michael."

"Who's Michael?"

"Michael is the one who started all this," I explained, "Michael is a ghost that has been haunting my house since the beginning."

"Is he dangerous?"

I waved my hand, "He's an idiot or something. Ignorant of his surroundings and things like that. He walked into the bathroom the other day and–" I trailed off. *Go ahead, Luke, and tell him what you were doing that day.*

"Look," I said, catching myself, "just come in for a few minutes. Humor me."

We entered my humble abode, the disgusting mess of a home that was composed of scattered beer bottles, bundles of clothes, and misaligned furniture. At an earlier age, my parents would have scolded me for my lack of care and proper maintenance, with extra commentary regarding the reactions that visiting company would have and the opinions of me that would spread among the community. My response all these years was a big 'Fuck you' in the form of not giving one ounce of attention to their lessons. *Would you even care if they were here, ready to scold you again? Or is it the fact that you have no idea where they are right now?*

"You live like a pig," Southway said.

"Yeah, thanks pops. From what I recall, your place wasn't much more organized."

"You live like a pig," he reiterated, "Just taking a quick look around the place tells me that someone of considerable negligence and ignorance occupies a space here."

"No one brought you here to judge, pal."

"And yet here I am as a witness to the existence of a miserable life."

I glared at him, muttering, "Let's just move along here."

"Sure, just point out the bottles so I don't trip over them and break my neck."

"You know, for a professor, you're too much of a smartass to take seriously."

"That's what the school board said when I applied for a teaching degree. But they eventually relented."

Michael hadn't made an appearance yet, an idea so common to me, but completely alien to Southway. Thus far, I was the one with the crazy ghost roommate, the nightmares, and having died once before with the knowledge that I had died. I still didn't know if Southway could see him, but I had to give it a try, out of curiosity.

"He should be around here," I said.

"Where, Luke?"

"Over there, actually."

Michael had been leaning against the refrigerator, a sight that only caught my eye upon entering the kitchen. He was simply leaning against it, but his body was transparent, meaning that pieces of him were cut off by the refrigerator door. I quickly considered spending the next hour throwing out any and all pieces of food left in there, but just as quickly reconsidered how long Southway's patience would hold up.

"Where, actually?" Southway interrupted.

"Right there, leaning against the refrigerator."

"I don't see anything, Luke."

"He's there, trust me."

"Where does he come from?"

"I have no idea. He mostly just showed up on his own accord one night."

"Uh huh. Does he jump out of corners, pop through walls?"

"He's a pretty shitty ghost. The quickest movement I saw him pull so far was standing up a bit faster than his usual. But he was the first strange thing I noticed. Dunno if he was the cause of my fun times being chased around by demons and shadows and shit or just a bother sent to annoy me by someone or something else completely."

Michael finally realized that two living humans were conversing nearby, so he peeled himself from the refrigerator door and took a few steps toward me. He stood less than a foot away, a fact that I conveyed by raising a hand to him and taking a few steps back. Michael complied with the boundary I had set up, taking one step back himself. Southway looked on quizzically, eager to see what I would do next to prove my story.

"It's good to see you, Luke. How was your trip?" Michael said, nearly at a whisper. He was awfully soft spoken for a supernatural freak.

"Rocky. The flight was short enough, but I already regret the trip."

"Why's that?"

"I think I'm going to have to take a longer trip."

"This may be the most convincing performance to date. You have not ceased to amuse me, Luke, however I don't believe I can entertain this ruse much more."

"What? What do you mean?" I asked.

Professor Southway rubbed his eyes, and then explained, "I wasn't too sure what to make of your sudden appearance at my door, and I still do not know who gave you my address or where you found the patience to continue this charade. But I can no longer believe you. I mean, I am standing in your kitchen, watching you speak to the plain air as if you were holding a two-sided conversation, when I can plainly see you are insane."

"Don't say that, Southway. You need to believe in this. I need your help."

"No, Luke, I don't believe I am rendering assistance to you any further. I was convinced by your fits and spasms, but this last act is clearly just that. I should've known to ask you where we were heading. This whole adventure is just a ruse."

"No! I need your help or I need your book without you. I don't know if I can finish this on my own, but, if you're going to leave, just leave me the tome."

"And why should I give you my property? Perhaps you are trying to trick me out of a rare volume."

I looked at Professor Southway carefully, and then said, "Professor Southway, you don't believe that book has any value. You told me you wanted to leave it with the vendor. Don't quit now. Please."

"I am sorry, Luke, but you've wasted my time."

A marker began to rise from my counter, gliding slowly across the kitchen until it stopped near a wall. To Southway, this is the event he witnessed. To me, I could see Michael carrying the marker in a standard, human way. Michael uncapped the marker, and then began to scribble on my wall:

"Professor…South, you need to believe in Luke. He is telling the truth."

"Did you have to write on my wall?" I said.

"I apologize. I didn't see paper anywhere."

I moved over to the kitchen sink, spun the roll of paper towels, cut off around six of them, and ran them swiftly underneath running water. I made my way over to the marker on the wall, where Southway was studying the message, hand upon his chin in a thoughtful way. With the paper towels in hand, water dripping onto the tile floor, I rubbed at the marker, creating a large mass of black ink in the wallpaper and destroying my home even further. I cursed at myself quietly, throwing the paper towels angrily in the trash bin.

"First, I had to deal with the blood on the carpet. Now this. I can't win," I sighed.

Southway glanced my way, unsure of his upcoming decision. "Let's continue this adventure, Luke Thornton."

"Did I convince you, finally?"

"Not entirely. I am a man of fact and science. But I'll humor this idea further because of what I've seen."

"How can you not believe what you saw?"

"Oh I believe I saw a marker write itself on the wall. But I don't know if I want to delve any deeper into this madness you've dug for yourself. Let's find the third book. I'll decide if I want to go on after that."

"I'll have to take that as a win."

I decided to re-pack my things for a much longer trip than before, in the event that I would not be returning home for quite some time. Rather than just clothes, I decided to pack a throwing knife into my bag, a precaution against any sort of creatures I may encounter along the way. *Not that you've had much practice with it, Luke.* Before taking off, I had asked Michael if he was able to leave the house, an idea that he confirmed as true. I attempted to ask why he didn't leave earlier, but I received a blank stare as a response. "It wasn't like I didn't ask you to before," I explained to him.

To further prepare myself, I wandered into the tool shed, throwing a number of items, including a hand axe and a shovel into the batch of supplies we had gathered. I found a first aid kit from my bathroom and introduced it to our collective luggage in the living room.

"Now we need a source of transport," I told Southway.

"What did you have in mind?"

I called over Tracy, who was more than ecstatic to see me once again. She hurried over to my house as soon as I hung up the phone, much to my chagrin. Tracy barely drove, due to a crippling fear of interacting with other human beings at speeds that could kill you (or so she proclaimed to me once, randomly), but I managed to convince her over the phone to bring her car over. Soon enough, I saw her silver four-door pull into my driveway. She nearly left the engine running in the excitement at seeing me, but managed to pull out the key before she leapt out the door.

"I'm so glad you're okay," she said.

"I'm, uh, glad I am too." I shot a glance to Southway, who seemed to be under a false impression of our relationship. I told Tracy that we needed a car, which saddened her a bit and nearly brought another tear to her eye.

"You're leaving again?"

"Well…yeah I am. I'm not quite done with what I started. I need some time and a way to get around."

"Oh."

"Yeah, so that's that. And don't worry about your car. I'll get it back to you as soon as I can." I waved at her as I pushed Southway towards her car and got in myself.

"Who is that girl, Luke?"

"Just a bit of a stalker problem I have."

Southway stared at me, and then said, "You are borrowing your stalker's car."

"Yes, that's the truth, as a matter of fact."

"You're taking advantage of that girl's interest in you," he replied.

"No I am not. I'm procuring a method of transport for us. Besides, she owes me a favor anyway."

"She owes you a favor? Does she really?"

"No, but if you don't shut up about it, you are more than welcome to walk yourself the rest of the way. As for me, I have a car to drive."

Southway conceded. Glancing up at the rear-view mirror, I saw that Michael had planted himself in the backseat in the interim. He smiled at me, and I shot him a look of disgust. I turned my attention to the bag I had packed and removed the knife from a side pocket. This I deposited into the glove compartment.

"What is that?" Southway asked, pulling his knees to the side to allow the glove compartment to fall open.

"Just a bit of insurance."

Starting the car, we began the next step of our journey.

The car rolled along the dirt road for about a mile. Neither the Professor nor I said anything the entire way; we were just eager to get off the road.

"We're getting close," he said.

"Yeah, I can see that," I said sarcastically, glancing at the GPS on the dashboard. He shot me a dirty look, like a look of the "it is completely your fault we nearly died" variety. So a look you've probably never seen before. Brad Pitt told me that 'You have arrived at your destination.' I slowed the car and looked around.

All that we could see was a sea of trees in the headlights, and a forest to the right and left. I glanced at the rear-view mirror, looking for a way out. All I found was Michael sitting in the back seat. The GPS device began its shut down process, with Brad Pitt reminding me to stow it in an unseen place, like the glove compartment. I obeyed. The Professor and I opened our doors and stepped onto the road.

"There is nothing here," the Professor stated.

"No shit, Tesla," I quipped. The Professor took a few steps toward me, *probably to shove my head into the dirt*, but thought better of it and looked around more.

"Look over there."

In the distance, I could barely make out a chain-link fence on the horizon. We both jumped back into the car and I hit the gas. The car sputtered and died. I took two fingers and put them to the side of my neck. Pulse was still slow. I then lifted my right hand, made a fist, and slammed it repeatedly into the dashboard.

"Show it who's boss," the Professor interrupted.

"Hey, fuck you. What are you gonna do about this?"

"Walk." He opened the passenger door again and began walking ahead of the car. *Lazy bastard didn't even close the door.* I jumped out of the car after him, and then remembered we had left someone behind. I jogged back to the back window and knocked on it. Michael turned to face me, poking his head through the glass.

"We're going up ahead, watch the car."

"Okay."

"Okay?"

"Yeah."

"Good. I'm going now."

I caught up with the Professor some ways ahead. Together, we walked up to the chain-link fence and saw a rather crude, dark green sign, much like the kind you'd find on a highway but slathered in orange-gold lettering, hanging above it.

"Farmingdale Dump?" I questioned, angrily, "The next book is in a dump?"

"The next **guy** who has our book is here."

"So, the….caretaker? The dump curator….guy?"

The Professor just shrugged his shoulders and walked up to the entrance. The odor was foul, repugnant and a war crime against the sense of smell. I thought of the number of scents one accumulates knowledge of throughout life and came away with the conclusion that it reeked of dead skunk dipped in raw sewage. Or, I would describe it as the kind of smell you'd expect when looking at a picture of a dump. Go to one, take a deep breath. I'll wait; books don't go anywhere when you're gone.

We didn't have a direction to go in. Rather, I just followed the Professor's lead, hoping he would stumble into something that would let me finally go home. A pigeon pecking at one of those plastic-can holders turned to look at me and then shrugged its shoulders. A little bit further, a little more trash. There were numerous, filthy plastic containers of microwave easy food and the occasional college-poor noodle cup. I managed to spot a dirty magazine in one of the piles and felt a bit disgusted at the fact that I made an effort to get a look at the cover. It was a low-budget, low-audience porno mag for lovers of the heavier woman, adorned on the cover by the image of a heavyset dark woman spooning what looked like vanilla ice cream onto her chest.

I slammed into the Professor while I was distracted. He took a look at me, brow furled, then at the magazine I was staring at. Then he turned back to me, making a disgusted face, like he was my dad or something.

"What?" I said.

"Nothing. Let's keep looking."

Never in my life had I imagined how much shit people throw out over time. The piles of garbage stacked high, liquids and solids all crushed into sickening goo. It was amazing. Some of the stuff people tossed weren't even garbage. I scoped out an antique lamp sitting atop a stack of old newspapers. The lamp was not a huge oddity in a place like this; I could imagine many old pieces of décor and furniture being carelessly tossed into the garbage for the simple reason that "it clashed with the color theme of the living room." I stopped in my tracks. Something was bothering me about it. The lamp was placed too conveniently. It couldn't possibly be a coincidence, and I could not see a sanitation worker taking his well-deserved break propping the lamp up atop a stack of discarded books.

"Plus it has power," the Professor interjected, breaking my stride.

"I was about to think that," I responded.

"Sure you were, Luke."

"Dick."

He was right, though. The lamp was getting power, illuminating a short area on the stack of garbage and barely making it to where we stood. Someone had apparently turned the dump into his, or her (got to keep this politically correct), personal sanctuary.

"We should be careful," the Professor said, never letting me finish off an internal thought, "Who knows if this guy is dangerous."

"Sexist," I probably blurted to him. My memory is a bit hazy; I may have just slurred an insult at him. What I do remember, however, was taking a stroll past the Professor to look up ahead. A hollowed-out car frame at the top of one of the piles began to slide down its side, pushing up used napkins, paper towels, and banana peels into the air. I turned quickly to my left to anticipate its eventual destination. Thinking I could outrun the car frame, I took three big leaps to my right. Lifting my head back to the avalanche, I watched in horror as the car hit a bulky refrigerator and catapulted directly towards me. I screamed like a woman.

I had my eyes closed the entire time, hands curled up to my face. When I heard the crash of the car frame, I felt a rush of air move past my body. I looked up from my fingers to see the edge of the car frame directly in my vision. I looked around and saw the entire frame surrounded me. Grabbing the top, I pulled myself up and over the frame, hitting the ground on my left arm. I stood up and rubbed it.

Before me was the car frame, lying on its side. Apparently, it had managed to land directly on its side, with my body standing perfectly straight through the driver and passenger side doors. The Professor had run up to me, startling me a bit. Although, when you have that unfamiliar awareness that you have just passed from this world and into another, any sort of stimuli is liable to freak you out for a minute or two.

"You were almost…well…"

I knew what he meant. It was the same as the car crash back home; one of me had climbed right out of the wreckage. The other guy was enjoying the wonderful sensation of being pulverized by a couple thousand pounds of American fiberglass and metal.

"Let's not talk about it," I answered.

"I…think that's a good idea," he responded.

A bottle soared through the air and landed with a crash, not two feet from where the Professor stood. He looked up, unfazed, into the eyes of the mad bum who had come to see the commotion. He was wearing a plain blue shirt underneath some teenager's old Downshallow hoodie, free advertisement for a long defunct rock band from the eastern seaboard. His jaw held onto a one-foot beard, brown, which was scarcely decorated by a splatter of food or crumb bits. Atop his head, a beanie, with the embroidered words 'Fashion Passion' in a red bubble-letter font, sat.

"Get out of here!" The bum yelled.

"Um, sorry about your…car?" I said, confused.

The Professor walked past me and thrust his hand out from under his coat, toward the bum. Then he introduced himself, "Professor Southway. Pleased to meet you."

"Ah," the man replied, "I see at least one of you has some manners. Well, welcome to my home. I've got a mini-fridge hooked up to my generator off there in the living area and some seats strewn about around here. Ah! Here's a recliner," he continued, "for the nice Mister Professor. And for the clumsy one, I have a lawn chair." He brushed off a layer of dirt that had caked the chair. It didn't look too inviting, but I sat down anyway. The Professor did the same.

"I take it you want to know how I came to live here?" the bum asked.

"Actually, I-" I started to say, but Professor Southway raised a hand toward me. Evidently, he had wanted to hear him out. *Not like you're in a rush or anything, Luke. Can't wait to see how Saarlathesh feels about us listening to this guy's life story. I thought about how little time a human life appeared to take for an immortal god.* I chased away the thought.

"You're right, clumsy one, we haven't traded introductions."

"I'm Luke." When he approached me, I could smell the dirt and grime he had accumulated from living in the dump, which took me aback considering I was now around that same filth. I did my best to not cough or gag. He didn't notice either way, so I quickly gave him a handshake, one of a very limp variety. He returned to his seat.

"I'm Harry. Harry Breck. Yup. Been living here for quite some time now. Used to live in that town you passed through, some ten or eleven years ago. A decade ago, I found my wife sleeping with my office manager, trying to convince him to give me a promotion. She figured she'd have more money for clothes, and I'd be a happy little husband. So I quit. Lost my job. Lost my house. Divorced the wife. So I came to live here in the dump."

"What a tragedy," Southway commented, with feigned sincerity. Feigned, but very convincing to Harry, it seemed.

"Wait, how did you go from homeless on the streets to homeless in a dump?"

"It's not so bad," he said, holding his hand up, as if I was going to interrupt further after I had stopped speaking. The raised hand was specifically for me, because he was facing my direction and looking into my face.

"It's amazing the things you can find amongst the discarding of common people. Things to live with, things that'll keep you warm at night, things that will keep you entertained, things to make things bright, and things to, well, build a shack out of."

"Look here," he pointed at a vase, taped or glued or both. "This vase holds the plants I collect in the forest just outside the fence. Look at the roses, the violets. How well they mix together under the moonlight and lamplight. Look over here," he moved over to the previously mentioned mini-fridge, "this generator here gives me enough power to keep some food stocked up for a long time. People sometimes throw out food just because a funny little number tells them it's no good anymore. But they don't even try to taste it. Give a scrap of food a chance, y'know?"

The Professor and I just nodded. Harry Breck moved around the living area of his makeshift, outdoor shaft, tidying up knick knacks and brushing dirt and garbage off of his furniture.

Professor Southway coughed. Twice.

"Hm? Oh, pardon me," Harry replied to him, "it's been so long since I've had…real company. I had forgotten you were here. Sometimes, I catch myself talking to no one but myself. Now, as I was saying, human beings living in the city have thrown out some wonderful things out here. A moose head's antler breaks off after falling in the living room, the family will throw it out and buy a newer, fresher one. That moose went through that type of story," he cocked his head toward the back wall (a large bit of plywood) of his shack. The moose head was downright creepy, especially in the nighttime light. It was indeed missing a good deal of itself, a portion of the left antler about two feet in.

Harry spat into the ground, then carried on, "The trouble with living on a day-to-day basis, where moose heads can be replaced as easily as buying another, is that there is no true value to any possession. When I find a treasure hidden in the mounds of this junkyard, I give it a proper home among all the other treasures in my shack. Tell me, Luke, what possession have you spent hours over, searching for the perfect position? For the perfect view?"

"I don't know," I said, "My pillow?"

Harry frowned. Professor Southway clasped his head into his palm. I looked around awkwardly, but Harry still had his eyes on me.

"Southway?" I uttered, escaping my own comment.

"Yes, it is about time we discussed our visit, Harry," the Professor stated.

"The reason for your visit? Were you not just visiting a bum in a landfill?" Harry joked, taking me by surprise.

"No doubt you already know that we have come a long way to share something with you. It was quite a drive, but, from the look on your face, I would say that you know exactly what I am referring to."

Harry turned to face Professor Southway. He smiled, and said, "Little guy in a suit, strange and weird? Talked about some important crumpled paper in my garbage pile?"

"Ask Luke. I didn't have the pleasure to meet the stranger."

Harry turned to me.

"I was in a car accident, I woke up in a hospital with some important book," I told him, "We're on a quest for the complete collection."

He walked over to a plywood desk that was slumped against the shack wall, originally an industrial sized piece of plywood. He pulled open a drawer, which caused the one below it to fall out. This apparently was the intended result, as Harry dipped down and scooped something from the second drawer. It was a piece of yellow notebook paper, *college-ruled*, with a **ton** of writing scrawled on it. He lifted the paper in his hands and turned it, front and back, towards us, like a salesman offering the latest product he had to offer. He completed the act by smiling and mouthing some inaudible boast about its features.

"This," he told us, "is nothing but junk. But that strange man told me to find it in a pile on the far end of the yard. Exactly where he told me in a dream, I found it. I was ready to chuck it away, but decided to keep it. Just in case that fella needed it for something."

"May I see it?" the Professor asked.

"No," Harry pulled the paper into his coat pocket.

"I need to see what's on it."

"It's just gibberish. Gibberish. Drivel. Lines on a paper. Not even letters."

"It's not in English."

"It's mine."

"Can we stop arguing? Why are we arguing?" I jumped right into the fight.

"Luke, we need that paper from him. It's important for what we need to do," Southway said.

"So the stranger visited Harry. Maybe the book is just somewhere nearby. Let the man keep his paper."

"Luke, you told me that we were to meet someone here. You're the one who is being told where to go and who to talk to. The stranger is talking to you, giving you directions," Professor Southway was trying to regain his composure. His hand was at his temples. "Luke, I told you back in London what I could decipher of the book I have. Your tome isn't that different than mine in style and the ideas they share. I'm starting to think we need to stop something from happening, but that might just be a wild sense of adventure. Maybe these pieces of literature aren't anything but a strange collection that some stranger wants in his library. But we don't even know if the stranger is *human*."

"Yeah, but who says we can't just give this up, right here and right now?" I replied.

"Because we have no idea what far reaching consequences that kind of action might bring us. I'd rather we play along until we get something concrete about these books or the stranger. Then we can make a move," Professor Southway reasoned.

"What if this **is** nothing but a wild goose chase? For some freak art collector?"

"What if it is? Do you really want to go back in that car, head home to your small town? Run screaming one night from your house while something chases after you? Don't you want to see this to the end? And, at the very least, make sure that we're not just handing over something we really shouldn't be?"

I stopped trying to fight the Professor. He had a point. All this shit had something to do with the stranger in the tuxedo, with the demands that he asked of us, of me. Maybe he had a way to get rid of the ghosts in my house. Maybe he was the reason they were bothering me in the first place. Maybe I would strangle him with my bare hands when I see him again. Maybe…if I knew where we were going from here.

"Luke, I know you don't want Michael to become your permanent houseguest," Southway added.

"You're right."

"Who's Michael?" Harry said.

It took a number of tries, but Southway was able to convince Harry to hand over the scrap paper in his jacket. While we walked back to the car, Southway pored over the details of the scribbles. I filled in Harry on everything we knew about the strange man in the tuxedo and Michael, being sure to portray myself in a bit more heroic light in both regards. He seemed doubtful at first, but said he was willing to accept my wild tales because we were taking him for a drive. Harry hadn't been out of the dump and into the countryside for some time; it would be his first return to the "civilized" world in a while. I didn't bother to argue that this wouldn't be a nice walk in the park because we now had him aboard.

Professor Southway and I took a few gulps of fresh, pine air, recycling all the sewage in our lungs with a breathable replacement. I took my position in the driver's seat, and Southway sat himself in the passenger side. Harry Breck decided to take the backseat behind Southway, which I had to remind him was currently occupied by Michael. Harry had a few words for the ghost, loudly proclaiming that Michael was free to take the seat next to him. I rolled my eyes and turned back to face the steering wheel.

"Where to?" I asked.

"It's a map!" Southway interrupted.

"What? What're you yelling at?" said Harry.

"A map of what?" I said.

"It's not in another language like I believed or a cypher of any kind. It's just chicken scratch. This is very clearly a map to some kind of digging spot," he continued.

"A digging spot? It's a treasure map?" I joked.

"Not too far from it," Southway answered, "It seems to me that the dump is the starting point. It must be somewhere in town. Luke, turn on the GPS again for me."

"Got it."

Professor Southway traced his finger along the screen, referencing the map whenever he encountered a turn or a bend in the path. Eventually, he settled on a point in the nearby suburbs, on or near 1125 Campbell Drive. The location was about twenty eight minutes away. We set a course, and the GPS found a signal, which Brad Pitt confirmed with a holler.

"Can you please change that?" Southway demanded.

"No."

CHAPTER SIX
The Final Tome

Normally, a treasure map leads to some sandy beach in the middle of the Caribbean. Or some form of seaside cavern, full of lost treasures of Some-Beard the Pirate. Other times, a treasure map crosses entire oceans and continents and brings any aspiring relic hunter to a lost city in the Sahara. Further still, a group of kids can find a map that directs them to the town park, a giant, black cartoon X marking the ground underneath the monkey bars. Normally, this kind of stuff is expected out of an adventure flick or an indie comic.

Where the three of us found ourselves parked was none of the above. Doubting Southway, I parallel parked between two cars, awkwardly and crooked, while looking up at the one-family home of 1125 Campbell Drive.

"This can't be right," I suggested.

"We followed the map," Southway said.

"Maybe you're just not reading it right," I said.

"No, this is definitely where the map leads."

"Must be buried in the backyard. Sounds to me like a good time for digging," Harry offered, from the backseat.

"Harry, do you think you can find it out there?" Southway asked.

"Woah, wait a minute. We can't go tearing up someone's backyard with a shovel because some map told us to," I said.

"We don't have much of a choice," Southway replied. He turned around in his seat, and then said, "Harry, open up the boot. There should be a shovel in there." Southway turned back around and nearly ripped my GPS from the holster on the dashboard. "Take this with you. It'll pinpoint the location as close as possible. The scrap of paper has what looks like coordinates written on the margin. Try typing that in."

"Roger," Harry said, taking both the scrap of paper and my GPS.

"No!" I interjected, "This is definitely not a good idea."

But Harry was already out the car door and rummaging through the trunk. I closed my hands firmly over my face, pressing two thumbs into the inner corner of my eyes.

"We just don't have to get caught. It'll be like grave robbing. We'll dig up the backyard, find what we're after, and replace all the holes with dirt," Southway said.

"I am not okay with this. What are we gonna do when the family wakes up to a bunch of patches of dirt on their back lawn? We shouldn't have come here."

"Do you forget who drove us here?"

"I didn't know it was going to be someone's house! We can't just dig holes into someone's land and hope that, if they wake up, we just explain that we're looking for an evil book of the dead and he should just go back to sleep!"

"And if it had been inside of a closed store or private property? What then? You're overreacting. No one is going to wake up.

Harry will find the book in the yard and we'll get out of here as soon as we can."

Harry had already returned to the driver side window as Southway finished trying to reassure me. He had made a preliminary search of the residence, scoping out the front yard and taking a glance into the front windows of the house. I had noticed that he was repeatedly returning to the GPS screen, comparing his location with the book's position. I rolled down my window, which he partially ducked his head into.

"What's wrong?" Southway asked. Harry had a doubtful look on his face, one that I didn't care very much for, but Southway seemed unfazed by.

"The GPS says it's not outside. The point is definitely in the house," Harry explained.

"Great!" I said.

"Relax, Luke. Harry, can you get inside?"

"No, absolutely not. No, no, no, no, no," I complained, starting to become upset at the trio of adventurers we had become even though we hadn't gotten very far since picking up Harry. *Drive home, throw your book in the lake, Luke. Both of them, yours and Southway's. I'm sure that Southway won't mind losing his book and returning home where he belongs.*

"Luke, will you try to not make a scene of this? How else do you want to finish this? With only two of the three books?"

"Can we? Can we just not have any books at all? Pretend like we never met and this never was a possibility we were considering?"

"Nope," Harry said.

Southway volunteered to watch from the street (naturally), promising to send a message to my phone if there was any trouble.

"I'm not giving you my phone number."

"Luke, you are seriously endangering this entire situation. We need to be smart about this."

So I gave Southway my phone number, feeling that I had given up more of myself than I was willing to in the first place. *He now has your name, your phone, and your job description.* Harry went with me, leading me to the small, concrete stepping stones that made a path through the back gate and into the yard. Beyond the neatly trimmed grass, the yard boasted an aboveground swimming pool, a swing set for a small child, and a bird bath, most likely made of plastic and designed to replicate a marble texture. Harry casually strolled up to the back porch, the wood creaking with each step up the stairs.

I pulled at his sleeve and said, "Shhhh! Do you want someone to hear you? Why don't you run up the stairs, then?"

Harry swatted my hand away and said, "Get off of me, Luke. I'm warning you."

"Jesus. Both you and Southway are tense."

I released his sleeve, and then followed the same creaking method up the wooden steps, which led to a glass sliding door. We both peered inside, unable to see much beyond what could have been a kitchen counter.

"No dog bowl," I mentioned.

"What?"

"I don't see a dog bowl. That means they don't have a guard dog or a pet dog. Y'know, like a yappy Chihuahua."

"Sure. Or a bulldog."

Harry reached into the pocket of his pants, wherein he fumbled with a few contents and succeeded in pulling out a small switchblade after dropping a few coins onto the deck.

"Shhhh!"

Harry ignored me, then knelt before the sliding door and began fidgeting with the lock, twisting and turning the knife handle this way and that way. I knelt down next to him, attempting to conceal myself in the dark with relatively light blue jeans on. *Smooth outfit for sneaking.* The lock audibly clicked out of place, which put such a smile upon Harry's face that you'd assume he either never thought the knife would do the trick or he was reminiscing on a previous lock he had jimmied open. Along with Southway, I had no interest in digging through the dark corridors that probably lined the halls of Harry's past. I was content with never knowing how he learned that trick.

"After you," he said.

I performed some kind of strange shuffling walk, as I was still kneeling low to the ground but unwilling to crawl into someone's house in the dark. Harry simply stepped into the kitchen casually, sliding the door behind him until it eased into the frame. He locked it.

"What did you do that for?" I whispered from the floor.

"In case they do wake up. Nothing will seem out of place and we can hide until they go back to bed."

"Lower your voice. You might as well dial the house number and tell them the night janitors are here to clean them out."

Harry didn't seem happy at this; his jaw clenched visibly, even though the nighttime darkness surrounded us. I looked around and took a gulp. Slowly, I rose to my feet, watching for any signs that someone already knew we were inside. If they did, I had every intention of leaving Harry behind to take the blame.

"Let's take a look around. They have to have a bookshelf or the book lying around somewhere," I said.

"Would you take a look at this bullshit," Harry said. I turned to face him again, seeing that he had casually dug into their kitchen trash, shifting through its contents. Much like in the Farmingdale Dump, I had the slight feeling of nausea rise in my throat.

"I know you live in the junkyard, but are you kidding me right now?"

"Look at this," he said, producing a bottle of half-finished orange juice, gallon sized.

"Orange juice?"

"Luke, read off the expiration date."

I peered through the dark, squinting in a failed attempt to have them dilate faster. From Harry's hand, I snatched the orange juice and brought it close to the sliding door, using the moonlight to illuminate the label. "Okay, so it's today's date. So?"

"They threw out perfectly good orange juice."

"And this helps us…?"

"Luke!" Harry said, not necessarily loud, but in a fatherly way that made me want to slug him in the face and call our mission a failure right then and there. My fear of having a right hook with the force of a small child prevented me from doing so. Harry continued, "This is the exact thing I was talking about back home. People wasting good food and throwing away useful stuff just because a couple of numbers tell them it's beyond use. Why, a man could find a decent meal in the wasteful refuse bins of the ignorant."

"I don't get it, Harry. You like to drink expired juice?"

Harry unscrewed the top to the gallon, taking a huge gulp from the rim and swallowing proudly, with a smile on his face and a fire in his eyes.

"That is seriously sick. Don't even dare pass that to me to try."

"This orange juice is tasty, Luke. Tell me, who decides that the juice will expire on this exact date?"

"Well, the people who work in the orange juice industry, naturally."

"And how do they know the exact time that orange juice expires?"

I shrugged my shoulders, "They make an educated guess based on how long someone else tells them it lasts?"

"Because all orange juice is made the same, right? Because no other factors affect it? If this family even has five members, they could've had this juice for breakfast instead of leaving it to truly expire in the trash."

"Can we just get on with this? You're freaking me out. Put the damn juice back in the trash and help me out here," I said, turning around to face the blackness of the interior. I looked into the hallway, making sure that no one was standing there with a gun, ready to figure out who was arguing about orange juice at two in the morning. *Jesus, it was like fighting at home back when I had what resembled a family.*

Harry began to wander beyond the kitchen, taking a right turn around the counter and disappearing into a room beyond. I chose to walk through the kitchen and into the hallway, being precautious enough to slide my feet across the carpet, muffling the sound. It wasn't long before I reached the front door; the foyer of the house was much wider in size than it was deep. Turning to my right and checking out the stairway leading to the bedrooms above, I crept into the living room.

The living room floor connected the carpeting from the hall. Around the area, I spotted a large TV ahead of me, with a number of game systems and media devices hooked up. A shadow that I thought moved was just a mess of wiring and cords behind the TV set itself. In front of the entertainment center sat a single, four person couch, green and white-striped in color and holding a few pillows of different sizes. Turning right once more, further into the living room, I spotted a computer atop a desk and the bookcase I was searching for. The computer was sitting in the corner to my right, the bookcase to my left, and a darkened doorway, in between the two, directly ahead of me.

From the doorway, the frightening, soot-filled face of Harry Breck entered through the darkness. From my chest cavity, the bones of my body played a rhythmic tune to the tempo of my quickly escalating heartbeat.

"Jesus," I whispered, "did you have to?"

"Sorry, couldn't resist. The bookcase is here."

"Yeah."

The bookcase was made of plywood, a do-it-yourself contraption that surprisingly was one of the few homemade projects that manage to look exactly as the image on the box it came in. It was colored a plain black, but the Technicolor explosion that graced the covers of the books gave a pleasing appearance to the entire piece. Below the books, three rows of film cases were stacked neatly, arranged, from what I saw, in alphabetical order. I began to look at the selection when:

"Hello? Luke? Is the book on the shelf?"

"Sorry, Harry. They have a good collection here."

"Do they have *Casablanca*?"

"How old did you say you were again?"

I scanned the binding on the shelf until I happened across one of the books that seemed to fit the style of the ones held by Southway and myself. Reaching up towards it, I had to balance myself on the bookcase with one hand; the book itself was directly on the top row, higher than the height that God had decided to give me during puberty. When it was in my grasp, I pulled the book out from the tight wedge it had made for itself between two others. The bookcase shook a bit as I jumped back and it wobbled in a concerning way, which prompted Harry to move in front of it and brace both sides of the shelf with two hands.

The bookcase ceased wobbling. I sighed in relief, as did Harry, who was still holding onto the bookcase with his head facing the floor.

"What are you doing in my house?"

I spun around just as soon as I heard the "you" in the man's voice. Before me, a young guy was standing about three inches taller than me and wearing nothing but a sleeveless A-shirt, a pair of white and blue striped boxers, and a bath robe, which was open. The open bath robe exposed and revealed to me that this guy didn't have the time to button up his boxers or had just taken some time to use the restroom recently. *Also, Luke, you seem to have a problem with wandering eyes.* In his hands, I noticed, with a large helping of fear, a wooden, signed baseball bat, more or less authentic and likely to be the real deal.

"Oh, hello," I blurted, trembling with the book nestled against my chest by a forearm.

He looked down at the book. "You're ***stealing*** from me?!"

"No?"

Harry split the second that I had uttered the stupid word, dipping into the doorway that he had scared me from. I looked back, as if hoping he would spring back out and grab me, but Harry had bolted as fast as he could through the kitchen. *That bastard is leaving me behind to take the blame. That was my fucking idea.* I heard the sliding door open in a rapid slam. By the time I turned back, a baseball bat was hurtling at my face with a speed I could only guess was quick by the gust of wind that hit me in the face. My knees found themselves willing to bend without my command, causing the bat to fly beyond my body and into the bookcase that I had removed the book from. The man's grasp on the handle did not falter, and he wound up another blow.

I wasted no time in scrambling through the darkened doorway, into an adjoining hall, where I crashed into the wall with my left shoulder. Pain raced through the muscles and shocked me into scrambling further into the hall, which saved me from the crushing strike that embedded the bat into the drywall. It did not take a struggle for the homeowner to wrestle it free from the newly-made hole, so I wasted no time myself. I managed to place the soles of my feet on the ground, gaining traction and speeding into the kitchen. Throwing my body over the counter, I fell to the floor in a heap, failing to land on my feet.

The young guy was quick to follow, although he didn't try to leap the counter as poorly as I did. Sliding against the tile floor, I pulled myself up with just enough energy to make a leap at the sliding door. To which I found that Harry had somehow dropped the lock behind him. *Shit, shit, shit.* I was now standing, turning to see the homeowner had been winding up a third swing. It hit me right in the gut with enough force to send me through the glass sliding door and had me tumbling across the deck with dozens of shards of glass. My body continued rolling until I reached the few wooden steps; I agonizingly slid across each and every step with the left side of my rib cage. Coughing and rolling onto my back, I looked up to see the stars in the sky.

My moment of rest was cut short by the homeowner walking into my eyesight, cutting off a perfectly nice view of the moon.

"Man, can you just, like, move aside for a second before you bludgeon me?" I coughed out.

The man responded by raising the wooden bat above his head. I barrel rolled across the grass as the bat connected with the ground where my body had been. The force of the strike had sent tremors through the guy's hands, splintering the bat and cutting across his palms. He yelled, which was followed by lights kicking on in the neighboring houses. I was sitting on my ass at that point, but I wasted no more time sticking around the neighborhood. At full force, my legs carried me through the back gate, across the stepping stones, and straight into the driver's seat of the car that sat parked in the same location I had left it.

I threw the book into the passenger seat on top of Southway's lap, floored the accelerator, and we were flying down the block the next second.

"Turn left here," Southway said.

I didn't argue. It was a dirt path leading into the deep woods, somewhere far from the house we had just robbed. None of us had said anything since I got back into the car, and, for most of the way, I was clutching at my stomach and ribs, trying to push away the excruciating pain. Southway had watched the cars pass through the window, leaning his head against the glass, Harry sat quietly behind him with a look of worry on his face, and Michael... Michael stared at me through the rear view mirror, saying nothing and doing nothing.

After a sufficient distance into the woods, which I determined by the fading sounds of police sirens speeding through the neighborhood, I pulled the car over to the side. I pulled the key from the ignition, and then sat for a few minutes in silence. *That was way too close. This whole trip has been a mistake from the start.* Aggressively, I threw open the driver side door, then walked beyond the car.

"Luke!" Michael said from the back window. I turned to face him, but it took me a few seconds to realize that he had stuck his head through the glass. I rubbed my eyes and hoped I was dreaming. *Nope.* Southway also got out of the car, but he leaned on the open door with his forearm.

"Where are you going, Luke?" he said, then rested his head on the arm he had placed on the door.

"I'm going for a walk, I need fresh air."

"Alright. Harry, get out of the car. We could all use some air."

Harry obliged him without complaint, and even Michael floated through the door. We were all standing around quietly, when I turned away and began walking through the woods. I made sure not to take any turns, in case I found myself too deep and in need of rescuing. So I simply walked straight down the dirt path, hands in my pocket and head to the ground. I thought about my friends, off at college and attending frat parties without me, making new memories with their new friends in their new surroundings. I thought about the fallen car at the dump, the memory sending a surging shiver up my spine.

Southway had told me on the trip back that I shouldn't think too hard about my "near-death experiences," on account that I, he suggested, most likely have been having them for a number of years. It was true, to an extent, that the amount of near misses in traffic, or close calls with falling objects, wasn't a small number. Driving, on any day, was a string of near misses and close calls. Danger lurked on every lane of every road, be it in the form of a person failing to signal or another attempting to merge their car with my own because of sheer boredom. The only difference to me was the fact that the stranger had taught me the truth; that every near miss is a death in one universe, and a transfer of my consciousness to another. *Between this and talking to yourself, they should have you—*

"AHHHHH NOOOOO!"

I didn't finish the thought. I had reached the end of the dirt path sometime before my inner monologue distracted me. I was lost in my thoughts, too stupid and too reckless to see that I was walking through crunching leaves, a pile of which had been camouflaging a nice deep descent down a hill. My body quivered on each blow as I tumbled lower and lower down. I felt my ankle catch fallen tree bark, which spun me clockwise and resulted in my back slamming against a standing tree. My trip didn't stop there either; the impact on the tree bounced me past it in some direction, and I spun again, tumbling through rocks, sticks, and leaves.

Eventually, I finished my roll to the bottom. The wind had been knocked out of me. I turned myself over onto my stomach, and then grasped at the leaves around me. *Fuck, I'm in a lot of pain.* Then, the world stopped. I felt frozen, a fact that was confirmed by the leaves, kicked up from my fall, remaining in place on thin air. The foliage around me seemingly drained of all colors. The land beneath me quickly opened up, leaving nothing below me but a black void peppered with stars. I fell into the void and screamed.

The fall was very short. I had landed painlessly onto an invisible piece of floor above the familiar blue-violet stream in the darkness. I looked up to see the face of the stranger, who was making his way slowly towards me. He offered me a hand, which I begrudgingly accepted, then lifted me to my feet.

"Do you need a hand, Luke Thornton?"

"Obviously. So I died again, huh?"

"It appears so. I believe your spine was broken on the second tree. Let's return you there, shall we?"

And with that, the world came back in between a blink. I looked around, saw that I was sitting against tree bark. The stranger was kneeling in front of me.

"Please spare me the details, will ya?" I rubbed at my back, finding that it was still in one piece in this universe. "I finished getting your books for you."

"Yes, my master and I are quite pleased."

"Can I give them to you?"

"If it were so easy. He has commanded that you bring them, and the two men with you, to a place not far from here."

"Of course. What about the ghost?"

"Of which ghost do you speak?"

"Michael."

"I'm not familiar with him."

I eyed the stranger carefully. *He doesn't know who Michael is, Luke. Michael isn't involved after all, you shouldn't have brought him.* I told myself that it didn't matter, that Michael didn't have to worry about risk or danger. He was here just for the adventure.

"Where do we bring the books to?"

"There is a shrine not too far from here, which in the old days saw much more use than it does today," he rose, then took a few steps away from me. He seemed to be surveying the woods.

"Can I have an address?"

"As per the norm, you will gain knowledge of that fact when our conversation has concluded."

"Tell me what you are."

"I beg your pardon, Mr. Thornton?"

"Like, what kind of creature are you? Where do you come from?"

He smiled, another cheap imitation of a human emotion, as I could see there was no emotion behind it. *Maybe he's a robot?* I dismissed the idea as too far-fetched. *As if this entire adventure wasn't ripped out of the mind of Jack Johnson for his shitty sci-fi show.*

"Why, I am human, like you, Mr. Thornton."

"Bullshit."

"I am quite sincere. You see, I serve my master, and I serve him quite well. I have been his servant for a long, long time. Those who serve Saarlathesh are handsomely rewarded for their efforts, gaining knowledge and a piece of his power."

"You're pulling my leg. Where do you come from, really?"

"It was such a long time ago…but I believe it was Colorado."

I couldn't believe such a lie. This had been the third time that I had spoken with the stranger; this time, I was in the middle of the woods, with no one else around to see me. How had he gotten here so fast?

"Here, let me show you." The stranger knelt once more before me, producing a small knife from his jacket pocket. He moved the knife over to his arm, which he placed against the skin carefully. "Watch." I was watching; I could do nothing else. With precision, he began to cut his arm in a calm way, exposing a calm river of red that gravity seized and pulled down the rest of his arm. From his jacket, he produced another object, a handkerchief, which he wiped the blood with.

"Well, you definitely bleed human blood," I said.

"As opposed to what?"

"As opposed to, like, bug juice or space-man green or something. It wasn't like the blood that's staining my carpet." I wanted to see how much he was involved in that particular scenario. In the hospital room, I deduced, and had plainly seen as fact, that the bee in my bedroom had been sent by Saarlathesh.

The stranger's face turned to frown, which frightened me. *For some reason, Luke, that looked genuine.* Then he said, "Regrettable, that you found it necessary to slay a messenger from Saarlathesh."

"A messenger? That thing tried to kill me! Maybe you should have a talk with your master. Both of you seem to be following two different playbooks."

"Mr. Thornton, do you remember how we first spoke? What necessary sacrifice you made to reach the master's realm?"

"Are you saying that I had to die?"

"Precisely."

I sat dumbfounded. They had killed me, dragging me along into this world of theirs. "Will it end? When I bring the books to you?"

"I am a man of my word. We will no longer require you. When the time comes, Saarlathesh will release you from the nightmares and from our employ."

"Your word better be worth something, or I'll kill you."

"That will not be necessary."

The stranger turned away from me once more, walking deeper into the forest. I sat against the tree bark and watched. I felt slightly relieved, yet uneasy at the meeting. It answered questions, but there was still the screaming voice in the back of my mind, telling me that I was in for just a bit more abuse.

"Mr. Thornton," the stranger shouted.

"Yes?"

"I've taken the liberty of fixing what ailed you. A bit of good faith, on my part. You will see that my word is quite genuine."

With that, he was gone. I moved my body, twisting myself and checking each and every crevice. I pressed down on my ribs, rubbed my back, and generally gave myself a good medical check. Everything seemed to be in order, cured and devoid of the sharp stabbing throbs that had been constant not a minute ago.

I rose from the ground, brushing the dirt from the back of my jeans, and then started to collect sticks around the place. After I had created a sufficiently large pile on a cleared patch, I produced a lighter from my pocket, igniting the bundle of firewood. It began to crackle slightly, which was helped along with the addition of a few leaves scattered around. In the end, I had a nice bonfire before me, so I sat next to it and placed my hands close. I threw the lighter deep into the forest, having used the majority of the lighter fluid to coat the firewood.

I wasn't a smoker, by the way. I was merely cautious enough to carry around materials in the event that they would be necessary. If my memory is still intact, the reason started, like most strange ideas, from a conversation that me and Jean had about the apocalypse. Not the zombie apocalypse or anything in particular, mind you, but any sort of apocalyptic scenario that could potentially spring up in the middle of a car drive home. Jean had argued that we needed to build a supply cache of weapons and things that could be used in the event of an emergency. I had agreed, as I often did with Jean, by adding in that, even without an apocalypse, you could never know when something could come in handy.

Raphael had added items to our list, and, surprisingly, Wayne even contributed a fair number of ideas that neither Jean nor I had thought of. In the end, I wound up carrying a lighter on my person at all times, a throwing knife (that I reasoned I could use as a dagger and which now sat in the glove compartment of Tracy's car), a good length of rope in my trunk, two rolls of duct tape in the trunk (the magic tape, as Raphael called it), a first aid kit underneath my driver seat, and numerous items that I had begun stockpiling in my tool shed one summer. Needless to say, regarding my car, I often raised the eyebrows of passersby, who never thought a harmless look into a young man's trunk would reveal a number of items that could be misconstrued as the toolset of a kidnapper.

I poked at the fire with a larger stick I had found. It was nearly morning by the time that Harry and Southway eventually passed by my campsite and found me falling asleep by the dwindling fire. I recall being lifted up by the two, and then pulled in a direction I did not want to go. They must've been stronger than I thought, or I was thinner, because they carried me all the way to the car. I was placed into the backseat, where I laid down and fell asleep. The car began to back out of the woods.

When I awoke, Harry and Southway explained to me that I talked quite a lot in my sleep, and that, barring the embarrassing details that I chose to share with them, I had mentioned an address to our next destination. I was spending the car ride lying down, which I regretted the one time that Southway was forced to stop short, sending me hurling face-first into the back of Harry's chair. I decided to switch to the seat behind Southway, placing my face against the window. Michael was also sitting with me, much to my disgust, staring out of the car window at the passing trees. *You just know that you were lying on Michael this entire time.*

"How far is it," I mumbled, hoping the only contact I made in the car was with the car seats and that I had not been on Michael.

"GPS says just a bit further," Harry said.

"We're close," Southway echoed.

The books had been collected and stored in my knapsack. A trilogy of cosmic reading material that was dangerous to the mind and hazardous to the soul. So, I lifted the knapsack from the car floor, removing the newest addition to our growing library. It was titled "*The Children of Saarlathesh*," and it seemed to be as dense as the other two books (a length of which I never read, having the attention span of an average teenager-turned-adult) and carried with it the familiar hardcover that they all seemed to share. I cracked open to somewhere in the middle, never being one to regret spoiling a story and read:

> The Ancient Greeks once appointed a number of gods and goddesses to be the bearers and avatars of any, and all, that they believed controlled the World. They had deities for farming, champions of war, festive gods of wine and dance, and the mother god of nurturing. To them, the many

faceted reality of our world was the product of good fortune and divine blessing that deserved worship through a humanoid figure, adopting the visage of the people he or she cared for.

The other gods, those lost to time or intentionally kept hidden from the persecuting eyes of the masses, see worship in a smaller scale, away from the golden chapels and weekly or monthly or yearly rituals. For these gods did not provide the necessities of life: they were not the cause of births or the bringers of rain, but the causes of death and the bringers of hellfire upon the damned souls, who saw fit to take up arms against creatures beyond understand and beyond the tangibility of our world. Yet, these gods are looked upon in the same manner as the Ancient Greek pantheon. These gods are the deities of the darker aspects of our world.

Saarlathesh, the great and powerful Insect King, as his namesake does reveal, is revered in the darkest circles as the lord of all insects, the phylum of Arthropoda, the smallest and most humanly-feared creatures of many eyes and many legs. Saarlathesh is the father of all that flutters and crawls, all those that leap through the air, and all those that cause women, and some cowardly men, to shriek at the sight of them. Yes, the human being, who on average rises to a height of five feet and three inches, cowers atop furniture from the lowly insect, a creature of mere centimeters.

The human race fears the insect for its appearance and for its ability to share a home with them. But humans shouldn't fear the lowly Earth insect; for they are but the lowest pawns of Saarlathesh, players in a grand scheme on such an atomic level that we can never hope to understand their true mechanisms. Saarlathesh, in the realm he has deemed fit to call his, has himself the power and command over much more terrifying insects; hybrids of the ones found naturally on Earth, but twisted and demented into forms that can, and has, produced death on those who simply witness them! But I shall not describe the entities here, lest I conjure images in your, the reader's, mind so horrible as to cause you much worry, turning days of your life into paranoid, schizophrenic shambles through doubt and fear.

And what a fear that humans can summon from within! Unnecessary fear, as it were, of the children of Saarlathesh, those winged demons and snake-like slugs who are a plague upon worlds hitherto unseen by the human eye! Yes, the Insect Fear is talked much in the circles of Saarlathesh's followers; those in the worship of the god find themselves in a state of exacerbated laughter upon the mention of it. For, when inducted into the secretive cult, the knowledge from elder times, from when the world was young and man still walked from place to place with no home, is imparted onto the new blood.

Some throw away their past lives, devoting themselves entirely to the will of Saarlathesh. Others remain important figures in society, but, when finding the opportune moment to do so, will escape from the festive parties and galas to venture forth into worship, away from the judging eyes of fellow governesses and officials.

Yet, the knowledge sometimes is too much for the young, innocent mind that often finds itself, as the phrase goes, "way in over their head." The path to finding the temples of Saarlathesh is simple for those who know his name and wish to invoke it carelessly. But the revelations bestowed upon them is hell; simply put, a concept so vile to the conscious, so corrupting in the concatenation of the words heard, that many do not go beyond the initiation. Instead, those who are poor in spirit find themselves catatonic if lucky…and utterly mad if not.

That knowledge is in no small part easy to explain on paper, as the concepts lack the human words necessary to describe them. Only a bit of that knowledge is known to be written. The understanding that man is neither alone in the universe, nor alone on Earth. That the cruel

machinations of beings so far beyond our com-
prehension control the world around us. And
finally, the information that has some screaming into the night, mad with regret for exposing their thoughts to such dark and forbidden
blessings: the admission that the human race is
not above the influence of Saarlathesh. That we,
with our sciences and pondering into late nights,
do not know we are the children of Saarlathesh,
much like the lowly ant or the horned beetle,
scattering our brood across the planet.

I stopped reading at the final line of the passage, feeling a
lump grow in my chest. Any casual reader, like the man whose
home we removed this book from, might happen to flip to this
page and assume that the writer had quite an imaginative head
on his shoulders or was having a bit of fun with the sanity of
his reader. *But Luke, you know better. You've seen it firsthand.* I know
I frowned, probably even laughed or giggled. Switching between
considering it a joke and accepting it as truth, I closed my eyes,
hoping that I wouldn't break out into hysterics or fits of crying in
the car. I decided to read on, hoping I could calm myself down
by shoving more of the garbage into my skull, reading it like a
fictional account.

Why? How? These questions are not even beyond
the sanest of our order, of our lowly cult. But
with the knowledge that the ritual of initiation
imparts, we are gifted with the reasons as well.
Human behavior, unlike that of a tiger or lion,
seeks out new lands to explore, not out of hunger

or need for resources, but out of the same drive that our cousins in the Animalia kingdom (the aforementioned fluttering fly and stinging bee) share. Insects, like humans, are commanded by the will of Saarlathesh to spread and multiply like vermin; to divide the planet amongst our brethren and choke out the contenders to our dark lord, the other gods whom also have interest in our world.

To our insect brothers, the call of Saarlathesh is overbearing and on the forefront. To us, it is buried by our ancestors, men who wished to cast out the influence of our creator. Those who rejected Saarlathesh were many, yet they did not realize that, spreading to different lands and establishing their new pantheons of gods, they have not escaped the subconscious command, the order to spread and multiply.

For the servants of Saarlathesh, that command is our holy word, our gospel. Our birth, our purpose, is as accepted as easily as a man or woman accepts that our world is three-dimensional. It is the natural way of things; to deny the command is to deny Saarlathesh himself. And to deny Saarlathesh himself is to welcome death and ill omen into your life.

I closed the book, wondering if I had just come to accept the fact, as the author said I should, or if I was far too tired of all the bullshit that was being fed to me. I rubbed my eyes for the millionth time this week, taking time to readjust myself to the paranormal bat-shit insanity that was my life. I had begun to notice that an argument was heating up between Harry and Southway in the front of the car.

"That's just ridiculous. You really expect everyone to just change overnight?" Southway was saying to Harry.

"What's going on?" I asked, butting into the conversation.

"Harry can explain it to you. I don't even want to talk about it any longer."

"What's the deal, Harry?"

"Remember what I said back at the junkyard?" Harry asked, "How people are so accustomed to throwing away things that still have use?"

"Like that carton of orange juice?" I asked.

"Exactly like that! We are a wasteful society. I was just trying to get Southway to see my point of view."

"I understand your point of view," Southway interjected, "but I don't think you understand people! Even if you get a whole bunch of people on your side, nobody is going to want to go out of their way to change 'for the better.'"

"And why not?" Harry asked.

"Because they are stubborn! Look, I really understand where you're coming from, I really do, but people are completely resistant to change! That's why we have fat Americans talking about their failed diets from behind an ice cream sundae. That's why, when people go around shooting other people and it makes the national news, there are those who hold tight to their guns when people start questioning the need for fully automatic weaponry! You can't take a gun away from a true-blooded American. Then how will they get a chance to shoot the neighbor they hate?"

"You're wrong, Southway. The biggest problem I can see is people like you who have no faith in other human beings. You're so critical and negative about change that you quickly take a stance of neutrality on the matter," Harry countered, "So now you become resistant to change. You're no better."

"Fine. I'm no better. I'm a monster and a terrible human being. Can we just get to this place without bringing this up again?"

"No, I want to finish this conversation. How do you think great men managed change? The greatest leaders of our time needed to herd everyone into one ideology. How do you think they did that?"

"I don't know, Harry! I really don't. So stop asking me that stupid question and get to your point."

"My point, dear Professor, is that people today seem to lack the motivation to change anything about their lifestyle and surroundings. It's why people seem to hate us so much, why their kids are becoming like ours. Rebellious. Uncaring. Self-righteous," Harry explained, counting those last three words on three fingers.

"How long was I asleep," I finally asked. Both men looked back at me, probably waiting to hear my input on the matter. I just blinked a few times, and then said, "Uh...Southway. Don't you think you should be watching the road?"

"I think I know how to drive, Luke," he replied, turning back in his seat to face forward. Harry shot me a glance, then darted his eyes toward Southway. He mouthed something to the effect of "This guy, right?" or maybe "I don't like him." Whatever the words, I got the intent. I had a bad feeling that we might be creating some strife in our little group, so I decided to change the subject.

"What do you think will happen when we get there?" I asked.

Harry looked at me, in a tired way, then answered, "We hand over these books and call it a day. Call it an entire year, in fact, and enjoy peace and quiet." Harry looked over at Southway, annoyed.

Southway caught his glance, responding, "Don't worry, you'll be able to go back home and no one will bother you there again. That's what you want to hear, right?"

"What the hell is that supposed to mean? It's the truth," Harry said.

"I don't know if any of us will just walk away from this."

"Hey, I made the stranger promise to leave us alone after all this. Don't worry, Harry," I said, redirecting my attention, "we'll be alright."

"Do you believe everything that strangers tell you, Luke?" Southway asked.

"…No."

"Then why do you seem sure about that?"

I didn't know. I was just being hopeful, after all. There were no assurances that we would walk out of wherever we were heading next without a scratch. We could be lucky, handing over the books and leaving within an hour. Or the stranger could very well feed us to the minions of Saarlathesh. I quietly pondered several scenarios in my head, but the exercise did nothing to ease my discomfort.

"We made it," Southway interjected, between my thoughts.

"What is this place?" I said.

"An abandoned asylum. Your friend picked a nice place for a closing act."

"He's not my friend."

"Let's go inside," Harry said. I looked over at Michael next to me, and he nodded agreeably.

CHAPTER SEVEN
Out of Luck

The four of us shuffled out of the car in unison. The asylum was decrepit. Vines had found their way around the exterior of the building, creeping into windows and cracks whenever they were in the way of growth. None of the windows, that I could see, still held their glass panes, save for one on the third floor. No, instead of glass, the windows were buzzing with activity; insects and bugs, of many types and legs, fluttered in and out of the old asylum. I could see more than a dozen worker bees off to the left in the shrubbery. Caterpillars crawled over the porch railings, around the windowsills of the lobby, around the asylum gardens, and everywhere else. Ants were numerous; a hill had grown in an exaggerated manner near the asylum's outer walls.

We took the first steps forward toward the hellish place. The gates of the asylum had long rusted closed, with a strangely fresh-looking chain binding the front. The image was complete with the large padlock fastened to it. Professor Southway inspected it for a second before placing it back against the gate. For a second, he looked through to the asylum grounds, scanning the place for something.

"Think there is a way in? Around the back?" I asked.

Harry answered by jumping up the asylum wall and grasping the edge of a stone block. With strained effort, he heaved himself up and atop the wall, where he now sat. He looked down, waved to us, and then threw his legs over the side, dropping out of view behind the wall.

"That's one way of doing it," Professor Southway said.

"I've got bad memories of high school gym class," I responded.

"Get over the wall, Luke," he replied.

"Hold on."

Before making my attempt, I ran back to the car as Southway stood confused or contemplating if I had given up and was going to drive away, abandoning the two men to whatever horrors laid within the decaying walls. I probably had given him a sigh of relief, however, when I moseyed over to the passenger door and dropped open the glove compartment. With care, I pulled out the throwing knife and the sheath it was contained in, shoving the weapon into the back of my pants. I threw my t-shirt back over, concealing it.

In the meantime, Southway had thrown himself at the wall, grasping at a stone block and heaving himself up with much difficulty. When he reached the top, he wasted no time throwing himself over and landing with a thud on the other side. I followed suit, walking up to the six-foot-plus wall, covered and constructed out of old, gray building stones. I reached up to the top of the wall and found myself just out of reach, my fingertips scratching at the side for more leverage. Bending my knees, I threw myself upward and reached towards the top, missing it by mere inches and feeling the nice and pleasant burn that accompanies scraping your fingers against uneven rock. I blew on my hands and shook them, admiring the newest cuts and scrapes of this adventure.

Harry and Southway looked on from the asylum gate; Harry had a doubtful face on, while Southway was pressing his palm over his face in embarrassment. Moving a few steps backward, I decided to make a running jump at the obstacle. When I felt ready (namely, when Harry's face grew bored and Southway already had turned his attention to the asylum grounds), I ran towards the wall and threw my weight upwards in a forward, leaping jump. My hands caressed the top of the stone wall, where I managed to grab on with my left hand, my right hand swinging wildly. Through the help of natural adrenaline, I swung and took hold with my right hand, then used all of my force to throw myself up and clear of the wall, tumbling onto my side from the six foot drop into the interior of the grounds.

"That was hard to watch," Harry said.

Michael, who had been a witness to the event on the outside, pushed his ethereal body through the stonework and commented, "That was very good, Luke." I softly wished I was transparent and easily able to move around. *So…dead?*

"Thanks Michael, I guess."

"We need to get inside," Southway said, as he was returning. While I was attempting my little exercise, Southway was walking around the front of the building, looking into the windows.

"What did you see in there?" Harry asked.

"Nothing but dust, cobwebs, and some covered furniture."

"Can we get in through the front door?" I asked.

Southway shook his head, "No. It looks like it was barricaded from the inside."

"Barricaded? With what?"

"Couches. Some dressers, from what I saw. Probably kids breaking into the asylum sometime after it closed."

Southway was almost one hundred percent on the money with that assumption. Between all the ghost stories and rumors that are spread worldwide by online bloggers, it's not surprising to find a written account of a night of terror, complete with claims of murderous apparitions chasing a group of kids out of a haunted and abandoned building. I don't know what it is with young adventurers these days, never understood the thrill of walking into a broken down house. What if someone got seriously injured because some idiot decided that leaving dangerous objects lying around, before closing down a business, was safe? What if one of the explorers let the dark corners and creaking floor boards get to their head, causing them to run screaming at nothing at all? What if there was a real killer hiding out in there?

Professor Southway tugged at the lobe of his ear, and then said, "I noticed there was a broken basement window around the side of the building. There isn't anything sturdy to land on, but it's our best chance to get inside."

Harry agreed, leading the group to the side of the building. Before I got any traction, Southway held my arm in place, waiting for Harry to disappear around the bend.

"Luke. I can see that things aren't going to be that safe for us much longer."

"Safe? Like me dying on more than one occasion?"

"I mean, we're getting closer to the end, and I think you need a way to protect yourself," he stated.

"Don't worry about me, Southway. I have my insurance, remember?"

I removed the knife from my pants, unsheathing it in a proud display of silver, shining metal. I turned it over and back again, presenting it to Southway like a blacksmith presenting his finest creation. The knife was decorated at the handle, an intricate design etched directly onto the metal as a unique signature of whatever online salesman Jean had worked up a deal with. Much like the novelty shocker, the items in my house that I labeled as "decorative" consisted of items of value and items so eloquently branded as "a waste of my fucking money." What they all shared in common was the simple fact that Jean had convinced me that I was in need of one.

"Do you know how to use one of those?" Southway asked.

"Do you?"

"Maybe," Southway said, looking back towards the rickety structure.

Harry appeared from the corner of the building, waving us to stop dicking around and follow him to the entrance. We shuffled across the grass, which at this point in time had grown much too high than grass should ever be allowed to, to meet him, and then we were directed toward the basement window that Southway had spotted. There were a couple of sharp pieces of glass still held in the frame, one of which I swore was stained with someone's blood but couldn't confirm as Harry brutally kicked the glass until it dislodged from the window frame.

"Heh," he chuckled, "I thought it would just break into pieces." It hadn't. The pieces of glass simply landed in the basement, sliding across the dirty, green-gray floor. We ducked inside, one at a time, while Michael performed his ghost trick of levitating through the building itself.

We glanced around the asylum, taking note of the cheesy, cliché gurneys casually brushing up against the wall along with small, feeble medical items, like gauze and medical gowns, strewn about the place. Like the closing of the asylum had concluded with a grand party between the patients, using the gurneys like surfboards, and the doctors, who threw off their scrubs and emptied the contents of the stock room all over the floor, the place had about as much clutter as I could picture.

"Upstairs," Harry said dryly.

The four of us moved cautiously through the basement, aware that the only lighting in the place came from the basement windows, clear enough to allow the daylight in. I paused at the steps leading to the first floor, noting to the others the complete lack of safety that they conveyed. The steps were wooden and poorly kept, time having a complete field day at ripping and tearing and removing chunks of the planks of wood that supported it. Harry and Southway decided to lead, careful not to break the stairs any further and completely ignoring the handrail, mostly because to do so was to avoid the eventual result of a nasty splinter pierced into the hand.

"Looks like the termites have gotten to it. Watch your step up, Luke," Harry said, as both he and Southway disappeared in opposite directions once they reached the landing.

"Hey guys! NO SPLITTING UP!" I shouted, then spoke to myself and Michael by saying, "That's like, monster movie rule number one, or two. The second you split up is the second you invite the killer to play a game of tag with his knife." I quietly reflected that I was the one in possession of the knife, and that I had no intention of stabbing anyone.

Michael didn't seem to mind, but I commanded him to stay by my side, a command which he obeyed, surprisingly. *Maybe he doesn't want to get lost in here either, or maybe he's scared of this place too.* I frightened myself by considering what could possibly send a ghost running in terror. *Maybe Saarlathesh.*

My ascent went swimmingly. When I reached the landing, I was greeted by an old-timey radiator against the wall. I was inclined to feel it and found it was ice cold to the touch. The walls were of standard hospital fair, even for the age of the building. *Maybe they renovated.* Lines color-coded the hallway, leading to different areas of the building. Not seeing Southway or Harry in sight, I chose to follow a green path toward the "Patient Bedrooms," disregarding all of the rules of monster movies and heading straight for the grand finale, where the revelation that the killer was a dead patient or former patient or mad doctor is found by the heroes just as soon as the killer finds them.

Along the way, I picked up a few pamphlets from the asylum itself, advertisements promising a new life and change for whoever joins "THE highest rated mental treatment center in the New England area!", and clipboards that still retained the notes of gibberish that doctors write to themselves and to other doctors who speak a similar dialect. Besides the level of complexity that accompanied medical notes, I couldn't make heads or tails of the random scribbling etched into the paper so many years ago. I discarded them as quickly as I read them, tossing them casually to the ground and returning them to their home on the linoleum floor.

In time, the green line I was following came to an abrupt end, finishing its path into the rectangular archway (door-less, as hospitals were inclined to have such archways) of the Patient Bedrooms. The name of the section, which was on a number of plaques followed by a directional arrow in the hallway, now adorned the archway in large lettering.

"Ready for a trip down someone else's memory lane?" I asked Michael.

"What is this place?"

"It's where the crazies were living when they spent time here."

"Oh. Patients, you mean."

"You catch on quick."

To my right, I caught a glimpse of the first bedroom I'd inspect, the number on the door reading "Patient Room No.9." I stepped inside to find a bare room, consisting of a miniature dresser, a box-spring bed with no mattress, broken window on the back wall, and a single pack of cigarettes sitting on an end table. I sifted through the dresser drawers, finding no articles of clothing or toiletries or a bible, and then proceeded to pick up the cigarettes. There were only two left inside. *There was a man staying here*, I imagined, *living day to day in this place, hating the fact that he was committed. He smoked like a chimney, something that bothered the other patients in the ward, so they moved him to the front of the patient wing. After breakfast was brought to his room, he would stand in front of the open window, watching the other patients in the courtyard and smoking his fifth cigarette for the day.*

I placed the cigarette pack back on the end table, then placed my arm across the top of the window frame, casually looking out the window as the man had done years ago in a time when the asylum grounds still held the laughter and cries and madness of the patients. *I should have myself committed after this is all over with. Just check into the nearest asylum at Empire and never tell anyone where I have gone to.*

I moved on to the next room, where I found not a scrap of interesting material, not a trace of a soul having even lived there. I made a quick mental note of the room (*The person living here was rather too neat and boring and his time at the asylum was as short as to not even burn a memory on the staff of the place. When asked, they would say that they had forgotten about Mr., um, Robert...man, being that his stay was short and uneventful*), and then found myself simply walking down the hall, tilting my head left and right as I passed open doorways. Papers littered this hall as well, although they were in piles like leaves in some places, which I joyfully nudged as I passed. I watched as they scattered about the place and soared a few feet before touching down again.

To my left, I spotted a room with a closed door, which I pushed open with my foot. The room had been furnished a bit more than the others. The miniature dresser, standard in each room from what I could tell, held a rather large mirror. An item that I didn't think had a place in a building that could possibly hold unstable patients. *A woman lived here,* I conjured, *one who found herself staring daily into mirrors for hours. At first, her family believed her to be much too conceited, a trait not shared amongst the others of the household and despised by the father of the family. Under his rule, there would be a minimum use of the bathroom to accommodate all the family, but the girl stubbornly refused to move her golden locks from the glass reflection. Her admiration became so great that, having previously thought the girl to be much too full of herself, a doctor was brought in to force a change of personality in her. Instead the doctor found her to be much in need of psychiatric help, as she held an unhealthy fascination with the curves and shape of her face and skin. In short, she was in love with her image.*

The doctor recommended this very same hospital, where the girl became a woman, spending time in front of the mirror and in front of the psychiatric lead, when it became necessary to try therapy on her. But the woman was too fond of her beauty, requesting a larger mirror to be installed in her room against the wishes of her family but in line with a doctor's attempts to cure her. To fool her, the doctor installed a fun house mirror in place of the norm, which distorted the image of the woman. Instead of recovery, these actions lead her to replace the love of herself with an unrestrained hate for her ugliness. Thus, the doctor was removed from his position and the woman was left to rot in her own prison.

But I couldn't know that for a fact. The mirror in the room was completely missing the reflective glass; instead, it was merely a frame. I removed myself from the room, continuing my journey through the decrepit asylum. In another room, I came across the etchings of a madman, who ticked off days on the walls in pencil, either mimicking something he saw in a film or being downright crazy to the core. *He was committed into the asylum against his wishes because his lawyer thought it was the only way to beat a criminal offense. His lawyer didn't believe in him or the evidence, something that aggravated him to his core.*

For all his trouble, he was locked away for, and here, I counted the tick marks on the wall, *about 234 days before they decided he wasn't the criminal they were looking for. He was released from his prison, then chased down his lawyer and bludgeoned him to death with a piece of 2X4 he had taken from a construction yard on the way home. The lawyer was found two days later; the man was chased down by the police and sentenced for murder to a maximum prison somewhere nearby. Now, he's etching the days in his cell with his fingernails, wishing for a pencil and wishing he had been committed. 'When they see these marks and my bloody fingertips,' he reasoned, 'they will send me back in there with all the other maniacs.' But they never did and never will.*

I shuddered at my own morbid imagination, but my subconscious blamed it on the eeriness of the asylum; the stillness of its rooms, the signs of decay and time long past, and the bothersome silence interjected by my movements and those of Southway and Harry, echoing ever so subtly from wherever they had lost themselves. In my mind, I considered if this place was as beautiful as the pamphlets made it out to be or if the asylum was more like a prison, full of tortured souls and mad doctors. As if fate needed to give me the answer, I watched as Harry turned a corner and called out my name.

"What's up, Harry? Where did you guys go?"

"I haven't met up with Southway, but check out this ledger I found," he said, handing me a dusty notebook, a detailed list of budget and expenses from the asylum's director.

"Seems like money was getting tight, according to the end of these notes."

"Yeah," Harry said, "Looks like the place was bankrupt. The doctors had to transfer all the patients out and lock the gate and call it that."

"A lot calmer than the idea I had," I said.

"What? Mad doctors and mistreatment?"

"How did you know that, I wonder?"

"You kids," he said, walking away and throwing a hand in the air, "always thinking in terms of horror movies and slashers. The real world isn't like that."

"Some places are."

"Well, I've never been to any."

"The idea has to come from somewhere, Harry."

"Yeah," he said, ducking his head into one of the rooms and out, "Some demented minds whose idea of hard labor is writing down stories for a living."

I scoffed. *Where was Southway?* I found Michael standing in front of the missing mirror of the previous room, moving his hair back with his ghostly hands to no avail. His hair was sloppy and uncombed. I couldn't decide if it reached that state from his general uncaring lifestyle or from whatever unfortunate death he met. He still didn't seem to be privy to the details of his own demise, and his attitude was such a blank that I didn't care to try to engage in a lengthy conversation with him about his history. The way I figured it, you transition into being a ghost and you just live that life like you never had another one. It's more peaceful that way, and I knew I would prefer stumbling about in confusion than guilt and regret over my decisions and choices.

Bees. I knew it before I opened the next room door, which had required some aggressive pushing to pry open, but I had heard them for sure. Bees. Dozens of little bees, unlike the one in my bedroom, were swarming in their hanging beehive above that room's bed. It was one of the biggest nests I had ever seen, but I stupidly had shaken it a bit from my charge against the door frame. The bees were getting restless and I was getting ready to scream. Harry heard me, pulling me out and slamming the door back into the frame. He yelled at me to run while he darted down the way he came. I elected to run back the way I came as well, through the Patient Wing and out into the hall again. As soon as my foot gained traction on the ground, I heard the door behind me burst forth, releasing its ghastly ensemble of winged demons, the swarm.

I tried not to perform the other monster movie cliché: looking back and stumbling like an idiot. So I looked straight head and forced my legs into overtime. Michael had been left behind in the room, but I knew the bees were only after me and Harry. I hadn't looked back, but somehow I knew that Harry was running just as fast as me, chased by the other half of the colony. I hit a corner with a slide, bashing into the tile-work of the wall. Some tiles broke free from their decades-long containment and crashed to the floor in small pieces and chunks. The bees were still on me, a collective hum of beating wings poised for the kill.

My feet found a hold in the floor, and I was up and running for dear life once again. It's a good time to pause now, to marvel at the sheer insanity of the situation. Yes, I was being chased through an abandoned asylum with a lump of fear beating the inside of my chest to death, but I just have to comment at the bizarre lack of dirt and grime that usually finds its way onto the floor of an abandoned building. Your mileage may vary at the reason of just WHY this particular location was devoid of grossness (considering it is a hospital-like building), but I elect to believe that there has to be a more divine reasoning behind it. Like, some other god, maybe even *the* God that everyone is so commonly worshipping these days, was sitting on his cloud throne and thinking: "Man, that Luke guy is sure running out of luck. Maybe I'll make it so that the floor he's about to touch won't leave a sliver of sludge around his palm."

But, of course, he, or He (depending on your perspective of the matter), would seem to be tragically missing the point that I would gladly trade a swarm of killer insects breathing down my neck for the chance to simply slip on the once-waxed floors of this asylum and happen to brush my hand casually across a layer of filth and disease. But if only I was lucky enough to have a supernatural being of such immense power and foresight to take a few moments of his day to worry about the mental state of a little worm such as myself. For now, however, let's get back to the matter at hand: my lady-screaming and a bunch of irritated, flying vermin.

So, being that I still was carrying around that aforementioned luck, I quickly recovered from my slide into the wall and sprinted further back into the halls. *Have to get away, have to run out of this place, get in the car and never look back for the rest of my lunatic-riddled, retail-working life.* I dared to look back at the swarm, seeing that I had seriously pissed off whatever royalty they had back at the hive. Considering that not three paragraphs ago I told you I was utilizing my keen, genre-savvy knowledge of horror movies (namely, DON'T LOOK BEHIND YOU), it is not at all anyone's fault but my own that I ran straight into the basement stairwell, tragically sprinting off the landing and plummeting onto the first few steps down. The staircase finally decided it had had enough of this maintaining-structure-thing and plummeted with me; a disgusting pile of rotted wood and splinters broke my fall. Although, the nice concrete floor decided to high-five my spinal cord.

"Luke!" Southway's voice called down to me from above. I threw my head back, pushing aside some chunks of wood blocks to look at him.

"I know this looks painful, but I feel kind of cozy taking a moment to lie down."

177

Southway crouched at the staircase, and then placed a hand on the floor. He dropped down to the basement level, having planned his fall and landed safely atop what used to be the wood railing.

"Look at this," he said.

I sat up slowly, making sure that no pieces of wood had pierced me in the side. Finding no injury, I turned to the pile of wood that Southway was pulling apart. Underneath the stairs, there had been a cellar door, no doubt leading deep beneath the asylum basement into the center of the Earth where Satan himself would greet me with a pat on the back.

"It's a good thing I didn't slam through it."

"Who knows," Southway answered, "You may have in another universe."

"You know, Southway," I said, rising up, "When this is all over, when I can be free to go home…I'm poking one of your eyes out."

"I've…never heard that threat before."

"Yeah, you bet your ass you haven't! Where's Harry?"

"He should be coming. When that little stunt you pulled down here had settled, the swarm turned around and headed back the other way. I'm sure he lost them by now."

"You saw them?"

"I was checking out the rooms on the second floor when I heard a woman scream. I found my way back here and saw you running with your head turned. You should really look ahead of you when you're moving."

"Just open this door with me," I said.

The cellar door, like everything else in this godforsaken place, creaked the entire way open. Below, a darkened, spiraling staircase had been carved out of the bedrock, unlit by anything. Southway pulled a match from his pocket, struck it against the bedrock wall and tossed it a few steps down. Whoever had created this place, he definitely built it with the mindset that a professor, a garbage man, and a slacker would have nothing but chills for the rest of their life when they got here.

"We're going to have to improvise with some of the bed sheets. It will be dangerous walking down here without any idea of whom or what is waiting around every turn," Southway said.

"We have no choice. Did you find the stranger upstairs? An altar or something?"

"No. Just some forgotten tools and possessions and probably a lot of forgotten memories. When Harry gets here, we'll make a torch."

As if Southway was the director, Harry made his entrance into the scene, jumping down from the stairwell and landing on a couple of wood chunks. He glanced down into the cellar door we were crouched next to, and then asked: "Are we going down there?"

"Looks like it, friend," said Southway, "Harry, grab those sheets and take my pack of matches. Give us some light."

The cellar door led to a descent in the form of a stone staircase, something carved out of the very Earth itself by idle hands, whose idea of a hobby was setting up cults in the darkest corners of the world. I trembled as Southway insisted I go first, but the descent was nothing more than a simple walk down the stairs. It was just that the walk was accompanied by the little brain cells in my head triggering images of death and despair and horrible monsters. Say what you will about how far the human race has come, we still can't overcome our ancestral fear of the dark. Some of us, at least.

As we walked in circles, down an unknown shaft, I began to notice that some bored cultist had turned the stone walls into his personal easel. From the tiny match that Southway had given me, and the brief light from the torch we had made, I could make out tiny figures dancing around a fire in one scene. They seemed to be ancient and primitive from the details I could make out. Above the fire, there was a great serpentine creature, with two eyes and an impressive set of chompers. Another scene was painted into the staircase further down, some form of luau between natives, offering up platters topped with human limbs to a familiar form. It was of no doubt to me that the image portrayed Saarlathesh, and the villagers worshiping him had no qualms with sacrificing their brethren in his name.

I hugged myself temporarily, as the air began to get colder the deeper we descended. It was also from the shiver that ran down my spine. *Good thing we didn't happen upon any cannibalistic rituals on the way here.* The thought did little to provide comfort to me; our journey didn't seem to have finished quite yet and my mind was only tempting Lady Luck to bite me in the ass just as I didn't need it. Southway nudged me forward when I had stopped, whispering something about needing to press on no matter the fear I felt. They had my back, he said. *Yeah, and when I get dragged down the steps and into the abyss, they'll have ample time to make a hasty retreat back up to the asylum.* The stairs seemed never-ending at a certain point, a fact that I sort of accepted. My body did most of the work in climbing further and further down, while my mind tried to find the path back to my happy place, a mental state that I had all but forgotten due to the intense PTSD I was sure to be developing as the journey continued.

When I was ready to fling myself down the rest of the steps and end my misery, my feet touched flat surface. We had reached the bottom and I had walked out into some kind of hallway. Stonework adorned the floor, ceiling, and walls before me. My match was far too dim to see beyond, however, so I reached for the fifth that Southway had placed in my pocket. I walked over a few steps to the wall adjacent to the stairs, striking the match against the tile work and hoping for the best. Defying no one's expectations by this point, the match failed to light when I needed it most, so I moved onto the next patch of wall, striking the match again. And to no avail. I reached out into the darkness, placing my arm outstretched so that my hand could feel contact with a better surface.

I felt something leathery touch my middle finger, so I placed my palm against it and rubbed. It was just the surface I needed, so I struck the match against it. The match illuminated the darkness, exposing the terrifying, giant praying mantis that I had just insulted. My face dropped almost as quickly as the match, and I spun around fast, taking off into the dark. The thing resembled another one of my dreams. It was definitely the same species as the one from Southway's home, the one that had pinned me to a wall and held me down for the stranger to whisper his words of wisdom to me.

"Luke! Run faster!" came Professor Southway's voice behind me. My feet clattered against the stone floor, echoing throughout whatever winding halls lay ahead of me. The sound was accompanied by the screech of the creature and its own footsteps; four legs rushed the demon forward toward me. After you've known you've died before, and have knowledge that you can have no problem standing back up, you tend to feel less threatened by the plain insanity that comes with chasing the shadows and finding that the shadows loved returning the favor.

Society is about staying in the light, spending life on a path of work, sleep, eat, and alcohol. You never stop to look into a dark alley, sure that you've seen something horrible and indescribable glance back at you. Society tells you look straight, avoid the dark places and keep good company. Because the second you decide that maybe you want to trade a life of number crunching for a life of adventure, maybe someone will knock you upside the head and say: "Remember that Luke Thornton guy? Got his ass eviscerated by some bizarre ass shit that no one should expose themselves to."

I wasn't about to become another unsolved murder, so I picked up the pace with my sprinting. The hallway was longer than I had guessed; I half-heartedly believed I would be slamming into a dead end somewhere around five minutes ago. As it stood, I wouldn't go down so easily. From my left, I noticed that a strange luminescence had entered the corner of my eye, so I turned my head and nearly lost my footing.

"Luke, what are you doing?" said Michael.

"I'm so fucking glad you're here and I can't believe I'm saying that," I said, through gasps for breath.

"Do you know that you're running in circles?"

I took a look at the wall around me, noticing that the cracks in the stone blocks had an odd familiarity to them. Michael may have very well been right. I didn't notice with the growling and roaring going on behind me, but I had been circling the same hallway.

"Find me a way out of here, Michael."

"I will, Luke. Let me scout ahead." Michael floated on beyond my sight, but just as quickly came back. "By the way, are you aware that something is chasing you?"

"YES! Yes, I am well aware, Michael! Get me out of here!"

Michael continued on his way toward my escape route, or so I had hoped. The thought did occur to me that, although I had been running circles, Southway and Harry had found a way out. I now noticed that I was passing the staircase we had descended from, probably for the fifth or sixth time. Professor Southway had used my distraction to slip into a doorway somewhere, no doubt.

Suddenly, Michael flew out from a wall ahead of me, almost as if he was swimming through the air. *Damn ghosts. Wish I could just run headfirst into a wall and find an exit. As it stood now, I would just lose momentum and gain a concussion.* Michael repeated this strange action, dipping and diving from behind the left-hand wall. I joked to myself that he resembled a dolphin, swimming along the top of the water and sometimes breaking through the surface. Eventually, he flew through the wall once more right next to me. I jumped sideways, as if he was in danger of running into me.

"Jesus! Don't I have enough reasons to collapse from a heart attack?" I said, my breath already labored and my legs in a state of gelatin.

"Sorry, Luke. I have found a way for you. Just run into the wall ahead as I do." From behind Michael, the creature screamed and I could feel him gaining much closer than before. Michael decided to begin to fly ahead of me.

"Wait! I can't go through the wall like you, you numbskull!"

"It is a false wall, Luke Thornton. It'll give way when you throw yourself into it."

I decided to give his idea a chance, although my subconscious tucked at me, telling me that I was putting my fate into the hands of an idiot. I witnessed the spot that Michael had pointed to, just as he flew his ethereal body through it. I swerved to the left and hurled myself against the stone wall, missing the spot through a tragic lack of coordination from my body and slamming into a spot to the right. Apparently, I managed to clip the right point on impact because the wall managed to shift in my direction, leaving a gap that slipped into a tunnel.

I crawled on hands and knees into the gap, just as the creature made an appearance in the corner of the stone, ready to grab me and drag me out. I goaded him on when I made it inside the tunnel, then kicked hard at the opposite end. The false wall swiveled back into place, jamming the claw that reached into the tunnel against the corner. The creature shrieked, dulling my sense of hearing. I clasped hands onto my ears, kicking harder at the wall. The claw was severed; the stone wall closed. I was left in a torch-lit tunnel with the severed arm of a hell beast and the ghostly apparition of a dimwit. I was ready to pass out from the exhaustion.

Unlucky for me, I knew that another second in this place could end in another run-in with some other demon. That or the creature behind the wall would figure out the trick and decide to enact justice, "eye-for-an-eye" style. Being that I was quite fond of my hands, I chose to walk down the tunnel, unsure of where it led. Several torches that hung there were fairly modern, something I took note of because of the relative dilapidation that had hit the majority of the asylum grounds. These torches had been lit recently, most likely in anticipation of my arrival. I found the end to the tunnel, which led to an open room, decorated with an altar, candelabras, and the smiling visages of both Professor Southway and Harry Breck. It resembled a medium-sized church, with tall stone pillars supporting the ceiling.

Although the place was meagerly furnished, I noticed that several wooden pews had been set up for followers, who, by the condition of the seats, must have long abandoned worship here. The entire place gave off a haunting vibe, a warning sign in the back of my mind that screamed "cannibals" and "sacrifice" and "devil-worship" as words that would not be out of place in a setting such as this. My mind turned toward some indie horror flick that I had seen once, where a virgin was sacrificed in a dark chapel for the devil. *Maybe they had secured the filming rights to this place because it sure fits the bill.*

"I see you took the long road," I joked, brushing the dirt off my jeans. "You know there was a shortcut right?" My thumb was extended in a direction behind me, back through the tunnel.

"Yeah, right," said Harry. Southway managed a chuckle, probably surprised at the absolute perseverance I had been displaying.

"Guess who's here," Southway said to me, gesturing in front of him. A column had been blocking my view to the right, so I hopped down from the tunnel entrance into the room. Standing in front of the altar was the stranger, the man in the suit that had led me on a hell bound journey for Saarlathesh. Both Harry's and Southway's tomes were placed upon the altar, on stone blocks that were perfectly carved to hold them. I removed *The Compendium of Shadows* from my knapsack, walking up to the stranger like a child walking to the front of the class. I held the book close to my chest.

"Give it to me, Luke Thornton," he said.

"I'm trusting you," I said.

"You have nothing to worry about," he replied, taking the evil book from my hands and holding it close in the same way I had. "You have reached the end of a dangerous and tiring journey. Go join your friends and we can begin."

I moved back toward Southway, taking a position to his left. Harry was a bit further up, closer to the altar and the stranger. The stranger himself was placing the final tome on the altar.

"*The Compendium of Shadows*," he stated. Then he turned to the book on the left, saying, "*The Children of Saarlathesh*. Again, he turned his attention, this time toward the book on the highest pedestal, in the center, and said, "*Saarlathesh, the Dark Almanac*. The power of Saarlathesh grows, as his property is returned to him. Listen to his cries of joy as his voice reaches out to all of his children and rests in their hearts." The stranger threw his head back, spreading his arms out.

"What's he doing?" I whispered to Southway.

"Being a nutter," he replied to me.

"Stranger," said Harry, "what happens now?"

The stranger put his arms back down and turned around. He looked over the room, more specifically at the three of us, and then said, "Now Saarlathesh will give us our next command. You three have been given a task and succeeded. You must join with us now and take upon another task for our Lord."

"What?! No, I'm done here!" I yelled.

"I would have to agree with Luke," Southway chimed in, "We did our part in this, it's about time we left."

"No, you seem to misunderstand the need for you to be here. Did you not think that there was a greater purpose for you, a greater need than to gather some trinkets for an all-powerful god? Did you not think he had other agents that would have found them?"

"You asshole! I haven't left my home in years," Harry said, "Why did you drag me all the way out here?"

"Harry's right. I flew all the way from England to meet you here. Now you say that I could've been left to myself and my studies?"

"You mean," I said, defeated and not willing to argue, "I…I didn't have…to die?"

The room grew a bit quiet at my comment, most likely Southway and Harry realizing that I had given the most for this moment.

"You see, gentlemen, the books were needed, as they will be used to teach and spread the word to non-believers, children who have lost their way in the world and seek guidance from those such as myself. But there was a much more important task that you all completed wonderfully. Namely, you've done the bidding of Saarlathesh and he is pleased with you all. He has more for you to do. Saarlathesh has many plans, some that have just been created and others that have long been set into motion."

"But why?" I asked, "Why bother bringing me into this? You must have known that I would want nothing more to do with Saarlathesh. Especially after what I've been through."

"Because you three have been selected, chosen out of all the people in the world and the agents of Saarlathesh himself, to be part of something wonderful. With me, the four of us are to bring the word of Saarlathesh to all peoples of this planet. To set upon a worldwide reclaiming of the realm that belongs to the Insect King. We have the gifts of knowledge, and we now have the leaders necessary to spread Saarlathesh's might."

"You're mad," Southway said, "I want no part in this. I had suspected that the return of those retched volumes would lead to another harebrained plot by your supposed god. What is your angle on this? Where do you sit in 'reclaiming the lands of Saarlathesh'?"

"My dear Professor, who do you think will lead this conquest? Certainly not yourself, no. I will lead the agents of Saarlathesh in enacting our master's plan, and you three shall be my closest advisors. You have already made it this far, do you not seek further enlightenment from the powers far beyond yours? There is much to learn from us, much that we can teach you of the world and the…other worlds."

"I wouldn't agree to that," Southway said.

"Come now, Professor. Do you not think it is futile to carry on in this way? You were selected by Saarlathesh, as he told me, to be a part of this. You cannot simply walk away from him, as if you can hide from his all-seeing presence. Saarlathesh has agents everywhere. If you choose to walk out of here an enemy, you must be prepared to face Saarlathesh himself, which would be quite an unbalanced match, I assure you."

"You don't even know that your god exists. He's a legend, a fragment from a long forgotten cult that you and your followers have dug up in recent years. I believe in facts, sir, and the facts tell me there is no Saarlathesh. Just a bunch of outcasts with nothing to do. You, and your 'followers', are all thrill-seekers, not much different from rebellious teens. You worship Saarlathesh because you believe you are part of some secret and important cult. But all I see are a group of idiots dancing around fires, calling out a name whose meaning has been lost to history."

"How can you say that, Southway," I finally added, "when I have explained everything that has happened to me? How can you explain away the things that I've seen?"

"Because I'm done playing this game, Luke. It's ridiculous! A god with that much power…where is he? I don't see him here to defend himself."

"You bring misfortune into your life, Southway," the stranger said, "by tempting fate in the way that you do."

"Fuck faith," he replied.

"Southway, what the hell, man? Have you gone crazy?!" I exclaimed.

"Southway, I don't think this is the right way to do this. If what he says is true, you've just damned yourself with your outburst," Harry added.

"Honestly, Professor, do you not see that Saarlathesh merely wishes to take back that which is rightfully his? He planted the early seeds on this planet. The first of your kind are of his brood. Humans have far out stepped their bounds, spreading to all corners of the globe and choking out life wherever found. It is funny that many of you consider insects so repelling when they are brothers to your species."

"Southway, he's right. It's in the last book we found. All of what he says is in there," I said, "I don't like what this means either, but we shouldn't go about this the way you're acting. We don't need to make enemies with something we can't fight."

"Shut up, Luke. The power of suggestion won't work on me. I won't be threatened by a fairy tale. I won't be threatened by this cheap man in his cheap suit full of his cheap lies."

I could see a look of concern on Harry's face; his mind was absorbing the information around him. At first, I thought he was in shock, but then I witnessed a hand raise to his beard, which he was stroking with an open palm. Whatever Harry was thinking, his attention and his eyes were resting upon the stranger. *Maybe Harry has a better way out of this.* If Southway was putting himself in danger, I had hoped that Harry had a plan for getting us all out of harm's way.

"Look, it is about time that something was done to reign in the homo sapiens," the stranger continued, "About time that you all stopped fighting your nature, stopped fighting the call that Saarlathesh has made since the earliest years of your ancestor's lives. Eventually, the sheep have to learn to listen to the shepherd and return to their pens. So many have been lost for so long, but we can lead them in our master's wishes!"

"He's right."

I had to make sure for a second that another person hadn't stepped into the room to speak out loud. That statement had undoubtedly been uttered from the mouth of dirty old Harry Breck, still standing near the altar and inching a bit closer to the stranger. Southway gave him a look of absolute disgust.

"My wife never ran away with an office manager," Harry explained, "It was the chief of police that she slept with. I used to be a cop, Southway. A good one. My wife decided I was too low on the ladder to care for any longer. They are both scumbags. And the things I've seen people do in my line of work, Southway. The amount of terror they would be capable of afflicting on another human being was beyond words. I don't like the human race. I don't even feel a part of it anymore. So why don't we go along with this man's nice little plan. His boss went through all the trouble of setting it up. It seems like a shame to waste an opportunity to teach humanity a lesson."

The Earth shook. I had felt some vibration shoot up my leg, but I had thought it to be just a case of the shakes. I was wrong. Something was happening for sure, and I could tell by the look on the stranger's face. It was confidence. Harry had moved just a step back, still within arm's length of the stranger. I pondered what sort of trickery Harry had devised; still believing he was on our side.

"Saarlathesh beckons, Professor," the stranger said, "Are you prepared to ignore the call?" The stranger threw his hands up once more, taking in something unseen to either me or Southway or Harry. After a few moments, the trembling stopped. The stranger opened his eyes, lowered his head towards Southway again. But now there was a different look on his face. He looked menacing, for once, in a way that bothered me more than ever. With a start, he reached into his own pocket and produced a silver-lined gun, pointed straight at my chest.

"Woah, what the fuck?!" I asked. Or more accurately, I pleaded.

"He chose you!"

"Who? Saarlathesh? He chose me to lead?" I asked, "Well, that's not so bad. So I lead instead of you. No need to get your panties in a bunch." *One day, Luke, you'll manage to say the wrong funny line to the wrong guy and get your chest blown out.* My subconscious thought was right; this was as poor a day as any to be joking around.

"No!" the stranger screamed, "He has chosen you as his avatar." He lowered his head in defeat, but kept the gun trained on me. Tears were forming in his eyes. "This was never about some great conquest, he told me. It was about finding a vessel for him. A vessel to absorb the essence of Saarlathesh. Don't you see? He's planning to walk the Earth...he's coming..."

"What?" Southway blinked a few times, taking in what he was saying, "What did you say now?" Strangely, Southway seemed bothered by what he had heard, and I could only hope it was his regard for my safety. It was as if a switch had been pulled, some keyword that fit some puzzle piece together in his mind. I could only wonder why, but I was a bit more concerned with taking lead into the chest.

"Me? A vessel? So, like, sharing a body with Saarlathesh?"

"No," the stranger answered, "Saarlathesh's essence would consume you in the experience. Your body would be made fit for his corporeal form. Saarlathesh doesn't exactly fit the model of a human being, you know, so he has to make...adjustments."

I tried to picture the body of Saarlathesh coming to encompass my own, but all I could picture was the winged demon in my nightmares bursting forth from my body, ready to subjugate the world under his rule. A being that had no place in this world, with the mere sight of him inducing the same reaction I had felt when I had taken in his image in the other dimension. To every human who would see him, madness would follow. Harry turned to completely face the stranger, placing his body in between the two of us.

"I said that I was upset with the human race, that the things I've seen have completely ruined any chance I had at giving a fuck about anyone anymore. But I lied. I have seen horrible things, but I've also seen communities come together for a noble cause. I've seen strangers give up their time and possessions to help the needy. I've seen strangers with good intentions, guy, and I'm not about to let you get away with your plans."

Harry lunged toward the stranger, grabbing onto his wrist and attempting to wrestle the gun from his hand. Before Southway or I could move, the gun fired, dropping Harry to the ground in a single shot. Southway and I backed away at the sound of the shot, pressing our bodies against nearby columns for cover. We ducked and weaved between the columns, putting as much material between ourselves and the stranger as needed to interrupt his aim. Southway had been on the opposite side from where I stood, the center path to the altar dividing me from reaching him. The stranger was standing on this path, poised to shoot at the mere sight of either one of us.

"Luke," Southway said plainly.

"What?" I was startled by his calm nature all of a sudden.

"Do you remember your insurance policy?"

"Yeah. Yeah, I still have it."

"Well, you're going to have to use it."

I removed the knife from the back of my pants quickly, removing it from the sheath and lifting it up to my face. If Southway and I were remotely lucky, we'd each get a quick bullet to the brain. If I was lucky, I'd be the first to go, and Southway would be able to settle his differences with Saarlathesh and his pawn without me. I supposed that it was likely I would end up in another universe again, having 'gotten lucky' due to the stranger's gun 'misfiring.' In which case, I would simply walk out of the altar room and through the asylum grounds and on my way home. But, I guessed that Southway would be a little more than upset with me if I left him alone.

So we stood our ground. Saarlathesh really knew how to get in a person's life, mangle it up until it didn't even resemble a sane man's idea of hell. I hated the bastard for not choosing one of my customer's or one of my high school bullies for an avatar, but I guess my luck was shit and he liked that. Or maybe I had a bit more worth than I had given myself credit for. Or maybe I was just happy to do his bidding, eager to leave a life of TV dinners, bad friends, and long hours at the comic shop.

"I don't know what you two think you can do from there, but I still have more bullets in this gun. Your friend didn't fare too well, Luke, so I suggest that you remove yourself from behind there."

"I…I don't think I can," I replied.

"Why?"

"Because trusting you not to shoot me in the face is like handing my money over to a thief and expecting him not to run away with it."

"Southway, talk some sense into him. You're intelligent. You can see that there is no way out of here. You both either face me or take your chances with the lives that lie beyond this room. Lives as enemies of Saarlathesh," the stranger said.

Southway darted from his column across the room to one much closer to center. He nearly took a bullet to the chest, as the stranger's pull of the trigger released a shot into some darkened corner of the room.

"Luke," Southway called softly.

"Yes?" I replied in a low voice.

"Gentlemen, if you cannot remove yourselves from behind those columns, I shall assume you have no intention of giving up.

And, if that be the case, you can rest assured that you will not be leaving this place alive."

"Luke, you have to get the drop on him," Southway near whispered.

"How am I supposed to do that? I've never killed a man. I've never even stabbed one before."

"He's not human, remember? How can he be in so many places, known where we're going? If Saarlathesh is real, then what makes you so sure that this guy isn't one of his little demon buddies in human form?"

"I've seen him bleed."

"Bullshit. When?"

"In the forest, when I fell down the slope. He appeared to me. I saw him bleed, Southway."

"You said he just appeared to you? Then by all means, teleport us away from here, Luke, because I had no idea that humans could do that. You were delirious, pissed off even, and you believe what he showed you was real? Put it together. This manipulative bastard hasn't told us a single truth. His boss even seems to have trouble telling him the truth. He killed Harry, for god's sake."

Southway wasn't letting this go without a fight, and I had to agree that he argued a good point. When I died in the forest, it wasn't ridiculous to think that the stranger had pulled me into the other world, dressed it up a bit to look like the area around me. It's where I had first gotten the book. It's the realm where my dreams were venturing into. I felt that now, more than ever, was my only chance to end the nightmares. And it only took some bravery and more arm strength than I believed I could muster.

I thought about the promise the stranger had made, the promise that I would not be tormented any longer by Saarlathesh. It was a promise he didn't keep. I used that anger to work up courage inside me. Peeking out of the corner of the column, I realized that the stranger had been arrogantly walking slowly towards our hiding places. The gun was not pointed towards us, but I knew that he would be able to pull off a shot before I could get anywhere near him. 1 motioned to Southway, without a plan in mind, but he seemed to have one of his own. Southway moved from his cover, ducking low and hiding behind one of the church pews near. With a careful consideration of the stranger's view, Southway crept alongside the pew, out of sight.

The stranger continued to walk down the lane until I found that he was just three large steps from the column I hid behind. And he was getting closer.

"Luke, come out from there."

At the stranger's comment, I heard Southway leap from his position, howling some calamity that caused the stranger to quickly turn and fire. Looking around the corner, I saw that Southway dipped below the pews swiftly, just barely enough time for the stranger's bullet to fly into the wall behind him. I took advantage of the situation, circling around the column and taking abundant strides to the stranger's position. Although he attempted to turn in my direction, I plunged the knife at him in a reckless manner, managing to catch the stranger in the throat. Blood flowed out of the wound and from his open, shocked mouth.

"Lu...waaay...hav...you..." garbled the stranger behind a mouthful of blood. He took several steps closer as I backed away, my hand still clutching the knife protruding from his neck.

"S-s-s-stop it! Get away from me!" I yelled.

The stranger's gate became labored; his body stumbled and fell upon my shirt, staining the fabric with a disgusting, ever-flowing fountain of bodily fluid. I found myself catching the stranger with my other hand, staring into eyes that were slowly losing any focus. With a spurt of more blood, the stranger's body finally chose to quit fighting the inevitable and passed in my arms. I was left clutching a lifeless, bloody mess of a man, whose eyes were transfixed upon my own in agony.

"Don't look at his eyes, Luke. Drop the body!"

"Y-y-you said he was n-n-n-not hu-human, Prof–," I stuttered, sweat forming fast at the brow. I let the gun slip out of his hand and hit the floor. I flinched when it made impact, but it did not fire.

"Luke, hold yourself steady. It's over now. We can get the hell out of here."

Southway pried the stranger's body from my hands, tossing it aside carelessly as if he were merely throwing aside a rug or blanket blocking his way. My body grew limp and fell. I curled up on the stone floor, sullied with blood, feeling its cold touch caress my cheek. I wanted more than anything to simply lay there in silence. To close my eyes and pretend I was going to wake up back home, having fallen asleep reading a comic book with the TV on.

"Luke, don't move from this spot. I'll get you out of here," Southway said. I heard his feet clatter behind me, moving toward Harry. I turned to see that he was checking him for a pulse. Although he faced away from me, I witnessed his head drop along with his grasp on Harry's wrist. He moved back to the stranger, picking up the gun from the floor. He returned to me in good time because I felt like my body was going into shock. My hands were shaking, holding onto my arms. Southway rubbed at my shoulder, yelling something at me.

"Get up! I'll take your arm and we'll walk out of here."

When I understood his words, I obliged him, slinging my arm over his upper back and attempting to walk out on my own two feet. We hobbled through a doorway, then down a short hallway.

I had to push away from Southway as a pool of bile erupted from my mouth, bringing some much needed decoration to the cavern's wall. Southway pulled me back up, repeatedly assuring me I was going to be fine. We continued down the hallway, with Southway checking around us and behind us for any sort of resistance.

With time, we had slowly made it back to the circular hallway that I had turned into my personal marathon room. Southway left me in a heap by the entrance, taking the gun in both hands. I heard that familiar shriek of pain, from the creature I had amputated, echoing from somewhere beyond. Southway's footsteps were the next sound I heard, followed by another scream and a hail of gunfire. A death rattle softly permeated my skull before Southway's footsteps grew closer again. He pulled me up on his shoulder, returning the two of us to the staircase.

Michael, who I had all but forgotten about, met us at the top. He was holding open the cellar door, which I'm positive that Southway still could not see. I asked Southway to stop.

"It's over, Michael," I said.

"I know it is, Luke Thornton. I was worried."

"Yeah…well…we got them, I guess."

"It looks like you have. Where's Harry?"

"He didn't make it," answered Southway for me. I choked back a feeling of loss, of regret over Harry's sacrifice.

"Are you coming back with us?" I asked.

"I'm afraid not, Luke. I like it here. There are other people like me here, they were just hiding. I think I feel at home…it has an air of…familiarity…"

I let Michael wander off from us, and then motioned to Southway that he had gone. With much assistance, Southway and I struggled through the basement window. The blood on my hands had proven to be slippery: my grip on the windowsill was lost more than a few times. When Southway had grown weary of my attempts, he personally hoisted my body up and through the window. I felt the cold air touch my face, a cool breeze that did nothing to erase the look of terror on the stranger's face. The final breaths he took were the result of my attack; I had taken his life in a brutal manner.

Pushing myself away from Southway a second time, I ran over to the asylum's outer wall and puked once more against the stonework. My addition to the property did little to improve the appearance of the place. I turned to face Southway, who was rubbing his eyes with his head facing the dirt. When he looked back up again, he was able to witness me stumble a few feet forward and collapse onto the grass with a thud. I blacked out while the cool breeze skated across my hair.

CHAPTER EIGHT
Lut Agonnox

Professor Southway and Luke Thornton made their way back from the Midwest to the East Coast, being sure to take only major roads and to spurn any strange occurrence along the way. This was a decision made by Luke solely; a decision that Southway repeatedly called 'paranoid,' 'schizophrenic,' 'cowardly,' and other such adjectives that may or may not have had an effect on the tempest raging in Luke's mind. Even if said comments did enter Luke's earlobe and remain inside his cranium for a time, he was sure to show no gut reaction, no quick snap of his jaw into a frown. Luke simply sat in the car silently for the duration of the ride.

On Luke's request, Southway never stopped at any particular location, barring the required stop for gas (wherein he was left to purchase snacks at the shop while Luke sat with his head against the passenger seat window) and when it came time for Southway to sleep and Luke to command the wheel. Luke's mind raced during this time, an unnecessary burden resulting in almost three car accidents, four cases of driving nearly off the road, and a single case of pulling over and crying over the steering wheel. All of these incidents met the same end: Southway was forced from his sleep and took over driving duties for the time being.

"You have to get over it," a worried Southway had said, neither believing his words to be true nor feeling guilt over pressing the matter. But, to these words, Luke paid no attention, catatonically staring out the passenger side window into the forests on the side of the road.

"In time, you won't even worry," a bothered Southway later commented, eyes focused on the road rather than the depressed heap of a man sitting next to him. He was very tired, but keeping Luke away from the steering wheel kept him awake.

"I think you should rest for a while, get your bearings and realize that your life in your small town at your comic shop is about to go back to normal," was also said, with little to no assurance as to the validity of such a claim. How would Southway know, Luke must have pondered (and we must assume he pondered for the purpose of this line of thinking) if all the nightmares would truly stop? How compassionate would Saarlathesh be, having had his chosen vessel murder his most devout follower?

In time, Southway found his way toward the Thornton residence, which at this hour was surrounded by the darkness of nightfall. Nary could a light be found in the Thornton house, neither from a room nor from a single, neglected lamp that had been burning electricity for the past few days. All was quiet. Luke stepped from Tracy's car, quietly promising himself that he would return it to her in the morning. Southway imparted some words of wisdom to him, but the words were meaningless and did nothing to assuage the guilt that pumped through Luke's blood. His clothes were stained and ragged, his eyes were very close to bloodshot red, and his sneakers were darkened from the gravel, dirt, and grime of the adventure.

Southway joined Luke inside the house, inspected the first floor for any poltergeists or paranormal creatures and made use of Luke's telephone to phone a taxi. He gathered his things from Tracy's car, said farewell to Luke (again, wishing him good health and a good life), then departed toward the airport.

Before getting into his taxi, Southway, having just deposited his belongings into the trunk, returned to Luke. With an arm wrapped about his shirt, he revealed the gun that the stranger had been using.

"I think you should have this, Luke," he said.

"Why?"

"You killed someone important to Saarlathesh. That must mean something. We definitely have disrupted his plans, but I'm worried that there may be some retribution for our actions. I want you to be able to protect yourself," he explained, "And you'd be better off not getting close and personal again."

"Thank you, Southway."

"I found another magazine on the stranger when I searched his body. It should be fully loaded. Take care, Luke Thornton."

"You too, Professor."

Luke watched the taxi speed off into the distance, and then closed the front door to his home, escaping into the bedroom. He sat upon the bed, turning on his cell phone and inspecting his text messages. He had no intent to answer or send one out himself; he merely stared at the screen, the only light in the darkness except for the shimmer of moonlight that finds its way in through a shuttered window.

As he sat on the bed, Luke shifted and felt a weight on his lower back. There, tucked in his pants, was the handgun that Southway had given him. The gun that had killed Harry. Luke felt the weight in his hand, felt the heavy sting of regret and bad decisions that is often associated with lesser things, such as lying to a loved one or drinking a few too many before work in the morning. Today, regret most closely resembled the harsh reality of having taken something that didn't belong to him. Something that wasn't his to remove from the world. A life.

Luke looked over the black metal cannon in his palm, and then gripped the gun carefully. He placed the end of the barrel under his chin, sweat gathering and ready to drip from his pores. And for just a moment, he felt a bit of peace. A split second of lifted burdens and a flash of absolved consciousness, as if the entire living world pardoned Luke of his crime. But the thought running through his head the most was: *Man, I guess this carpet is about to get a whole lot worse.* One trigger pull later, and he was right. Luke's body flew back onto the bed, spilling a crimson river onto the sheets, which dripped on the floor. And for yet another moment, there existed a moment of peace; throughout the Thornton residence, there was nothing but silence. Not a footstep, not a cough or sneeze. Not even the common hum of electric current, buzzing through the wires of the TV set.

Professor Southway told the taxi driver to drop him off about two blocks from his house. He thanked the driver, handing him a crumpled bill that he produced from his coat pocket. With a wave and a thank you, the taxi driver made his way down the street, turning right and disappearing. Carefully watching his surroundings, Southway made his way to over to the next block. He was careful. Careful to not be seen in the neighborhood. He broke into a jog at the corner, stopping at the front door.

Southway slipped the silver key into the lock, and then struggled to fully push it in all the way. He pulled back his hand, bringing the keychain up to his face. Quickly, he flicked the first key aside and returned to the keyhole with a second. The key fit this time, unlocking the front door to the house. Professor Southway slipped the keychain into his pocket, and then slipped himself through the doorway. The study was still as messy as the day that Luke rang his bell. Books littered the carpet near the door, as much as they littered the entire house. Southway bent down to one of the stacks, picking up an encyclopedia with a blue-green cover.

The book was relatively new, Southway realized as he surveyed the cover, in a way that seemed to betray that he had never seen it in his collection before. He placed it carefully atop the pile again, and then looked to the kitchen. The refrigerator was still running on a rather cold setting; the contents were slightly iced. Southway moved aside a pitcher of lemonade and a gallon of water to reveal a couple of American beers, hiding in the back of the rack. Digging into one of the drawers of the nearby counter, he produced a bottle opener. Throwing back his head, Southway chugged the bottle.

"Delicious," he said.

Nestled in the hall towards the back of the house, exactly between the bedroom and bathroom, was the basement door. It was this door that Southway was now opening, exposing the darkened steps that led down into the cellar. Southway looked to the right, spying the light switch on the wall. With a stiff index finger, Southway flicked upwards, bathing the entire stairwell in light. At the bottom of the stairs, sprawled across the basement floor and the bottom two steps, was the body of an older man. Long, gray hair stretched wildly across the floor, covering most of the head. From underneath the body, a burgundy puddle hugged the cracked composite of stone tiles.

Southway was not shocked at the discovery. In the same calm and professional manner that he had exhibited earlier in the week, Southway looked on the event as if he was surveying a painting at a museum. His feet began their descent down the creaking, wooden boards. Down to the scene of a crime. He stopped at the body, . crouching down to pull the hair back from the dead man's face.

The man had seen decades gone by; either he had experienced a long and demanding life, or the wrinkles of his skin had increased at an early age. Southway brushed the hair from the man's forehead, in an almost father-like way, caressing a child that slept. He touched the man's shoulder, pressing his arm firmly forward until the man turned over onto his back. A knife protruded from the man's sternum at an angle, piercing the right lung. It had been an excruciatingly agonizing death, a final dance for life through labored breathing and chest pains.

"Poor, old man Southway," said Professor Southway, "It was fun being you for a while, but I'm afraid the ruse is over. You are free to take back your identity, Professor. I shall not need it in the future." The man laughed. Professor Southway remained on his back, knife in the sternum, where, no doubt, some stranger or authority would find him. The man who had killed him rose from his position near Southway, and then turned further into the basement.

The basement was barely furnished; its most prominent features were a washer-drier combination in the corner beside a stainless-steel plated, brass faucet. Above the man, pipes of many different shapes and sizes zigzagged around the woodwork. Some led above the ceiling and into the bathroom above. Others stretched across the ceiling and crept down the wall until they dug beneath the floor. The killer walked to a darkened corner of the basement. Here, a power drill laid atop a tile, cord still connected into a nearby wall socket. Beside the drill and cut out of the foundation wall was a slightly-less-than-man sized hole. The man stuck a foot in through the gap, and then ducked his head inside.

After three steps down, the man found himself in a darkened laboratory. A number of tabletops stood upright around the room, while others with broken legs leaned like ramps alongside the wall. Glass was scattered across the tile floor in abundance. Atop a nearby desk were even more textbooks from the above library, pencils of assorted sizes, loose-leaf papers that were written upon, and a trio of beakers, each holding a clear, violet-tinted liquid. The man smiled.

At the far wall, a lone table sat. It held a number of slightly-used candles, which sat upon tea saucers from the kitchen. In the center, a strange, carved idol composed of hardened clay sat; it had the form of a burning dragon circling an empty throne. Beside the throne sat two carved humanoid figures. A man wept into the hands that he held up to his face, and a woman reached out toward the dragon, eyes wide and mouth open in a scream. Above the clay figure, on the wall above the table, was a message written in a quart of blood from the late Professor Southway. It read: "We call upon the Lut, for we do not know the terrible wonders of the Earth, nor do we have the power to face them."

Southway's killer removed the satchel that had been slung onto his back since the start of his adventure. From it, he produced Luke's copy of *The Compendium of Shadows*. He placed it to the left of the idol. Again, he reached into the satchel, this time producing the stranger's *The Children of Saarlathesh*. He placed this book to the right of the idol. The man tossed aside the satchel, which landed in a heap of broken glass.

"Oh, Lut! Speak with me. The avatar of Saarlathesh is no more!" the man who killed Southway proclaimed to the idol, arms outstretched in a V. The idol sat quietly in attention. The ground shook. The floor beneath Southway's killer trembled as if in a tempest. The fragmentation of the floor tiles increased in size, some splitting into halves, while others split into pieces. The man braced his feet upon the ground, as his arms stumbled and waved in an attempt to regain a semblance of balance. From outside, the faint blaring of car alarms could be heard, raising a calamity of noise and cacophony, waking the sleeping populace of the town. Behind him, the man could hear the metal grinding of pipes scraping together. One of the pipes detached, leaking a steady stream of water into the room.

From the idol, a distortion of many voices began pouring forth, in resemblance of a large crowd all speaking aloud at once. The voices grew louder and louder still, blocking out the rumble of the earthquake, drowning out the concert of car alarms, and deafening the splash of the broken pipe's contents. When the sound became too much to bear, the voices stopped. The man heard nothing, saw nothing. The silence gripped his subconscious, slowly eroding the comfort mankind finds in the buzz of electronics, the chatter of passing humans, and the noise of life. And all at once, a singular voice spoke out.

"We are aware of the status of the avatar."

The man licked his lips and swallowed, "My friends, the deed is done! Saarlathesh's plans for the Earth are no more! It will be long before the Insect King pines for control of this realm for a second time. I rejoice in our victory." He dropped to his knees, pressing his forehead into the floor, which still rumbled.

"Yes…yes, the dark lord has not taken it well, it seems," the voice replied.

"The Lut people know! Oh, how glorious is the wealth of knowledge you share. If only a miserable human, such as I, could be gifted with the superior cognition of the Lut! Glory to your people, Voice of the Lut! Glory to the success of the Lut!"

"And what of the mortal, Luke Thornton? How has he fared since your last encounter?"

"He is broken, oh Voice! Broken by man's subpar brain! A mind broken because he lacks the clarity of the Lut and the righteousness of our actions."

"Hmm, you will see him again in your future travels," the Voice said.

"My future travels, Voice? Do you have another task for your servant?"

"Are you ready, mortal, to receive the gift of the Lut?" the Voice replied.

"The gift?"

"For services rendered. You will become the avatar of the Lut deity, the one we worship as Lut Agonnox. He from which we are named." The man began to slowly retreat from the idol. "Do not be fearful, mortal, for you have been chosen to embody the essence of a god! You will walk where he walks, speak when he speaks, and do when he chooses to do. Saarlathesh's minions are routed for now, and it is time for Lut Agonnox to take possession of the Earth."

The man's happiness slowly eroded, as if a bullet had pierced his brain. He felt it. The warmth. The slow, creeping heat from the forceful entry of Lut Agonnox into his mind. The heat became the sun; it seared at his flesh from the inside. The man screamed as he fell to the ground. His body convulsed, preparing itself to be the carrier, the avatar. The hair on his head pulled and tugged away from his scalp, falling like leaves onto the tile floor. The rest of his body hair followed; tufts lying in heaps next to him. The man tossed and turned, screaming and kicking at the air.

His scalp began to peel itself. The skin tore in half, like an unseen force was ripping open his flesh as easily as one rips a paper. The skin tore itself away from the man's face, exposing muscle and bone and bulging eyes, full of terror and pain. The man's tears burned as they dripped down his unprotected flesh. Slowly, his lips tore themselves with the skin, revealing a hellish set of screaming teeth. The body finally collapsed to the floor with a loud clatter. The shaking around the vicinity of the house had ceased; the car alarms were, one by one, switched off by their respective owners. The pipe in the room ceased its flow of water, slowing down to a short buildup of moisture that dripped in evenly spaced intervals.

Minutes passed. Eventually, an hour. The body of the once living man was sprawled on the cold, concrete, tile floor. His clothes had left him; all that remained was a bloody bundle of muscle and bone that neither stirred nor shifted. Just stillness. For the people outside of the Southway Residence, the temporary earthquake was a random and confusing mistake of nature; a natural event that had no business waking up the good people of Dartford from their collective dreams, which consisted of their waking days and the strange, twisted dream logic that one encounters in the deepest throes of slumber.

But the man in the pool of blood did not dream. He remained still. Still in body and mind. Still in his soul, which no longer was a possession he could claim as his own. His soul had been replaced, wholly, by the eldritch being inside of him. For this is the result of tampering with the unknown; the horrors of the world are meant to frighten children in stories, told to them by parents to groom them into well-behaved, and fearful, adults. But by adulthood, the horrors are over: the boogeyman replaced by the daily grind of a nine to five job, one that was chosen out of necessity and not interest. In essence, the ghosts and goblins fabricated by the imagination of a child slowly fade into obscurity, while the very real fear of death grips their later years.

And yet, the man with no skin sits in a puddle of his own noxious fluid, charred and torn skin, and strands of hair. If only the world were able to fit into this basement and see the true horrors lying, waiting, in the corner of darkened master bedrooms across the globe, perhaps the boogeyman may last well into the golden years of one's life. But this is not possible. It is beyond society as a whole to see the true capability of the universe around them; to function properly, a society must believe only in what scientists call the "real" and "tangible." It is for the unfortunate few that such a revelation appears, tearing the fabric of their world and leading to a descent into chaos and lunacy.

The real and tangible skinless man, lying in a pool of his blood and surrounded by his skin, disturbingly began to shift his seared, fleshly palms until they were flat against the ground. With both hands, the body pushed itself upwards, revealing the contorted expression that the killer had left on his face before his passing. The skinless man rose further, placing one knee on the ground to support himself and pushing up further with his arms. It was kneeling. With a start, the body rose onto two feet, creating a sickening ripple in the crimson pool. It lurched forward, reaching the broken wall of the hidden basement room with a number of stumbles and falls. The room had become decorated with strands of the body; scraps of skin and hair still clinging to the damp muscle rubbed off onto the tables and floor around the place.

With a slowness of movement, the body lifted a leg and moved forward through the wall, and then ducked its head inside. The body of Southway was still on the bottom of the steps, where his upturned face exposed an apparent look of dread; although, if from the killing blow or the frightening skinless man before him, it is unclear. The skinless man continued past Southway, up the steps in a slow pace. Step by step. Foot by bloody foot. At the landing, it flicked the light switch down, casting a foreboding darkness upon the ghastly events that had transpired in the basement of the Southway Residence, Dartford, Kent County, England.

In the bathroom, the skinless thing had found its way. Ripping open the medicine cabinet and leaving behind a rather sizable hand-print, it found itself three sizable packages of medical gauze. With a careful precision, it began wrapping the body, beginning at the soles of the feet. When it had reached the abdomen, somewhere close to where the man's stomach would have been, the skinless creature stopped to view itself in the medicine cabinet mirror, turning its head from side to side as if there were some semblance of beauty that needed to be maintained. But the only image to see within that mirror was an abhorrent entity; a gross remnant of what used to comprise a man, sans the outer components that common society requires. Namely, skin. When the wrapping had completed, the result of which left most of the body wrapped besides the eye sockets and the fingers, the thing walked out of the bedroom and into the hall.

The bedroom of the Southway house lit up in an instant, illuminating the queen-sized bed in the center of the room. Besides the bed, the room saw fit to house a nightstand of rather unappealing style (wood, with a single, book-sized drawer), a lamp adorning the aforementioned nightstand (of white plastic, crudely shaped to resemble some form of expensive ceramic alternative), a rather tall dresser (of the same color and design as the night-stand), and an open closet (complete with shuttered doors) that betrayed a rather pitiful collection of button shirts, ties, and two kinds of coats (one that was thin for the spring air, the other heavy for the winter frosts). A single, five-foot mirror hung on the wall between the bed and closet. The frame was of the same brown wood fashion as the other wooden furniture pieces.

The skinless thing heaved heavily, as if the body itself ran on the very human need to intake air into the lungs. But the body was no longer in control of its previous master. To Lut Agonnox, the body was much like a puppeteer's favorite marionette, dancing to the tune of the puppeteer's skillful hand. Scratching at the bandages, the skinless man stood before the poor selection that was Southway's wardrobe. With prudence, it removed a few garments of clothing, which it began to fit over itself in a typical fashion. Having long since destroyed the man in possession of the body, the body failed to flinch at the tug of the cloth against the bandaged muscle, even though the nerves still screamed messages to the brain to stop.

Once the dressing had been completed, the skinless man stood before the mirror, admiring the simplicity of a pair of beige slacks, slightly polished business-casual shoes, and a navy blue button down shirt, which, on a second thought, the creature buttoned all the way up to the neck. To complete the outfit, it pulled at a box above the hanging clothes and produced a rather dull flat cap. With this article, the skinless man placed it atop its head, pressing down slowly to fit the skull. This was accomplished, without much pleasure to describe, with the accompaniment of a low, but reasonably audible crunch from the creature's cranium. Concluding that the task of dressing was complete, it grabbed the heavier coat from the closet and put it on. Looking into the mirror, it flipped the collar upwards to conceal as much of the bandages as possible.

Upon the nightstand, it spotted the wallet of the late Southway, along with a passport (used recently for travel to the quiet countryside of Alsace in Eastern France), a silver watch, and a small, silver lighter. Taking these four items into possession, the skinless man filled the pockets of his pants, placing the passport in an inner coat pocket. If the effect was possible, the appearance of a grin, smug in nature, may have been seen upon the visage of the creature. It turned away from the nightstand, returned the bedroom into a state of darkness with a flick of the light switch, and then made for the front door, where it took one last survey of the Southway Residence before closing the door behind it.

CHAPTER NINE

Coffee with the Dead

As I sat on the bed, I shifted and felt a weight on my lower back. There, tucked in my pants, was the handgun that Southway had given me back at the asylum. The gun that had killed Harry and had brought a level of madness to me that I was wholly unprepared to experience. I felt the weight in my hand, felt the heavy sting of regret and bad decisions that is often associated with lesser things, such as lying to a loved one or drinking a few too many before work in the morning. Today, regret most closely resembled the harsh reality of having taken something that didn't belong to me. Something that wasn't mine to remove from the world. A life.

I looked over the black metal cannon in my palm, and then gripped the gun carefully. Hesitating, I placed the end of the barrel under my chin, sweat gathering and ready to drip from the pores that were found there. And for just a moment, I felt a bit of peace. A split second of lifted burdens and a flash of absolved consciousness, as if the entire living world pardoned me of my crime. But the thought running through my head the most was: *Man, I guess this carpet is about to get a whole lot worse. I should've tried harder to get the bumblebee blood out of it. But I guess that doesn't matter now.* One trigger pull later, and I was right. The carpet wasn't going to get any better, but I sure as hell wasn't adding anything to it tonight.

The gun had gone off with an audible click, failing to eject a bullet directly into my skull and proving that, at the very least, I was incredibly lucky. I pulled the gun away from my chin. Southway had been wrong, I realized. Suicide wasn't a way out of the recurring cycle of death; suicide had either transferred my conscious into another universe or I was having one hell of a dream. *It isn't a dream.* I considered for a second delving deep, mentally, into the consequences and effects that my recent suicide may have had, but I knew that no good could be had from putting my mind in that kind of state. I can't imagine that many people can recover so quickly from a suicidal stupor, but I reasoned I might just have gained a new lease on life and I wasn't about to give it a second go.

Although, I just killed myself in another universe to get to that revelation, so any good feeling I may have felt at that idea was quickly replaced with sudden horror. I threw my mind away from the thoughts, thinking instead of how I would have to open the comic shop in the morning. I walked through the living room and past the kitchen entrance, throwing open the back door and walking out onto the grass in my bare feet. I looked at the metallic killer in my hand, and then pulled my arm back in a pitcher's stance. With the crystal blue glimmer of the water of the lake as my witness, I heaved my arm forward, hurling the gun into the deep, drowning depths. *Good riddance.* It was time to get myself back to normal. To get my life back to normal. Returning back inside, I threw myself upon my bed and fell fast asleep.

A week later, I dreamt that I was standing at a cliff side, over-looking a waterfall spilling into the river down, down, down below me. I leaned over to survey the drop, seeing a figure at the bottom waving at me with a smile. I was eager to join him. My body stepped off the cliff, and I was falling alongside rushing water, which splashed onto my face.

I awoke with a start, tossed and turned, then fell into a state of dreaming again. In my next dream, I was standing in my local town, outside of a building that my mind told me was a school, but my subconscious had constructed in the form of an abandoned factory on the outskirts of town. Before me stood my three high school friends-Jean, Raphael, and Wayne, all wearing clothes out of my wardrobe. My dream self was running towards them, shouting some nonsense about having found a secret way into the principal's office. Jean, Raphael, and Wayne all looked doubtful, telling me that there was no way we could get into there without getting caught. But I insisted they follow me, and I turned back to the building.

When I looked back, I saw that none of them had followed. I was alone in the middle of a concrete sidewalk. From behind, a person tapped me on the shoulder. They had the face of an adult, but a soft voice, like that of a child.

She looked at me motherly and said: "Luke, you should go home. Your friends have gone."

"But what about the secret entrance? What about the fun we could have?"

The woman sighed and said, "There simply isn't time to go on an adventure. There isn't any time at all."

"But there can always be time."

"Life is about moving," she said, "and life is about finding your own way without looking back. Besides, you might trip if you don't look forward."

"But what if I don't want to move forward?"

"Well, then I guess it's always as easy as…CRAWLIN' IN MY SKIN. THESE WORDS, THEY WILL NOT HEAL…"

I woke with a start, realizing that the woman in my dream was singing a song halfway through her sentence. Without having to think, I switched off my phone's alarm, a song I had picked half-heartedly the night before but generally liked. I hadn't connected it in my dream, but in the waking world it was obvious that the alarm had found its way into my subconscious, causing the strange woman to mutter out those few lines of the song. I chuckled quietly, still unsure if the previous night had truly happened as I remembered. But this was a common occurrence already. I have found myself in truly unwanted situations, and then lied to myself that it was all a dream. But all of it was real, from the cross-country trip to the stained fabric of my bedroom floor.

After a moderately warm shower and a piece of stale toast for breakfast, I set out to the town center. I had already returned Tracy's car, greeting her with half a smile and managing to stand my ground when she threw her body at me in a warm embrace. She said she was glad to see me. I said I had some things to take care of, escaping from the situation that only way I knew how: by lying. I next went into town to put up a sign near my shop window, which said "Manager Back From Vacation - Will Re-Open Soon," with a lingering doubt as to how soon I intended to open for business again. Another week, though, seemed to be enough time to get my bearings back and return to the life of an uninteresting citizen of small-town-nowhere.

After that week had passed, I found that I currently possessed neither a car nor a bicycle, so I walked my way over to the comic shop. I dipped into Mama Hill's Express Station on a small detour. Mama Hill was ready and waiting to greet my from behind the counter.

"Luke! I had the most exciting trip. You have to hear all about it!"

"What trip?"

"Did you forget? The cruise I took. I told you about it…oh, but that was before your accident. It must've been the least important thing on your mind."

I scratched at the back of my head, and then said, "No, I remember it. Sounds like you had a helluva time."

"I did! Managed to relax and take it easy for an entire week! I collected some seashells for the store," Mrs. Hill said. And boy, did she collect a number of shells. They were all hung up on strings, dangling from the store ceiling. From the quick glance around, it looked like Mama Hill had spent more time collecting seashells for the Express Station than enjoying a vacation, but who was I to judge the way a person chooses to take it easy. My idea of a vacation had started with dying in a car crash, then assisting a demonic entity in taking control of my life and nearly inviting him to play houseguest in my skull.

"You look terrible, baby."

"I feel terrible."

"Robin had stopped in here when I got back. Told me you went on a little adventure of your own."

"It was an adventure, alright," I grumbled at her while my eyes were pre-occupied with browsing the food I would replace with my lack of a breakfast that morning.

"Maybe you should've taken my offer," Mama Hill joked, "those liners aren't full at this time o' year. It was like owning your own yacht with the space we had."

"Maybe." I finally made a decent selection, a diced chicken breast sandwich (prepared personally by Mama, as the logo on the seal told me) and paid at the counter.

"You take it easy, Luke."

"Ya," I said through the chunk of sandwich I had viciously bitten into.

I continued on my excursion to the entrance of the comic shop, carelessly biting into the sandwich as if I hadn't eaten for days. Thinking back, I wasn't even sure if I had. The bread crumbled with every bite, tossed into the wind for some pigeon to devour on his way to the nest. I thought about Harry's comments from back at the junkyard, something to the effect of people not realizing how much waste they generate individually. Then my mind drifted to those last few moments of his life, which consisted of a bullet lodging itself into his forehead. With my eyes clenched, I pushed the thought away, afraid to give too much of my time thinking about mistakes of the past and the climatic finale to my adventure.

Why had I even come back to this crummy town? It was filled with nothing but a boring routine of day-to-day assholes and drunken nights in front of the TV and that lingering sense of abandonment from living in my parents' house. Somewhere down the line, I had blamed all that had happened on them running out on me. But that was just a common scapegoat, blaming my trouble on a couple of worthless human beings who took a look at their teenage son, said good enough, and then departed on a quest of their own. Wherever life had taken them, I had hoped that the guilt ate at them.

I had eaten my sandwich, tossing the wrapper into a refuse bin, but having the wind goaltending caused it to flutter up and over the top. I cursed at the plastic, and then began whistling as I walked away. The sign on the comic shop had quickly been vandalized, a fault of my own for placing it on the outside of the shop rather than on the inside of the window. It now read: "Manager Back From Hell - Will Re-Open To Your Displeasure." I had to laugh a bit inside myself at the cheap shot from whoever had run by the front window with a black marker and terrible handwriting. I ripped the sign from the door, tossing it to the ground much like I had the wrapper. A passing police cruiser changed my mind, which led to me diving after it.

My clothes were ruffled from the pavement, so I brushed them down and placed the sign into the refuse bin. I was still patting myself down when I caught Robin walking in from the corner of my eye. I looked up in his direction, then back down at my clothes.

"Hey, Luke!"

"Hello, Robin," I said, still patting away at some dust on my sleeve.

"You're back!"

"No, I'm away. This is merely a hologram. 'Hello, kids. Management will return soon to give you your fairy tales and men in tights.'"

"That's not funny."

"And yet I'm dying inside," I said to Robin, without an ounce of laughter in my face.

"How did it go?"

"Peachy."

"Well…you look like hell."

"I am hell," I said quickly and without thought.

"What?"

"Never mind. What are you doing here?"

"I came to see if the shop was open again."

"Craving another adventure with your rich foster parent?"

"Who?"

"You know…Bruce Wayne? Your name is Robin, you love *Batman* comics. I shouldn't have to connect the dots this often with my remarks, you know. It ruins the joke."

"Very funny."

"Again. I'm dying inside."

"You're still an asshole!" Robin shouted.

"Now I'm missing your point."

Robin threw his hands up in the air, once again upset at the runaround I gave him. Although Robin was probably the closest thing I had to a friend in recent years, I sure as hell didn't give him any indication of the fact. It's a sad truth you have to face when the only person who you can call a friend is just the person you see with most frequency. Somewhere, I hadn't cared about this truth and decided that a life of being an asshole was better than making myself out to be a good person.

"Are you here to open the store?" Robin finally asked.

"Tomorrow. I'm just taking down the sign."

"Alright. I'll be back here tomorrow."

"Of that, I have no doubt."

Robin delivered another dose of "You're an asshole, Luke" before departing from the storefront and strolling around the corner to the center of town. I made my way back home, expecting to find nothing to do but sleep till tomorrow. True to myself, I napped until dusk, and then forced myself to sleep some more until the morning.

I was able to make my way to the comic shop on time, having the indecency to skip both breakfast and a shower altogether. A quick shave, a change of clothes, brushing my teeth, and a glass of water were all that encompassed my morning routine this day. I stumbled into the shop right on cue, ready to start the day with a little more than a half smile on my face and about seventy dollars in cash in the register. One turn of the key and a pull at the front gates later, and Luke Thornton's comic shop was ready for business and ready to serve every dimwit, halfwit, and idiot that shuffled in at odd intervals.

I made it a point to give a nasty scowl to customers that I felt would only be in the store to argue. The majority of them took the hint, turning right back around and leaving the establishment to find a better class of shopkeeper in the town center. Others put on a look of confusion, deciding to browse a few minutes and scatter a number of comics into the wrong categories. I continued my scowl, specifically in their direction and making sure to make eye contact, until they too left the premises. The final few people did not understand the meaning behind my deterrent, choosing instead to remain in the store in order to punish me for not wanting to work this day.

As should be obvious, I found it a lot easier to handle customer questions and transactions when the people asking the questions had spent the better half of their childhood reading comics any chance they got. When it comes down to it, talking to a comic shop clerk without prior knowledge of the subject of comics is like trying your hand at physics without first having figured out mathematics. The customer just ends up horribly wrong about everything, and I end up completely frustrated that I can't explain the simplest concepts without being met with "What?" "What's that" and "Wait, go over that again" as responses. On more than one occasion, I've encountered this scenario:

"I'm sorry. Can you explain that for the fourth time?"

"Are you serious?" At this point, I bury my face into my hand.

"Well, excuse me! I don't read this junk, how would I know?"

As everyone knows, the quickest way to not upset a specialty store owner is to jump at the product he sells.

"Yes, ma'am or sir," I would answer, "All of these items are junk and I'm selling them to corrupt your child/son/daughter/toddler/husband into being an immoral piece of shit. Tell me again what you were in here to buy?"

I am not a nice person. But neither is anyone else. I just have more trouble than most keeping it to myself.

An awfully large woman was busy yelling for a refund at the counter when I saw it. On the far wall opposite me, some strange spider was making its way across. It looked huge, even at the distance from where I stood, but that description was coming from a guy who Robin would say had declared war on insects since birth. The thing was strange; it's body was more like a scorpion than a spider and its head was a yellow, bulbous sac seemingly glued onto an abomination.

"..And the level of pornographic content on each page was ridiculous! Look at how low cut this woman's blouse is, how skimpy she is! What kind of business is this that sells smut to kids?!" droned the woman.

"Would you excuse me? I have to take care of something," I said, snatching a newspaper I had behind the counter. *Newspaper? Luke, you'll need a goddamn flamethrower to kill that thing.* My subconscious did nothing for my image as the mastermind of mass insect genocide.

The large woman used her body as a barrier between me and the shop floor. I looked up at her and, with disgust, realized that I could see the hairs curling inside her nose.

"You're not going ANYWHERE without giving me a refund."

I reached into my pocket and pulled out a ten dollar bill. I grabbed the woman's hand and said: "I'm sorry. Just leave the comic on the counter and have a nice day." I pushed past her quite easily now that she had lost her iron stance. The woman was speechless, but from behind me I heard the comic slam onto the counter. This was soon followed by the ring of the bell on the shop door, but I was too focused on the spider to worry if she had left or someone else had entered.

As I got nearer, the image of the spider on the wall grew more detailed. The thing made me sick to my core. It did indeed have a yellow, bulbous sac for a head, but now I could see that its body was of a strange color gradient. Its flesh was a fine mix of red, blue and purple that may have leaped straight out of a *Spider-Man* comic. The thing was moving back and forth in place, either building a nest on my wall or trying to plot its next step across to the horror section (where it honestly belonged). My next step was figuring out how I was going to goad this thing to and out the front door. It must have heard my thoughts because, after that last one, it turned its bulb to me and leapt into the air.

I screamed. The spider continued its trajectory in the direction of my face, and I threw the newspaper flat against it. The two connected, causing my newspaper to flutter into several pages onto the ground and the spider to fling against the wall, bursting its yellow bulb. The wall was stained with the disgusting liquid that was found inside, and the spider continued until it landed atop a number of horror comics that I had placed into the "Definitely Not Scary, But Stupid" bin, the sign of which decided to dislodge and float to the floor. There were a number of patrons standing around me at the time (it was one of the more popular areas in the store to find comics), and their faces conveyed the utter confusion and fear that I had just brought into their lives.

With growing anxiety, I watched the spider's legs twitch repeat-edly, as though the spinal cord still had enough juice within to men-tally fuck with me. As if the spider's body was saying: *Look at me, Luke. Come on over and led me leap onto your face and suck the look of horror right off.* With enough time, the twitching died down, and some of my patrons decided it was as good a time as any to start slipping slowly away from me. One guy, who was down the aisle to my left, slid against the table of comics until he reached nearly a foot away from me. He flattened his body to avoid bumping me, escaping the aisle and running for the door, which he threw open quickly.

I relaxed from my heightened position, a Kung Fu stance that consisted of my legs spread slightly apart and bent at the knee. The hand that threw the paper was extended with my palm open, and my other hand was placed gently at my abdomen. I noticed, looking behind me, that a child had begun to weep softly to him-self, huddled behind a *Miracleman* comic. From the look of terror on his face (which I annoyingly noticed was directed at me, not the abomination I had just murderfucked off the wall), he was close to peeing himself.

"Everybody. Outside. Now," I said softly.

Everyone obliged my order as if I was a maniac, holding a gun and making threats in a bank. When the shop became entirely quiet, I looked outside to make sure that no one else was near-ing the door. I rushed to the back of the counter, scooping up a dustpan and a number of paper towels. I went to work on the spider body first, pushing it into the dustpan and flinging it directly into the trash. With a twist and a knot, I closed the bag immedi-ately, not wishing to chance that the little bastard would grow a new head, gain two hundred pounds and devour me alive. Next, I scrubbed at the wall, much in the same way I had been scrubbing at the bloodstain on my carpet.

I looked at the comics that the spider had fallen upon, noting how deeply each was stained with its blood. I selected any and all that had a drop of the demon liquid, then tossed them away into a fresh garbage bag I had opened. I briefly considered burning the comics and the bag, then burning the wall, then burning the shop, and lastly setting myself on fire, but I knew that I wasn't thinking clearly. I'd need dynamite and a comically oversized detonator before I would ever feel comfortable standing in this shop ever again.

I re-opened the comic store after I had thrown out all evidence of my murder scene, greeting new patrons and old patrons back politely. I decided that business had taken a turn for the slow, so I reached toward the horror section, grabbing a comic whose title relayed to me that I was in store for a low-quality, amateur attempt at scares. Behind the counter, I flipped through five pages before hitting an ad for bubblegum, which ripped me from whatever little immersion the comic had generated for me. Throwing it aside, I turned to the registers, deciding to count the tills early in the event that no one currently in the store would purchase anything. It wasn't that farfetched an idea; for years, they had been reading my comics for free.

Robin, walking in later than I had anticipated but showing up nonetheless, sauntered to the counter around eight o'clock.

"Shouldn't you be having dinner?" I said.

"Who has dinner at eight? My family eats at six," he responded.

"Well, I tend to have dinner at around ten thirty."

"You get out of here at nine thirty. And you live by yourself. AND you think a packet of salty noodles and potato chips is a balanced meal."

"Yes. Truly, I live a life of freedom and midnight ice cream."

"That's not having freedom."

"Oh? Aren't you still in middle school? Like eighth grade or something? What do you know about freedom?"

"Probably no more than yourself."

I smirked at Robin, deciding that I have given this kid enough shit for days to come. It was time for something different.

"What can I help you find today, Robin?"

"What?"

"Do you want advice on comics, I'm saying?"

"Did you hit your head?"

"No, I just want to be helpful."

"Well don't do that. It's freaking me out. Stick with talking bullshit."

"Yeah, well, can't say I didn't try."

"So what happened earlier?" he asked. I bit my lip, saying that I just loudly killed a spider on the counter by whacking it with my shoe.

"See? There's the bullshit," he said, with a smile, "Tommy down the block says you freaked out and threw a paper at the wall. Splattered some poor fly with no remorse."

"THAT'S bullshit. That thing was a spider and it was large enough to tussle with an ox."

"Right."

"You should've been here," I said, lowering my eyes and pretending to count money when I merely was flipping through it quickly.

"I should have," he said, walking off to probably find a second copy of *Knightfall* to gift to a friend.

At about eight twenty, a man walked in to the shop who I had never seen before. He was wearing a full, brown raincoat and matching fedora, an outfit that befitted Humphrey Bogart or James Stewart more than your average American in the 21st century. He was out of place; a horse-drawn carriage in the middle of busy Tokyo, a medieval knight's armor on the battlefield of Normandy, an enigma in the middle of a comic shop. I surveyed his features, his stature, but I couldn't get a good look at the guy. His fedora crept over his face in such a way that, even in the shine of fluorescent bulbs, I could not see but a glimmer of white from his eyes, surveying the comics his two fingers flipped through. He had medical gauze around his chin, the only part of his face that wasn't concealed. *Must have taken a fist to the face.*

The man bothered me the longer he stayed; regulars to me had mostly consisted of large, portly children or men with greasy, stained shirts or those ultra-nerdy types that you can find dressed as *Archie* at a comic book convention. This wasn't a regular. He wasn't regular in any sense of the word. *No, the word for this guy is unsettling.* I watched him carefully, hoping that the punch in my gut was telling me he was a thief and not an eldritch horror about to burst into tentacles in the middle of my comic shop. *Who was he?* I could feel that he had come here with an agenda, and he was killing time to get me alone.

My intuition was getting so good I was worried I'd have to check myself for a menstrual cycle. The guy was meticulous in the way he avoided eye contact; I was full blown believing he was purposely trying to make me uneasy with the way he floated around the aisles. Eventually, Robin came up to me and offered up a hardcover of *The Killing Joke.*

"Again?!"

"I have never read this, Luke, you know that from my purchase history," he said, angrily.

"Bro, if I haven't sold you this comic at least four times, then what the hell have you been doing NOT reading it?"

"What do you mean?"

"Tell me you've heard of this before you picked it out."

"Yeah, I was looking specifically for it, Luke. I was just busy browsing other stuff."

"Jesus, man. Here," I handed the bag to him and his receipt, "For what it's worth, it's a good story, if you can believe I liked it."

"With all the shit you give me, I would be surprised if you liked anything that anyone liked."

"That's not true! I like *Tales from the Outer Darkside of the Twilight.*"

"That shitty sci-fi rip-off? You like that garbage?"

"Hey, what happened to your respect for my tastes?"

"It died around the fourth time you insisted on calling me Rob."

The conversation mostly ended at that point, as I don't want to fill a page of me and Robin going back and forth calling each other the lowest names imaginable. It was definitely a friendship kind of thing; that little comment of "Fuck you, good night, see you later" that friends understand as a joking goodbye, but strangers see as a fight.

Everyone had cleared out by eight fifty, but the man in the raincoat remained inside the store. I grew very uneasy at his presence, picking up the phone a number of times before setting it back down. *What if you drag some cops into some form of mess?* Cops are always dying in movies exactly once it looks like they can rescue the hero. The last thing I needed to add to my ever growing guilt was the life of an officer of the law. Plus, having a cop here would undoubtedly give me a boost of confidence that would quickly turn to horror the minute that a demon rushes into his flabby chest. *C'mon, Luke. Fuck off...do it yourself.*

"We're, uh...closing...soon," I near whispered to the man. He didn't even bother to let the words create any sense of reflex in him. Most people at least turn to hear the source of the little prick who was threatening to kick them out. Giving up on him, I managed to close the door in the face of a running couple, two nerd-lovebirds who had come to pick out a last minute bedtime story. From the experience, and the look on their two, heartbroken faces, I managed to feel a sense of joy replace my worries as I slid the lock on the door into place. That is, until I realized that there was someone standing directly behind me, peering into the back of my skull with a stare.

I rotated my body to see the face, or rather, the lack of a face on a man who very recently had seen some third-rate doctor about plastic surgery. The medical gauze wrapped his entire visage, but they had long ago lost their clean white appearance. Instead, the gauze was stained with dried blood. I squealed and made an attempt to push past him, but whatever creature this was grabbed me by the collar and held me off my feet. His fedora fell off his head as he turned it up to look at me.

"Luke…Thornton," it garbled out, blood dripping from the mouth of the creature.

"What the fuck are you? Let go of my shirt…It'll stretch." I decided my life needed an extra dose of comedy to go with the trauma, but it wasn't helping the fear from squeezing my chest.

"You're…coming with…me…to…"

I kicked at its chest, felt some form of bone or something in his coat crack. His grip loosened enough that I was able to wrestle free, falling to the ground on my ass. A pain shot up from my bone, nearly paralyzing me as I crawled away from the raincoat creature. He seemed to be recovered from whatever damage I had caused him, as I looked back to see that he was ready to follow. My feet kicked into overdrive, finding nice traction on the shop floor and propelling me forward to a standing jog. I jogged to the back of the place, and then realized that, if anything, I was boxing myself in.

"Luke…THORNTON!" the creature grumbled loudly, reaching out towards me in a strangling gesture.

"Get the hell away from me! What do you want?"

"Come with me…THORNTON!"

My hands scrambled for something to hit it with, but scattered in front of me were only the soft covers of hundreds of comic books. Finding no alternative at the time, I began flinging comics at the creature's face. An issue of *Punisher MAX* flew past his head without impact, flying to the floor and skidding to a stop underneath the front counter. I reached and threw an *All-Star Batman & Robin* without hesitation, clipping the creature in the face but not slowing it down in the least. Upon picking up the next comic, however, I recognized the cover and stopped myself from launching it at my assailant. It was an issue from Neil Gaiman's epic, *The Sandman*. In the bin next to me, I carefully placed the comic back into its rightful place. This seemed to confuse the creature, stopping him long enough for me to chuck a nearby copy of *The Amazing Spider-Man #544* with more disgust for the magazine issue than I had for the creature before me.

The graphic novel hit him square in the face, knocking him back a bit and causing him to put an arm up defensively. *About time that comic was good for something.* I shuffled through more terrible issues, throwing them as quickly as I could and slowly moving in a clockwise direction back to the front door. As I neared the last bin of comics, I pulled a handful, tearfully realizing that I may have picked up some gems in the pile, placed in by negligent customers too lazy to return it to its proper place.

"ENOUGH!" the creature roared, knocking me over with a gust of air. I grabbed and crumbled a handful of issues into my right and left hands, stood up, and chucked the lot of them at it. The creature's mouth unhinged, pouring forth a jet of flame that cut through the air and burned them to a crisp in midair. I dove underneath the table I stood behind, feeling the heat graze the back of my neck as I did so. The flame continued into the wall behind me, where the spider had made his appearance earlier in the evening. The plaster and crumbled tiles that made up the ceiling caught fire almost instantaneously, much to my anger.

Bastard is going to burn down the place if I don't do something. Not content to watch my livelihood go the route of my life, I elected to dive towards a fire extinguisher by the counter. It had seemed that the creature still retained a human level of intelligence, as he had anticipated my next course of action and caught me. I struggled once more with his freakish grip, kicking him square in the groin. Rather than be freed of the monster, he cocked his arm back and threw me against the back wall of the store. Looking up and attempting to breathe through both smoke and the wind that had escaped my lungs from impact, I recognized that my store was slowly burning to cinder. It was at this moment in my life that I wished I had a back door to the place.

The store was coming down fast. Pieces of ceiling tile were breaking off and setting fire to the bins and tables full of easily combustible comic books. This would be a time when I normally would complain about the cheapening of materials in the industry, but I was in the middle of a duel with yet another creature from hell. Only, neither of us had our hands on a sword or a gun or a sharpened pencil. Smoke choked my eyes and suffocated me, but I knew the only way I would survive this would be to make it out the front door. I attempted a running leap over a table once I got onto my feet, but the flames erupted out of control when I got near, causing me to instinctively recoil from the heat. I tried it again, finding myself a third time in the hands of the monstrosity that stood amongst the flames.

The fire had burned off most of his clothes, revealing a disgusting spectacle of forcibly removed skin. This creature was once a man like me, but he had lost most of what made him human some time ago. He was an abomination, with a sickening look and a sickening smell that made me wish he would chuck me in the fire to release me from the amount of bullshit I was putting up with for the past month. I wasn't so lucky, as the story continues to go. The creature wound his arm back one last time, chucking me through the pane of glass that held the front windows of my shop. I crashed and burned onto the pavement of the sidewalk outside, losing consciousness.

"LUUUKE!"

My body lurched up, in the way that your body kicks up at the sound of your mother calling you to wake up in the morning. I was laying my stomach, tasting the finest aspects of American sidewalk and there was an intense heat burning the soles of my shoes. I looked back to see the pitiful sight of my comic shop erupting into flames. I wondered to myself where the fire department was at, either drinking at Harry's Rest or flipping cards to each other at the station. Whatever the reason, they were taking their sweet time arriving in my time of need. I pushed my body up to a pushup on my hands, allowing my knees to take over in keeping my body off the ground.

This is where it was going to end, I told myself. If I was ever going to die, it needed to be at my lowest, having just spent the better part of a few weeks' vacation running around for Saarlathesh, killing a man who threatened me with a gun, and possibly blowing my head off in another universe. I had left high school not knowing what college I would attend, or if I even had the balls to finish anything I would have started. But I guess I was wrong about myself. I was about to see my life to the end, be it from the fires of the store or from the hulking menace who was surely going to come outside and beat me to death in front of my neighbors.

Although, sometimes God has his own plans and decides that even I'm not pathetic enough to just call it quits when I have no chance of winning. It's easy to sit on a throne in the clouds, not feeling threatened and making a choice in a man's life to prolong his suffering and call it a blessing. His blessing came in the form of a speeding car grinding to a halt in front of the sidewalk I was laid upon. The passenger side door swung open, and I lifted my head to greet the driver inside, the savior of Luke Thornton. *What the fuck is going on around here? Have I completely lost it?* If I had, my brain was getting too clever; sitting in the driver's seat of the black car was the stranger, the man whose neck I had decimated back at the asylum.

"Please just kill me now. Blow my head off or something," I said to him.

"You're not that lucky, Luke Thornton. You seem to be in need of a rescue."

"You can't still be alive."

"There may be other, more important things to worry about at this time," he said, raising his eyes and focusing on something behind me.

I turned in the opposite direction, witnessing the now-flaming man exit the comic shop as if he had strolled out of a frozen yogurt shack with a grin on his face. I wasn't about to be strangled by a burning corpse, so I dove headfirst into the car, landing on the crotch of the stranger. I pulled myself up and strapped the seatbelt on, and the stranger slammed on the gas pedal. We peeled off into the night, two men escaping the scene of arson. *Nightlife in town, a dance with death and a resurrection being the highlights of a good evening.* The last look back of my comic shop, on the remnant of my **normal** life, was in the side-view mirror of a dead man's car.

"You're hands are shaking. Can I buy you a coffee, Mr. Thornton?" the stranger said.

I held my hands close together and just stared forward through the windshield, unsure if I was planning a dive out the car at forty miles an hour or if I was going to allow him to drive me to wherever he was planning on killing me, one bullet to the head for one bullet to the head for my troubles.

"I'm buying, if you're interested."

"Pull over to the bar at the end of the road. Harry's Rest. It's on your right."

The car pulled casually to the right, until the stranger made a full turn into the parking lot of the best bar in town. I noticed that he had the decency to throw on a blinker, even though there were no other cars in sight. *So…what? He follows both an abomination from beyond the stars AND traffic laws?* We walked together into the place, the stranger holding the front door, a wooden affair that you can find sealing any bar, open for me. I stopped at the doorway and shot him a look of distrust.

"Please enter."

A young woman at the entrance directed us to two bar stools and asked if we required a menu or just a list of drinks. From the look on her face, she didn't exactly like the image before her: a man in jeans and a t-shirt, another in a tuxedo. I ordered a coffee, with milk and sugar, while the stranger simply asked for a glass of pomegranate juice. The woman stared for a second and needed to consult the bartender to see if the drink was indeed on the menu. And it was. We were served rather quickly, an impressive feat considering we had walked in to a full bar. Several college students, some of whom I recognized but would not recognize me in return, were drinking heavily on the opposite end of the bar.

"WHOOOOOOO! We need to see some ladies tonight!"

"Damn right, man. We gotta see some big ol' titties in our faces!"

"Too bad this town never opened a skin joint. We would've been there right now!"

I chuckled at the comment, wondering if a town like this even had the space or moral depravity for a business like that. But I guessed that sex sold no matter where you lived. It was possible to find an adult video store not too far from the next town over from ours. I've known some of my patrons to frequent that place as well, though I couldn't say that I ever visited out of curiosity. Things might have gotten lonely at home, but I had the computer hooked up for that sort of thing.

"What is your name? I never asked what to call you," I finally asked the stranger.

"If I am remembering it correctly, I believe that I was called Murphy."

"'If you remember correctly?' I asked him, "How can you not be sure?"

He sighed and said, "It has been so very long a time since I have come to be called that. You see, Saarlathesh does not call one by their name. I have been in his service for a many number of years, far longer than a human should have the need to live. There are so many tasks that my master had asked of me."

"So what does Saarlathesh call you by?"

"He simply calls, Luke Thornton."

I shifted in my seat, twisting my body toward Murphy. I asked, "How long have you lived, Murphy?"

"So very many years, Mr. Thornton. I can remember events no man living can claim they have participated in."

"That many, huh? Are we leaning toward a hundred or two hundred?"

Murphy seemed to be thinking for quite some time, but his face betrayed his answer before his words were able.

"I do not recall the number, sorry. When you are in the employ of the master, time seems to slip out of your grasp until you barely have possession of it at all. Things become…simultaneous."

"Simultaneous," I muttered, sipping at the coffee cup. I didn't ask what he meant exactly, but I could understand the gravity and weight of the comment. Murphy had been on Earth for a long time, serving a monster beyond understanding.

"So why this kindness now? Why rescue me at the shop and why hold the door open and why buy me a cup of coffee?"

"There is something I require of you, Luke Thornton."

I nearly rose from my seat as I said, "The hell you want with me?! I haven't done enough for you?"

"I would not exactly call our scores even, as it stands. You have stabbed me, remember. Killed me, even."

"Yeah, so? How is it exactly that you're still alive and breathing?"

"Simple. I killed you."

I stopped sipping at the coffee long enough to take the time to think about his last few words.

"What do you mean?"

"Again, it is quite simple. Somewhere else," he said, pausing as the waitress returned so that he did not say anything in front of

236

her. We waited for her to ask whether we were doing alright, and she sped off to a table away from the bar before fully hearing our answer. Murphy continued in a near whisper.

"In another universe, Luke Thornton, I shot before you could reach me. I simply crossed over to a world where I had not been so fortunate."

"So you're visiting from another dead-me universe. Great. How is it you can cross over at will?"

"Do not ask. I do not have the need to reveal that information. Come now. Do not fret, Luke Thornton, I have not come here for petty revenge."

"Then why are you here?"

He studied my face for a second, before he said, "I am going to help you free yourself."

"Free myself from what? Retail?"

"I do believe our burning acquaintance more than took care of that for you. No, I wish to free your soul from the grasp of Saarlathesh."

I stopped drinking my coffee completely at this point. *How in the hell does Saarlathesh own your soul, Luke?*

"How the hell does Saarlathesh own my soul, Luke? Uh, gah, I mean Murphy?" I blurted.

Murphy blinked, taken aback by my mistake. He said, "You picked a very poor choice after returning home. Suicide is always a dangerous game to play, especially once you become aware of the repercussions."

"How do you know about that?" I demanded.

"I work for Saarlathesh, Mr. Thornton, I know whom he directs and controls. I am privy to such knowledge."

"Okay, so explain to me how he owns me." I was becoming upset at the prospect of having to step foot outside this town once more. I knew it was coming, but I was willing to fight the truth, fight anything.

"Taking your own life is a surefire way to bring more danger into your life than you know. Your soul is thrown from your body. 'Up for grabs,' I believe is the Earthly term for it."

"So Saarlathesh has his claws in me…wait, where does a soul go without being up for otherworldly auction? Is there a heaven?"

Murphy simply shrugged. He drank some more of his pomegranate juice, wiping his mouth with a napkin in the way a rich bastard would do so. Proper and pompous-like. The bartender finally caught sight of his choice in clothing, looking him up and down with confusion in his eyes. Murphy smiled at the man, a big wide smile that you would not want to encounter walking home late at night. The bartender quickly returned to mixing the drinks at hand, being sure to break eye contact with Murphy and turn his back to our side of the bar. A guy next to Murphy began to call out to the bartender but to no avail. It seemed his drink had gotten low, and the day had called for more than he had consumed thus far.

"So…Saarlathesh has my soul. There's no need to tell me how bad that is. But what other mischief have I gotten myself into?"

"You now have a shadow-self."

"A what? I have a shadow? I know that already. I've been trying to get that bastard off my back for years," I half-heartedly joked, coffee cup clattering in my hand as my body shivered. I wasn't going to make this situation any easier, but I was trying.

"No, not a typical shadow. A shadow-self. Every suicide gets one, although I'm not entirely sure of the reason why."

"So was that him back at the comic shop? Burning my life to the ground?"

"No, that was something wholly different."

I thought about the burning man, then asked, "Murphy… what was that back there? What kind of being is that?"

"I have no idea. It is not something of Saarlathesh's design."

"Yeah, I noticed."

"You should be more concerned with your shadow-self, Luke Thornton. He will try to combat your actions."

"In what way?"

Murphy shrugged again, I muttered curses under my breath.

"Everyone's shadow-self acts a bit differently," he said, "Although, they all act as tormentors to the soul they belong to. They are reminders of the life that takes itself. They are the deepest fears and regrets and negative emotions that you feel, all wrapped up into a single entity. They exist simply to remind you of your faults."

"But for what purpose? Why do they exist? Who makes them?" I asked, and then added, "What makes them?"

"Do you know why parrots can imitate human speech?"

"I don't, but I'm sure some scientist has figured it out."

Murphy explained, "This is similar in that regard. Someone might know the answer, but you and I do not. It simply is until an explanation can be found."

I had finished my coffee and Murphy had consumed his drink. It was time for the two of us to pay, so Murphy motioned over the bartender, handing him a nice tip in addition to the bill. Both of us walked out of Harry's Rest escorted by the eyes of the patrons in the place, whose expressions were those of curiosity. A side effect of living in a world of constant flow of information is the incessant need for people to stick their collective nose into other business unrelated to them. Celebrities can attest to that fact, but, in this location, we were neither celebrities nor notable figures, just a gentleman in a suit and a slob in a t-shirt walking out of a bar.

"So what do we need to do?" I asked Murphy outside.

"We need to find our way into Saarlathesh's realm. Find an opening and take you to your soul."

"Hey, Murphy. If I exist in an infinite amount of universes, doesn't it stand to reason that we'll find my other souls?"

"We are only concerned with your particular soul, Luke Thornton."

"How are we going to find it?"

"Simple," he stated, "We will only have to look through half of your souls."

At this point, we had already reached the car, but I had stopped while grabbing the door handle. I looked over the roof of the car into Murphy's eyes.

"How do you figure that?" I asked.

"Because, Mr. Thornton, not all of your suicides were successful. We are only concerned with the souls of the ones that weren't."

"The fuck?" I responded.

Both of us dipped our heads into the vehicle. Murphy flipped on the radio, switching to a rather plain and boring classical music station, which was currently in the middle of an annoying composition of Bach. I left the radio on the current station, not because I had a respect for the driver's choice of music, but because I knew from experience that there was nothing enjoyable to find on radio stations.

"What happened to the Lukes who killed themselves," I asked, a surreal question, although it seemed right at home by this point.

"They simply will not be where we find the others," he said with a smile. I hated Murphy's guts, and I hated his smile.

"Just start driving," I said.

CHAPTER TEN

Into the Hive

I watched a solid yellow line bend and twist along the road for the next half hour, wondering what my parents would say if they had been still around. Something about me not being home enough, about how weary I looked. Or they would simply not care in the least. I was quiet since our time in front of Harry's Rest, thinking about the next journey in my future.

Murphy had believed that, although I wasn't responding to him, that I would be interested in him talking about where we would be going. I was just concerned with getting there in one piece. He droned on and on about the pathways to other realms, hidden just outside the view of the commoners who walked day to day through their lives with minds more concentrated on the future than the present. He joked that the best way (at least, to those that had stepped outside the bounds of reality and sanity) to hide something valuable, something important, was to place it directly in the path of a human being.

No one will notice the absurd and strange, he told me. *Why would they need to, Luke? Why should someone bother stopping to see that every day is just a slow crawl to death?* To this, Murphy told me that having a purpose in life was exclusively human.

"Animals do not need to have purpose, for they are simple minded," Murphy was saying, "and the day-to-day survival is distraction enough. Somewhere down the line, humans found the time to develop philosophy and critical thought. Suddenly, people found the need to occupy their time with classifying the things around them, with planning toward future events that may not come to pass."

"Uh-huh," I said, head placed against the passenger side window.

"If humans were ready to use their minds to explore around them, they should have first thought to prepare themselves for what they would find. It is no wonder that there are so many broken minds scattered throughout the world. Careless research can lead the soul to the wrong darkened corners of the globe. Sometimes, it is better not to know than to make the attempt."

"When are we going to make it?"

"We have just arrived, incidentally."

I looked up from the road, seeing that we had parked at some library.

"Where are we, Murphy?" I asked.

"North Arlington Library," he stated plainly.

"What, did you find yourself lacking some personal time to read? Had I known we were running personal errands, I would have gone to the bank first."

"Please stop jesting. We have arrived at where we need to go."

"I don't get it, Murphy. What game are you playing?"

"No game, simply looking for an entrance."

We walked silently up the steps of the building, passing the front desk after the double doors at the entrance.

"How can I help you…uh, gentlemen, today?" a librarian asked us. No doubt she was also filled with confusion at the wardrobe we had selected.

"No need for assistance, madam. Thank you," Murphy said.

"Oh, uh, okay...sir."

"What are we doing here?" I whispered.

"There's a door in the basement of this place," he whispered back, "For now, find a book and pretend to read."

Murphy broke away from me and disappeared into another part of the library. I threw my hands up in the air, noting that the librarian at the front desk was looking quizzically at me. *Yeah, lady, I'm a crazed lunatic who's going to rob the place. Just look away and save yourself the worry.* I walked over to the crime thriller section, perusing the book spines for a title that stuck out in my mind. I must have passed through two rows of books, holding no less than fifty books each, when I stopped at a copy of Agatha Christie's *And Then There Were None*.

I recalled reading the book before, some long time ago when I was still required to get up at six o'clock in the morning to attend high school. I was given a list of books to read for an English class, having decided in my lame teenage-angst-period of life that this book sounded cryptic enough to be a cool read. Flipping through the pages of the book, I decided to begin reading at page one, removing myself from the world around me and having each line in the book become a movie, played in my head at my direction.

Murphy interrupted my little escapism soon after.

"You have found yourself a book. Good work. A nice read, as well, but we do not have time for that," he said.

"What are we doing?"

"Come with me. Quickly, down these stairs."

We descended down the flight of stairs to the basement, hall of atlases, guide books, home improvement, and, for some reason, a small section of comic books, both Japanese and American. Murphy led me forward, dipping in between bookshelves and weaving out of rows. Without much thought, I let my body move along the path, while my eyes were transfixed on the words of Christie's novel. I bumped into Murphy, who scolded me slightly for reading behind him.

"I haven't read this in a long time."

"This is not the time for leisure, Mr. Thornton."

"It never is."

When we have weaved and ducked for a short time, we stopped in front of an old, wooden door that seemed to be bolted closed. I could see that a padlock was holding a plank securely against the doorframe.

"Do you have a key?" I asked.

"It just so happens that I do," Murphy said.

"And why is it that you have a key to this door?"

Murphy stood upright from the padlock, turned toward me, and said, "There are many doors much like this one, in old buildings that do not see much foot traffic."

"Who put them here?"

"Why, the owners, naturally," he smiled as he said this.

"And why do they all have the same doors and locks?"

"Well, how else do you expect them to travel to their master's realm?"

I took a big gulp, unsure if I was ready to enter the realm again.

"The owner of this library is a member of your little cult?"

Murphy said to me, "Mr. Thornton, it is one thing to not know of our secretive 'cult,' but it is an entirely other matter to assume that it can be called 'little.'"

"How many of you are there? How many call Saarlathesh 'mister?'"

"Thousands. A needle in a haystack that is the world, but enough to do his bidding."

Murphy opened up the door, which led to stairs much like the ones we had found in the asylum cellar. He lit a match from his pocket, igniting a torch hanging on the stone wall before he closed the wooden door behind us. He barred the door from our side, and then motioned down the stairs to me. I offered an extended arm toward the stairwell, not allowing my host to have the jump on me. I still wasn't sure if this was a trap, even if the man did offer to buy me a coffee.

Taking the lead, Murphy descended the spiral steps carefully, watching his footing on the crumbled stones. I did the same, not wanting to catch a torch in the eyeball. Eventually, I caught sight of the familiar violet-blue stream beneath a starry sky that had decorated Saarlathesh's realm on my previous visits. The stone steps merely ended instead of continuing into a walkway, but instead of a plummeting drop, Murphy began walking on air after stepping off the last stone. I followed, careful to feel flat, invisible ground before I took my other foot off the staircase.

In front of us, there was a single wooden doorway, similar to the one in the library above, that was surrounded by a building that stretched left and right to the horizon.

"Mortgage must be a bitch for the owner," I joked.

"You don't have to pay much if you own the realm," Murphy commented.

We walked forward toward the door, only for it to open slowly without our assistance. I readied myself for anything, placing a foot forward and one back, in another Kung Fu stance I had seen in a movie once. Murphy remained the stoic; holding his torch directly upright and maintaining his proper posture. The doorway fully opened, revealing a fly the size of a small child. It wore a tuxedo much like Murphy's, and stood upright like a human being. The fly moved forward to Murphy and took a bow.

"I see the lord has arrived," the fly said, in a human voice that ranked at a pitch that I could only compare to being halfway between a woman and a young boy.

"Yes, I have brought a visitor to the realm. Someone fresh."

"Ah, we are expecting two, yes," the fly answered.

"Woah, wait. What do you mean you expected us?" I said, my body pulling at my mind to turn back around.

"Take hold of yourself, Luke Thornton. The denizens of this place are expecting you, not the master," Murphy told me.

"Yes, this lord has informed us of his arrival," the fly stated.

The fly turned back toward the door, walking up to it and standing with one disgusting leg grasping the edge of the frame. He was waiting for us to walk through, and I realized that he was a form of butler for the place.

"Why does he call you 'lord'?" I asked Murphy.

"It is my title under Saarlathesh. His most important advisors are called such."

"How many lords are there?"

"Just two. I am his right hand, you know..." Murphy trailed off.

"Only two? What happened to the thousands of cultists at his beck and call?"

"They are not all at the top of the ladder," was the response.

After closing the door behind us, the fly directed us forward through a darkened tunnel, a sort of hallway barely furnished and resembling an old European castle interior. To my left and right, tall gaps in the wall revealed the outside realm, still a black sea of stars. I moved toward one, looking below and seeing the blue and violet stream, remembering my painful experience within it.

"Mr. Thornton," said the high-pitched fly, "we must continue down the path."

I turned back, disappointed that I hadn't been mauled to death and released from my madness yet. Our trio walked through a set of double doors, which were almost thirteen feet in height and slipped further inside the interior.

I was very confused at my surroundings, a fact that my body revealed by blurring my vision lightly and giving me a bout of nausea. Murphy extended an arm for my support, which I held onto tightly as the feeling passed. When I recovered, I looked back to see the doorway behind us was no more than the height of an average house door. The room we found ourselves in was not one of immense size; instead, I found that I was in an oddly furnished chamber, which was decorated with strange objects in a very strange way.

No furniture sat upon the floor, yet I could very well see that the room was furnished. On the wall in front of me, a mahogany desk, like the kind you would find in a CEO's office, was placed, defying gravity in favor of the owner's decorative taste. Behind the desk (or above it, depending on your perspective) was another fly, sitting in a computer chair and writing some unseen message onto a piece of printed paper. He looked up to see us, not betraying an emotion of joy or sadness or annoyance regarding our appearance. Although, seeing that he didn't even have a human face, I do not know how I came to that conclusion.

"Good morning, how can I help you gentlemen?" said the second fly. I looked around and saw that the butler had left us alone with the secretary. This fly resembled the previous, wearing yet another tuxedo. But his voice was much deeper than the first. Both Murphy and I had to throw back our heads to look directly at the seated fly. After just a few minutes, I knew that I would be feeling pain in the back of my neck in the morning.

"Um, hi? How are you?" I asked.

"…My lord, what can I help you with," the fly said, ignoring me.

"We are seeking his soul," Murphy answered, pointing.

The fly scratched at the underside of its head, which I guessed could be called its chin, and then placed his hands together with his elbows resting on the desk. The chair was rather short for the fly's size, so his hands hung above his face, nearly on level with his forehead.

"What do I call you?" I asked.

The fly scratched again, and then returned his hands to their places. He said, "I suppose if I am to have a name, you may call me 'Bzz'." He pronounced it as it would be read phonetically, which caused me to groan. The fly's many eyes seemed to be working in the way you might imagine; the nausea I had felt before jumped back into action. The thing before me was revolting.

"Can he go alone through the doorway?" Bzz asked Murphy.

"He will have to," Murphy answered.

I returned my head to a forward position, glancing at the door on the same wall as the desk. Thankfully, it was upright in my favor, so I wouldn't be climbing up and over in a pathetic display of American physique. I walked a few steps forward to reach for the handle when the fly interrupted me.

"No, no, no," Bzz said, floating down and upright from his office chair, "We are simply not ready for you to go through. Allow me to adjust your destination." Bzz removed a panel from the wall alongside the door, performing some strange action to whatever was behind it. His body blocked my way, so I could not see what he was tinkering with. I guessed that this was done on purpose, and I didn't care to find out that he was playing with cow entrails behind there. I turned to Murphy.

"Where does this lead?"

"Right now, somewhere you don't need to go. In a few moments, it will lead to where you need to go."

"Where's that?"

"The place that your soul can be found."

"What are we going to do when we get there?"

"We cannot both go. You are required to retrieve your own soul, and then bring it back to this lobby."

"How do I find it?"

"You'll know when you do. Just be prepared to face some nightmares. There is no doubt that you will find your shadow-self somewhere within."

"Great. I should have brought my knife."

The look on Murphy's face dropped into an angry snarl, which I avoided sight of by swiveling back around to face Bzz. Bzz was floating in the air, wings beating the space behind him, looking at the two of us.

"In just a moment, we will begin." I heard a faint grinding begin from somewhere beyond the wall, which devolved into a harsh metallic scraping that prompted me to throw my hands over my ears in protection. The mechanical whirring became some cacophony of mechanical and insect-like buzzing, almost as if a hive of bees was physically turning a large crank. I imagined a team of worker bees, all decked out in tuxedos, pushing forward with all their might. In time, the noise subsided, leaving us standing as we were before.

"It is ready for you, Luke Thornton," Bzz said.

"Good luck," Murphy offered.

"Right."

I stepped forward once more, looking towards Bzz and seeing that his thousand eyes were reflecting tiny images of me. I
scratched at my arms, grossed out at the unpleasant sight before
me. *Insects look bad enough at their Earth-born size*, I thought, *and I
didn't think they could get any worse.* I swallowed heavy, reaching slowly
toward the handle of the doorway to my fate. Twisting the knob,
I pictured a thousand different landscapes that could possibly
stretch before me. However, all that greeted me on the other side
was a red curtain, like one you would find in a cliché theater. I
walked through the curtain.

On the other side, I found myself looking at myself. That may
have seemed confusing, but, in this world, everything seemed perfectly
rational. Another Luke Thornton sat upon a wooden chair, seated in
the middle of an empty bedroom. The floor was wood, the walls covered in a lame floral design that you would find on an old lady's blouse,
and there was a single window peering into that familiar void outside
on the opposite end of the room from the door I had entered. The
drapes around the window were tinted that old-timey, translucent yellow. I could see that the wall to my left contained framed paintings of
silhouetted heads, belonging to people I could not recognize.

The other me in the chair didn't move; he sat staring at me,
with eyes that didn't blink and a smile that read "Sex Offender"
from cheek to cheek. I moved slowly across the room, being sure
to make a full circle as far as possible from the other me as I
could. I was practically pushing against the wall with the paintings,
sidestepping as if I was making my way across a cliff side or the
edge of a building. The other me followed my movements, never
adjusting his face in any way; just a creepy smile and a set of staring eyes accompanied me around the room. About halfway into
my journey, I realized that his head was rotating far beyond the
limits of the human body.

I continued forward, testing my sight and seeing that he was in fact nearly making a full one eighty turn around his neck. For laughs, or out of sheer need to alleviate my terror, I backtracked a bit and went forward again, mostly to see if he would still follow. He did, quite eerily. I eventually positioned myself near the window, with the seated Luke having finally rested his head in a full one eighty position. My back pressed against the glass, and my mind quickly searched for exits, finding them nowhere but at the door I had entered from. I decided it must be one of those tricks, the kind where an entering doorway would lead somewhere else when opened from the other side.

The theory never had a chance to be proven. From behind me, the window shattered in a rain of glass, as two hands reached forward to grab my shoulders. I struggled in vain against my assailant. I looked up to see the other me get up from the chair, head still completely backward. He began to slowly walk towards my direction, his legs working in a backward motion and his eyes transfixed on my own. Not wanting to see whether he was going to help me or kill me, I stopped fighting and allowed the arms to pull me back through the window.

I fell and fell and my eyes closed so that I could scream in the darkness. I felt my back make contact with the floor, but not at the speed that I should have hit it. I opened my eyes and found that I was back to back with another wall. I was upright and standing in another room. There were three duplicates of me in the room as well. One of them had been rocking back and forth, seated on the ground, until I had abruptly entered the room. Another was standing with his head previously in his hand, but he had raised it to look at the newest member of the collective. A third was standing with his arms crossed and facing the wall I was currently on.

"Oh, another one," said the Luke with his arms crossed.

"Welcome," said the other standing Luke.

"Uh….hi? Have I gone crazy yet?" I asked them.

"No," said the second one who responded, "And we all came here separately, so we already started distinguishing between each other in case any other Luke showed up. I'm Luke Alpha."

"I'm Luke the Third," said the Luke with his arms crossed, "Mostly because I was the third one to get here."

"And that's Bitch Luke," said Luke Alpha abruptly, pointing to the Luke on the ground, who was currently shivering.

"I told you I don't like that name!" said Bitch Luke, "Pick another one for me!"

"If you don't like it, choose one yourself. If you aren't going to bother, you better learn to deal with it," Luke Alpha said.

"It's nice to meet all of me," I joked. They all groaned. "Sorry."

"It's not that," said Luke the Third, "It's just that I said the same thing when I got here. After I freaked for a second and tried to fist fight Luke Alpha."

"My jaw still hurts, asshole," Luke Alpha said.

"Where are we?" I asked.

"We ask that a lot," said the three Lukes together, in a creepy unison. They all looked at each other, and then turned to look in three separate directions. Bitch Luke went back to looking straight into the wood floor. I took the time to survey the room, realizing that it was much the same as the previous except that the doorway now was directly in front of me and the window to my left. I was swiftly becoming disoriented of my location.

"Are you guys just pieces of my subconscious?" I asked.

"Fuck no," said Luke Alpha, "We reason that we're three different Lukes from parallel universes. You're just a fourth."

"So, we're all on the same mission?"

"To get our souls back? Yeah, I think so," said Luke the Third, "The way I look at it, we all might be the same guy, but souls are given on a per-universe basis."

"It makes the most sense," Bitch Luke commented from the floor.

"If that's the case, what happens when one of us dies and goes to another universe?" I questioned.

"I dunno," Luke Alpha said, "Either we start in a new, copycat universe or we meld minds with the Luke of the parallel world." All three shrugged their shoulders in unison with me. It seemed like a surreal dream. One that should be painted one day. *Sure, go up to a modern artist and ask him to draw this. I'm sure he'll turn up his nose and continue putting lines on a paper and calling it a painting.*

"Pssh, modern artists," we all blurted out, with the exception of Bitch Luke who said 'I wonder if they…'" and trailed off when he realized he wasn't leading the same train of thought as us.

"I'm starting to see the reason the universes can differ only slightly," said Luke the Third, echoing a thought we all must have been having at the moment. *Too fucking weird, let's hurl ourselves out the window, Luke.* I ignored my mind's call for a second suicide, considering that two suicides in one lifetime would only serve to further fuck me and not do anything to un-fuck me from my current situation.

"I'm going to find a way out of here," I said.

"We've been trying, there just isn't a way out of this room and that window doesn't look too inviting," Luke Alpha said. I peered out the window, noticing the same void that could be seen outside.

"What about the door?"

The three of them looked to each other, then back at me.

"We haven't worked up the courage to open it. The last room with the rotating head trick wasn't exactly pleasant, and we don't know what to expect next," said Luke Alpha.

I swallowed my anger and said, "Can you tell me when you got off the floor, Bitch Luke? Because I can't seem to remember you leav–oh, wait, no, there you are still on the floor. Maybe the two of you should switch nicknames."

Bitch Luke giggled into his arms, which were crossed against his head and balanced on his knees at the elbows. Luke Alpha gave me the meanest look, the one I usually gave to customers who thought "No refunds without a receipt" meant "Refunds for everyone!" He continued glaring at me until Luke the Third cleared his throat with an obnoxious cough, something I realized I hated when I saw other people do it. I hated it even more because I could see that I was a hypocrite.

Having had enough of this circus, I stomped my feet over to the door, throwing it open and immediately feeling what can only be described as an insect's feeler wrap around my chest. There was another curtain draped on the other side, so whatever was gripping me was hidden from view. Only the disgusting tentacle was seen extended at hip level.

"Holy FUCK!" one of me screamed from the room.

"Oh my god, he's going to die! We should have kept it closed! We were right!" came the voice of who could only be Bitch Luke.

The tentacle pulsed and tightened, crushing my abdomen in an excruciating way, like someone gave me a gigantic hug with beefy arms. It pulled at my body, but I held onto the doorknob, slamming the door shut into the frame. I held on for dear life, my body fully horizontal and parallel to the floor, one arm extended to the doorknob and the other dangling at my side. I tried to go to a happy place in my mind, somewhere I would like to retire, but another pulse meant the tentacle tightened around me once again. I let go of the doorknob and was flung backwards through the air.

My body crashed against what can be best described as a gigantic mass of hens on the wall of the next room. I looked at the impact sight, noticing that I had only slammed into a wall much like the others, only, on touch, the wall felt light as a feather. I could almost fall asleep on the floor as well; its texture looked that of wood, but it too felt like cushions. I closed my eyes, then that voice inside my head decided to return. *Hey Luke, maybe you should spend more time realizing that WHATEVER GRABBED YOU IS IN THE SAME ROOM AS YOU.*

I jumped up, startled and incoherent. I was in yet another room like the last, only the door was in front of me and there were no windows in this room. In the center of the floor before me stood another Luke Thornton. This one didn't look as friendly as the first I encountered and definitely was not one of the three idiots in the other room. No, this Luke wore a grin that was so sinister that I may or may not have tried to replicate the same look to see if my face could contort into such a shape.

"Stop making faces at me and stand up," he said.

I did so, asking, "And what can I call you?"

"Don't you recognize me?" he asked, placing a fist at his neck and cocking his head to the side. His hand unclenched itself and began to trace up his neck and onto his right cheek. His other hand joined the first on his other cheek; the image was that of a grown man looking like a school girl swooning over a guy.

"I mean what do I call you, you freak," I said.

"You can call me Shadow-Luke, because I'm that thing that you should be afraid of most," he said with a smile.

I felt sweat on my palms.

"Okay, so you're my shadow-self. It's good to know that I'm still better looking." My shadow-self still held that disturbingly wide smile, something that films usually use to tell the audience that this was the evil twin. I wondered how much of my pop-culture-riddled mind contributed to the appearance of my shadow-self. *Was it so farfetched to think I had some influence in his creation?*

"So you still talk to yourself?" he laughed.

"Yeah, it keeps my sanity in check."

He stopped laughing and said seriously, "You really aren't as clever and funny as you think you are."

"Yeah, I'm funnier than even that." I began to make the same clockwise motion around the room, circling Shadow-Luke. I had all the intent to spring at the doorknob and run into the room over.

"Where are you going, Luke? We haven't even had fun yet," Shadow-Luke said.

"Me? I'm not going anywhere, I'm just trying to get the drop on you," I replied.

"Drop on me? I'm not even human like you. I'm faster, stronger, and I can be anywhere I want in the manner of a second."

"Yeah, well, HYAHH!" I had thrown myself at the doorknob that was now behind me, throwing open the door and revealing the same three Lukes that I had left and a brand new Luke, as confused as I was only a few minutes before.

"I'm Alpha Luke and—" Alpha Luke was explaining, but he trailed off at the sight of me. I stood in the open doorway, looking at four copies of myself, when I heard the Shadow-Luke's footsteps behind me get closer. I ran forward into the room, ready to shut the door behind me, but I felt a shoe kick me in the ass, catapulting me back into the other room. I flipped and landed on my back, with a nice view of the Luke Thornton that had sent me back into my personal hell.

"Don't you bring that shit in here with us," Alpha-Luke said, slamming the door closed.

I felt a hand sharply grip the collar of my shirt and hoist me up onto my feet. Shadow-Luke let his grip go when I was firmly planted on the ground.

"You got all dirty from your fall," he said, brushing my shirt with his hand, removing dust and grime from it. I began to help him when he gave me an uppercut to my chin, sending me back down on the ground with a new bruise to show off to the boys and girls back home.

"Haha," he chuckled, "You are so WEAK!" The final word was said in a deepened, demonic voice that was definitely not within my vocal range.

"Get up, Luke Thornton. Get up and let's have us some fun."

Shadow-Luke wound up a kick, placing his foot directly onto my chest cavity. I recoiled from the pain, turning over onto my stomach. I began to grip the comfortable floor with my fingers, dragging along the rest of my body with both hands. Shadow-Luke grabbed the hair on my head and slammed my forehead into the soft, relaxing wood. It was oddly relieving. He turned me over, straddling my body and bringing his face close to mine.

"What's the matter? Can't go further on like this? Certainly this isn't the worst you've faced so far, is it? What are you waiting for? An invitation or a freebie?" He stood from his position with me, gripped around the collar, same as before.

"Go on! Hit me! It's on the house," he said with the devilish smile. I pulled my arm back, mustering all my anger and the little bit of arm strength in my muscles, and then thrust my fist forward. Shadow-Luke swiftly ducked my punch and returned one into my ribs. I keeled over and collapsed on the floor again. He kicked me over onto my back with his foot.

He laughed heartily, then asked, "When will this get boring for me?! We are having so much fun, aren't we? AREN'T WE?" The same demonic voice boomed from his lungs. Then he said, "Yes, we are. We are having fun, Luke. So put a smile on, you can't have fun with a frown on your face."

I didn't comply with his command.

"SMILE, damn you! Smile for ME!" Shadow-Luke said, kicking me in my ribs repeatedly. I groaned, letting out a half-smile for his amusement.

"Hoo hoo hoo! Now we're having fun! I'll tell you what. I'll stop. No tricks!"

I glanced up at my shadow-self, wondering when the pain would stop. But I could tell that it wouldn't. Not for a long time if I didn't get out of here.

"By the way, I've decided to join you on your little quest here. I think I can be of use to you," he giggled, giddy like a child, "But you have to let me come with you."

"Fuck...you..."

"Now that isn't PLEASANT for you to SAY!" Another kick, another surge of pain. "I'm not giving you a choice!"

I felt his hands turn my head to my left side, then grab a hold of my right ear. I tried to struggle free, but he slapped my hands away from his. His fingers, sharp as talons, began to pull at my ear, sending a shockwave of hurt throughout my head cavity. I felt like I could die. But he wasn't about to let me. First, he put a foot into the space he had created into my ear. Next, he pushed my ear farther open, placing another foot within. Finally, he began to push his entire body down, deep into the side of my skull. I screamed in pain as he cackled madly.

Eventually, I felt my ear return to normal and the pain was slowly beginning to subside. I pulled myself off the ground, sitting up and cupping my ear with both my hands. The pain was finally gone after a few agonizing minutes. I wiped the sweat off my brow, unsure of what would happen next. *I'm going to burst out of your chest cavity like in that space movie.* That wasn't a thought of my own, I realized to my horror. *Yes, Luke. I'm in your thoughts! Spooky shit, right? Like Saturday evening late-night shitty TV frights. Hey, I think that line rhymed!*

I was in an otherworldly hell, with my doppelganger somewhere inside my brain, and I had no way out of an insanely small room. I looked to the door, wondering if opening it again would lead to a new room like before. *Yesssss! Yes! Run back there! Run back over to them! We could have some fun.* I kept ignoring the voice in my head, trying desperately to think clearly with him overpowering my thoughts. I thought of running into the next room, an axe in my hand, and slaughtering the other Lukes in there. It wasn't a daydream of my conjuring. I looked around, remembering that a window was still not an option for escape.

In my attempts at finding an exit, my feet moved softly over the still odd floor until I reached a corner that made a completely different sound, the sound of a light piece of plywood. I stopped and looked down at it, seeing that the floor texture did not match the rest. *Oooo, what have you got there, Luke?* I ignored him once again, trying to pull up at the plywood guarding god-knows-what. Using my fingertips, I was able to pull up and toss aside the floorboard, exposing a man-sized hole that lead into another room that was similar to this one. *Jump! Land on your head and DIE! Hahaha!* I jumped and landed on my feet.

You're such a killjoy, Luke. You would have just woken up in a parallel universe. Maybe. Hahaha! The Shadow-Luke was getting to me, twisting my thoughts and fucking with me in a serious way. I needed to find a way to rid myself of the shadow, to end the damn voices. *You can't! I'm here for life! Look Ma, I've got myself an apartment!*

"Fuck you, dude. I'm gonna find a way to get you out of there and then I'm going to beat the ever-living shit out of you. Y'hear me?"

Talking to yourself is one thing, talking to yourself out loud is a mental illness, Luke.

This room was finally different, a change of scenery that I desperately sought in this mad realm with its mad citizens, its mad architecture, and its mad god. A part of me realized that I was just as mad as the rest, mad enough to belong in a place like this. Mad enough to buy up real estate and call it home. The other part of me that still was keeping me rational informed me that this thought had gone on too long.

"Fuck you, Shadow-Luke!"

Hahaha! What are you blaming me for?! Man, do you go off on a tangent, haha! Once again, I took a look at the room, noting that it was a full cushioned white, much like the inside of a mental patient's favorite room. I casually strolled over to a door on the far wall, knocked on the one glass window there, then waited.

"Could I get this door open, please?" I said to whomever or whatever was waiting on the other side. To my surprise, a security lock buzzed and I heard the familiar sound of an electronic lock being opened. I tugged at the door, finding it opened easily and swiftly. I made my way out of there. *That was far too easy, Luke. You got lucky this time.*

"Yeah, or maybe somebody up in heaven had taken another liking to me."

The hall I had entered was a long corridor, reminiscent of a doctor's office, less the one the crazies go to and more like the family doctor in town. I strolled down the way, noting the strange names that adorned the plaques on the side of each door I passed. When I had gotten a good few feet down the way, the floor collapsed beneath me in a crumble of wood pieces, dropping me down some darkened shaft into a probable grave below.

I had lost count on the amount of times that this adventure featured its star actor plummeting. Here I was, nearly about to be the recipient of more spinal cord damage than I was willing to endure, far more than my body would even want to handle. But then, a thought entered my skull, a small light that maybe, just maybe, I would land in another room like pillows or find myself just saved in the nick of time.

My body slammed at terminal velocity into a concrete pavement, both surprising me and letting me down in one instant. I bounced upright immediately after impact, and then fell over to my side, placing a hand on my back. I didn't know where I was, some black room only illuminated by the ceiling I had just come crashing down from. A bout of nausea hit me in the throat, and the complete list of contents in my stomach spilled out from my mouth. A larger piece of whatever bile decided to make a reappearance pushed its way up through my esophagus.

First, a shoe pushed through the back of my throat, popping out of my mouth. I struggled to breath, standing and tumbling over to what looked like a countertop. I slammed into it coughing roughly and watching the appearance of an ankle and, soon after, a shin, protrude from my wide open mouth. The muscles on my face resisted the stretching, but my lips were being forced to part further, allowing a thigh muscle to bulge out. To my horror, I soon saw the edge of a pair of pants connected to the rest. I gagged and pushed at my throat, not intent to choke to death with some demon's crotch in my mouth.

"How did they find him?" an officer would ask a frightened couple.

"He…he simply fell…from the sk-k-k-y, from above. The poor soul," they would answer.

"This is too weird," some rookie cop would comment.

With one final cough, an entire leg, up to the hip bone, was dislodged from my throat. I stared at the limb, and then flung it forward. I took the time from recovery to scope my surroundings, noticing that this area of the room was furnished like a kitchen, without the appliances and decorated with countertops and cabinets only. Another revolting hiccup told me that more was to come. Again, I pushed my hands against my throat, forcing out whatever body parts were left. The details need not be said, but, in all, I expelled another leg, a torso, a torn arm, the other half of the previous arm, the second arm, and the head of Shadow-Luke. I was left leaning against the counter, having thrown the bits somewhere into the kitchen area.

My body was slumped against the counter, support I needed to sit upright. My legs were stretched out before me, and I could tell that I had a look of pure exhaustion and relief. It reminded me of a particular bad night of drinking that Jean and I had participated in one summer. It ended nearly the same, although I expelled fluids and chicken from my stomach, not a whole human being. I looked over to my left, noticing that the half-an-arm was crawling by fingertips across the kitchen linoleum. I dove to my right, rolling across the floor like a failed action movie star.

Standing upright, I could see that Shadow-Luke's body was attempting to put itself back together but failing completely. The body seemed more intent to bunch together in a ball, leaving his head pinned to the bone of his knee, which jutted out from the skin. The head and the knee bone snapped together with a disgusting crunch, and then his eyes snapped open.

"Fuck that hurt."

"No kidding, asshole. Did you enjoy the trip up?" I replied.

"I'm gonna kill you, Luke."

"And how will you manage that? Roll me over? You look like a Halloween edition of silly putty."

"You son of a bitch! Wait…what is that? What is that?!"

Our little conversation was put on hold for a moment, as the building we were in was rumbling, and I could hear the distant shrieks of whatever insect monsters populated this place. I thought I faintly heard the voices of Bzz and Murphy, yelling something about getting out of the way. Then I heard a familiar growl, calling my name and getting nearer. I ran past the ball that was Shadow-Luke, opening one of the kitchen counter compartments. I removed the cooking supplies, pots, pans, and cuttings boards rapidly, spilling them over the floor. When I found I had enough room, I ducked my head inside and closed the door to the compartment. Then I heard its voice.

"LUKE THORNTON!"

It was most definitely the voice of whatever creature had burned down my comic shop. I held my breath in the cabinet, hearing some crashing sound emanate through the place. Then, the kitchen wall burst outwards. I took a peak out of the door, being sure not to move too quickly, when I saw the burned man standing before the mass of Shadow-Luke. The expression on Shadow-Luke's face was one of terror. I got a better look at the burned man, seeing that he had left himself in the oven of my store a bit too long. He looked like the remnants of my failed barbecue party last holiday.

"LUKE THORNTON!" the burned man screamed at Shadow-Luke.

"No! No! I'm not the Luke you're looking for! I'm his double, I swear it. I swear it on my left arm!"

"LUKE THORNTON!" the burned man screamed again, grabbing hold of Shadow-Luke's body, casting it into the nearby kitchen bag. I heard the pounding and the crunching of Shadow-Luke being packed into the tiny canister and the screams that echoed from within. I slowly closed the cabinet door after seeing the burned man pull out and tie the bag closed, slinging it over his shoulder like Santa Claus. He left the room out a doorway ahead, so I dipped out of the cabinet, tossing pots and pans aside with my feet as I shuffled out of there.

The hole in the wall was about the size of a bulldozer, so I easily walked through into the adjacent room, which was empty save for the window that was so familiar by now. I shuffled across, hoping that something else wouldn't surprise me and thanking my luck that I was able to escape both Shadow-Luke and the burned man in one cowardly move. In the next room, I could see the faint glow of two candles, whipping back and forth as though some unearthly wind commanded them to do so. They were placed alongside a strange altar, an almost coffin-like slab like the ones you'd find at a Viking funeral. And atop the slab, was the ghostly image of myself, cast in a strange, transparent-green glow.

My body was lying motionless like a cadaver. Both hands were crossed across the chest, prompting me to wonder if I had become a ghost and a vampire in this realm. I mentally swatted away these ideas, understanding that this was most probably the soul I came in here looking for. I briefly contemplated pulling out my cell phone and dialing home, hoping to get Michael to pick up my soul and drop it off someplace else. Then I remembered he had chosen to stay back at the asylum. I pondered for a few minutes, considering that the burned man's distraction had given me the time to do so.

With hesitation, I decided to try to pick up my soul, holding it like a new bride or a dead body. I thought that my hands would just slip through and cause some form of strange reaction, but I was delighted to find that I could hold it like a tangible thing. I used my back to hoist up my soul, then quickly placed it back on the altar awkwardly. I reached for my back, pushing a fist sideways into it a few times. *You're getting old.* I cursed and told myself that I knew that already.

Bending with my knees, I tried again, managing to lift and hold onto my catatonic soul. As I did so, I felt the weight that I had put on over the years, or I felt the neglect of visits to the gym on a daily basis. My soul was quite heavy. I turned back around, walking back the way I came, when Murphy met me at the doorway.

"Murphy! Look what I got!"

"There is no time for humor, Luke Thornton! We must get you and your soul out of here. Things are becoming dangerous in this realm."

"Dangerous how?"

"Well, that creature from your shop is back–"

"I know!"

"And he is through with grinding up your shadow-self's body. It has realized that it may have made a mistake in identity. It is looking for you again, battering the guards back and forth." I decided against asking him what the guards of this place looked like.

"What about the other versions of me? The ones I encountered in those rooms?"

"Do not worry about that right now. I need you coherent and not in a state of confusion. If I were to explain who or what or how they are, we could be here for more time than we have."

"What else do I need to worry about besides finding an exit right now?" I asked, deciding to trust his advice and wanting to avoid any unnecessary surprises.

"Oh…Saarlathesh knows you are in his realm. He is going to be sending his minions after you."

"Why are you doing this, Murphy? Why go against your master?"

Murphy smiled his inhuman smile again, and then said, "I meant what I said back at the asylum. I have slaved for Saarlathesh for many years, and I will not see you replace me as his most important disciple."

I looked down at the soul in my hands, saying, "What was he planning on doing with you?"

"I am going to guess that he was waiting to claim you upon your natural death from your world."

I swallowed, then asked Murphy to show me the way out. I followed his lead as he moved through rooms and passages. We darted from one area of the building to another. I was sure that, having had the time to draw a map of this place, I would find myself drawing over lines I had already made. It was then that I heard a voice, my own.

"He'll be fine living alone. He's already a grown man by most standards."

I didn't know where it came from or why; I certainly didn't have the thought at the moment, but I was disorientated for a second. Still holding onto my soul, I leaned against a nearby wall and closed my eyes.

"Luke, there is no time for rest either. I should not have to tell you that," said Murphy.

"I heard myself speak some words. Something strange," I replied, opening my eyes.

"Hmm....it must be from direct contact with your soul. They say that touching your soul gives you a glimpse into some truths you keep hidden. Hidden from even your conscious mind."

"Great, I needed a roadblock."

I lifted the body higher up on my arms, then continued to follow Murphy through a long, nearly endless hallway. There seemed to be that same starry void in the distance; the image was not from a window but a gap in the building's architecture. Like the builders had just one more wall to put up and decided that a lunch break was a better idea.

"I hate all my friends for leaving me behind and going to college. It was our time to relax and enjoy life, and they chose to leave me!"

My body bumped into the wall to my right, my shoulder taking most of the force. I stopped for a second, adjusted my soul again, and then continued forward. *You weren't abandoned by your friends. You didn't go off to college because you were unsure of what you wanted to do with your life.*

"You didn't know what you wanted to do with your life because you thought it would be too much work to decide. So you fell into an easy daily cycle that got you nowhere," said my soul, eyes now open and directly talking to me.

I didn't stop jogging along with the body, but I decided now was not the time for a heart to heart.

"Can we do this later, please?" I said, struggling to keep my arms from dropping to my side and calling it a day.

"It's always about later, Luke. Never about figuring things out now, never about making something of it all."

"Luke, we have almost found our way out," Murphy said, turning back to face me.

"Your parents thought you would find a way out," said the soul, "They knew that you were destined to be a slacker when they left you. Maybe they thought that you needed to be on your own to learn a lesson. But you didn't learn. You just went with the flow."

"Luke, don't quit now!" came Murphy's voice.

My legs were giving way, dropping down from a jog to short stumbles forward. I was really pressing myself, trying to reach the end of this insanity. *They didn't leave you out of kindness. They left out of their own selfish choice. Luke, you know they did.* I told myself this was the truth, but I was currently at odds with the supposed "inner truths" that my soul was telling me. The whole thing was rather dream-like, and I thought again about whether I had passed out in front of the TV in the middle of an episode of *Tales from the Outer Darkside of the Twilight.* Of course, I knew that the writing on the show still wasn't particularly good, so any ideas for the events surrounding me would have to come from somewhere deep inside. And I knew that I just didn't have the brain to come up with so much bullshit.

"You wanted to have this adventure," the soul said, "You love living in a world of fiction, taking you away from a boring monotony of retail, manufactured microwave dinners, and loneliness. Look at all the friends you have invented, all brought together by yourself and your need to be important."

I stopped in my tracks. This was the best argument out of any that I was responsible for this nightmare. Maybe I got lost in the excitement of being chased and punched and nearly set on fire, and I began to love it. In retrospect, it made a kind of twisted sense that I would turn my life into a living hell, just to get away from the real hell: a limbo-like existence in a shit town with shit people.

"Luke! Why are you waiting?" Murphy called from the gap in the wall, seeing that I hadn't made it as far as he had.

"Either none of this is real or I just don't give a damn anymore. I'm kind of tired of all this."

Murphy walked right up to me, and then gave me a punch to the face that caused me to stumble. Strangely, I still held onto my soul without dropping it.

"What the fuck was that about?!" I demanded, spitting blood from the newly-made bite mark in my cheek.

"I wanted to show you that the pain was real, so this is real."

"Goddammit! Couldn't you have pinched me or something? Like they do on TV? Fuck…I know this isn't the ideal situation for that, but…Jesus, man. Warning next time."

"I am sorry. Shall we continue?"

At that moment, I heard the call from the burned man from somewhere within the building, echoed off the twisted architecture.

"Yes, let's get the hell out of here," I said.

I followed Murphy out the gap in the wall, allowing him to test the waters first. He showed me that there was an invisible floor here too, so I took a step up onto it and began walking across the void once more. In the distance, there was a single, white-painted door sitting in the middle of the air. Both of us walked over, with Murphy twisting down the door handle and revealing a strange, small room. It was larger than a closet, but not by much. It didn't contain anything other than a familiar blue wisp cut into the air. The same I had encountered in the barn at the start of this journey.

"This is one of the pockets out of here," Murphy explained.

"Yeah, looks like the one I took to get in."

"There are a few of these scattered about your realm and ours. Maybe one day you will step through and pay us a visit."

I looked at Murphy with tired eyes, and then looked down at the soul, at a ghostly duplicate of me in my arms. I looked around at the realm of Saarlathesh, the starry sky and the blue-violet stream that, I knew, flowed back to the master of this place, the Insect King. For a minute, I was quiet, reflecting on all that had happened. On the people I've met and the turns my life had taken.

"Fuck. That. Noise," I said to him, taking a step into the closet and through the blue portal, disappearing back to Earth with my soul in hand.

King of Weevil, Wasp, and Fly
We ask for guidance
We ask for knowledge
Give us new life to serve you

Creature of Teeth, Wings, and Black Eye
Your enemies are many
Your enemies strike fear
Give us new life to serve you

Saarlathesh, the Old One
We spread your terror and dread
Give us the tools to do your bidding
And engulf the Earth with your spawn

Saarlathesh, Saarlathesh
We worship your realm from ours
Meld the two worlds, Great King
And release your disciples from their mortal coil.

–Excerpt from *The Compendium of Shadows*,
as recovered and translated by Prof–(the rest is illegible)

The preceding passage was found scrawled upon the wall of a cave, located on an uninhabited island in the South Pacific. Although thought to be the remnants of an ancient people who once crossed the ocean from New Zealand (losing course on their way and crashing upon the island), the island has had evidence of human visitation from more recent times, as evidence by shoeprints molded into the mud near the cave site.

Was it written by an old band of lost prehistoric men or is it graffiti by vandals in more recent times? Or is it the rough scrawls of a mob of reclusive, secretive cultists? The source of this passage is uncertain. However, the drawing accompanying the passage is a wonder of its own. It is a depiction of a great insect-like being lording over kowtowing humanoid figures, which are surrounded by many smaller beings like the creature itself.

–Excerpt from *The Compendium of Shadows*

Afterword

It is best, I think, to begin this small section with a bit of idol worship. That is, there are a number of influences in my personal life that I can label as an "influence" in the writing style present in the preceding text, which I most certainly hope that you have enjoyed reading. I find that it would be a disservice to the works of my influences if I were to not throw in an important acknowledgement to them. Yes, if I were to simply release this book as is without taking the considerate time to thank them properly, I will feel as if I have ignored them.

To those that know of his work, H.P. Lovecraft is the absolutely seminal writer I aspire to replicate the style of with this novel; it is no secret that my love of the macabre stems from numerous readings through the complete catalog of Lovecraft. I have often read, and re-read, two very unique stories, *The Colour Out of Space* and *The Music of Erich Zann*, both of which are high on the list of my most treasured Lovecraft tales. I will not deny any influence from Lovecraft's gods, most notably Cthulhu and Shub-Niggurath, in the creation of my very own eldritch abomination, the title character of Saarlathesh. In a way, I feel as though Saarlathesh and countless fan-made creatures belong to the Lovecraft universe.

Johnny Toxin

Undoubtedly, Lovecraft is the master of the cosmic horror story, and I believe that it should be expected of all writers who cherish his work to give the proper respect to his craft.

The second author that I must acknowledge is David Wong, pseudonym of a Mister Jason Pargin, for two of his works, *John Dies at the End* and *This Book is Full of Spiders: Seriously Dude, Don't Touch It*. While Lovecraft is responsible for the cosmic horror elements of my story (and, indeed, of Mr. Wong's as well), David Wong's books contain such a great, fun, comedic sense in the face of inter-dimensional beings, a living drug, death, and a cast of characters put through one hell of an adventure. And it is his work that convinced me to put pen to paper and craft the story you hold in your hands.

I spent, and spend, my time writing short stories and concepts, but *Into the Hive of Saarlathesh* is the only idea that has turned into a full-on novel. I owe David Wong for convincing me to chase after publication, even though I doubted at first that I could ever write enough material for a complete tale. But here it is.

As a final acknowledgment, I must thank each and every one of my Kickstarter backers. These men and women are all responsible for their support and their funding toward publishing this work of literature. You all (and hopefully you are reading this right now) deserve my eternal gratitude for getting me this far. Thank you for believing in me, for donating, and for taking the time to read this little word of thanks. You're the best.

Full List of
Kickstarter Backers

Austin Worst
Evan Rodrigues
Tom Etzel
Ana Figueiredo
Angela Ferreira
Cristina Ferraz
Justin J. Bowen
Ilda Vitorino
Christopher Romano
Lidia Ganhito
Ramona Martinez
Maria De Lurdes
Steve Cerqueira
David Di Fabrizio
Tom Toynton
Daniel Fiore
John Ferreira
Jonathan Zazula
Jason Cooper
Chris Mihal
Gerald Bernardin
Lisa Hogya
Matthew Martin

Sandra O'Hare
Frank Moreira
Ana Paula Silva
Alex Fernandes
Liz Schettino
Maria Cardoso
Elvira M. Vieira
Jeff Balla
Maria DeVito
Joe Louro
Terry Pacheco
Ana Paula DePaco
Morgan Hay
Arthur Lazarus
Michael DeRisi
Thomas VanDermark
Maria Ruivo
Lila Caamano
April Lanzet
Sam Perl
Brian Fischer
Steven Mentzel

About the Author

Johnny Toxin is a freelance writer and programmer who has an associate's degree in video game design. He loves fiction in all its forms, and has been writing short stories for seven years now.

His debut novel, *Into the Hive of Saarlathesh*, started out as a much shorter piece of fiction, which was slowly teased out as Toxin found himself relentlessly writing, until he created what he is proud to describe as "a weird piece of fiction, horror, and comedy."

As is evident in his work, Toxin enjoys having a laugh as much as a scare, and he plans to bring more of his unique tales to print as soon as possible. In the meantime, however, he sincerely hopes that his fans won't hunt him down in New Jersey.

Printed in Great Britain
by Amazon

17968926R00162